Windfall

Windfall

A Novel

James Magnuson

Villard

New York

Copyright © 1998 by James Magnuson

All rights reserved under International and Pan-American Copyright Conventions.
Published in the United States by Villard Books, a division of Random House, Inc.,
New York, and simultaneously in Canada by Random House of
Canada Limited, Toronto.

VILLARD BOOKS is a registered trademark of Random House, Inc.

ISBN 0-375-50210-6

Random House website address: www.randomhouse.com
Printed in the United States of America on acid-free paper
2   4   6   8   9   7   5   3
FIRST EDITION

It would be difficult to describe the avidity with which the American rushes forward the secure this immense booty that fortune offers.

—ALEXIS DE TOCQUEVILLE

Windfall

Chapter One

On a long hill just outside of Corsicana, Ben first noticed that he was losing power. Stepping on the accelerator felt like stepping on air. His speed dropped from sixty-five to fifty-five and then fifty. Two pickups and a small Accord with an A and M sticker in the rear window zoomed past him. Once he got to the top of the rise everything kicked in again; there wasn't a trace of a problem.

The moon shone over empty winter pastures and the drained swampland along the Trinity River. Katy and both children were asleep. He'd hoped to get back to Austin early enough to at least look over his lecture notes for the next day, but saying goodbye to Katy's family after a long vacation was not a simple thing.

For years they'd been spending Christmases on Katy's family's farm in Mississippi. There was no place in the world where Katy felt freer. The kids took care of themselves, roaming with their cousins, riding horses, going on long jeep rides over the fields, The family all gathered for the holiday—brothers, sisters, relatives from Boston and Chicago. Contrary to the nearly universally held opinion of Mississippi as a bastion of the unenlightened, these gatherings were as cosmopolitan as any Ben had ever experienced; there were folklorists and screenwriters, Harvard cardiologists and painters from Venice Beach. Sometimes it seemed as if meals for twenty were being prepared non-stop, but Katy loved it, working in the kitchen with her mother, organizing a pinata party in the garage for all the kids, black and white, who lived along the road, taking long walks through the pastures with her sister.

Their life in Austin seemed so small in comparison. On the long ride through Louisiana and East Texas a quietness would settle over Katy and Ben always felt an unacknowledged reproach in that quietness.

He heard someone stir. Glancing in the rear view mirror he saw Matt shift under his quilt, throwing his arm across his eyes, trying to go back to sleep. The headlights flashed across a shack with a hand-painted sign for barbeque tacked above the door; it looked as if it had been closed for years. The van's tires hummed on the asphalt. He reached down in the sack next to his seat and fished out a couple of stale gingersnaps. He turned on the radio, flipping through the evangelists and the oldies stations, trying to keep himself alert.

Then, on a long incline, ten miles east of Mount Calm, it happened again: the accelerator suddenly going soft as a bean-bag chair, the van slowing down—sixty, fifty, forty—and this time the motor began to backfire. Katy woke up, turning sleepily to him.

"Is everything O.K.?"

"Everything's fine," he said. Ben was a man who kept his worries to himself.

As soon as they hit the top of the hill all difficulties vanished; once again, the van was running like a top. Katy was asleep in another minute, but Ben was utterly awake.

This was all they needed. Maybe it was something small, a dirty filter in the carburetor, but when was it ever small? The van had eighty-five thousand miles on it and they couldn't afford a new one, but the truth was they couldn't afford a three hundred dollar repair bill either.

Every time something like this happened it seemed to push them to the brink. In his twenties and thirties Ben never thought about money, more or less what you'd expect from a scholar whose specialty was the Transcendentalists, but now, in his forties, trying to raise two children on a thirty thousand dollar a year salary, it was all he thought about.

There wasn't an ounce of trouble the rest of the way in. In the blackest of moods, Ben sped up the ramp onto I-35 at Waco, merging fearlessly with the thundering trucks and the shiny bright sedans of returning college students.

They pulled up in front of their yellow, two-story house in South Austin a little after ten and roused the sleeping children. As he shoved open the front door he heard the slither of two weeks of mail piled inside. He carried the two heaviest suitcases into the bedroom and checked the phone messages. There were a couple of invitations to New Year's parties they'd missed and a half dozen calls from the kids' friends, but it was always less than you'd hoped for.

The kids handled coming back better than he and Katy did. After a couple of trips to the car to help carry things in, Abby was soon ensconced on her bed reading Sassy Magazine and Matt settled at his computer, installing the newest version of Wing Commander that his uncle had given him for Christmas.

When Ben came into the kitchen with the soggy sackful of snacks and half-eaten apples, Katy was already on the phone with her mother, letting her know that they'd arrived safely. Ben put the boxed fruit juices in the refrigerator, unlocked the back door and stepped outside.

It was cold and a wind had come up; the weatherman had said they could expect a freeze. The moon, shining through the gnarled branches of the live oaks, cast ghostly shadows on the brick patio.

He retrieved the sack of catfood from the toolshed and poured some of it into Dusty's metal dish. He gave a low whistle, rattling the bowl. When there was no response he called out three or four times. Still there was nothing. He unlocked the patio gate and went around the side of the house, calling as he went. Dusty had a habit of disappearing over Christmas vacation. It was her way of punishing them for abandoning her.

He left the dish of catfood on the back steps and went inside. Katy was still on the phone with her mother so he went into the bedroom to use the other line. He called Alice, the ten year old down the block they paid a dollar a day to feed Dusty while they were away.

Alice hadn't seen the cat in three days and she sounded as if she was near tears about it. "I put food out every day, just like you told me, and petted her," she said. "I don't know what could have happened . . ."

"But Alice, when you came over in the morning, was the food gone?"

"No. Not for the last couple of days." Ben's silence only set her off again. "I'm really sorry, Mr. Lindberg. My Dad and I went out looking for her yesterday . . ."

"It's not your fault, Alice," he said. "Please. It's just something Dusty does."

When he went back into the kitchen Matt was hunched over a bowl of cereal and Katy stood at the stove making a grilled cheese sandwich for Abby. They wanted to know who he'd been talking to and when he told them the story Abby was vociferous. He had to go out and look for Dusty. What if the Doberman that lived across the street had gotten hold of her? Their poor cat could be dying under some woodpile. Ben tried to argue that Dusty would probably show up in a day or two, like she always did, but it was hopeless arguing. He was outvoted three to one.

Flashlight in hand, he jogged down the front steps and out across the yard. At ten-thirty most of the houses were already dark.

They lived in a strange non-neighborhood, cut up by too many church parking lots. Their house was the nicest one on the block, a two-story Victorian, but they, like their neighbors, were renters. The man next door was a carpenter who seemed to split his time between working on his boat in his driveway and smoking dope with the musician who lived on the other side of him. Across the street was the woman with the Doberman. As he passed under her windows he could hear her arguing with her boyfriend; at least once or twice a month the police would come by.

He and Katy had found the house on a whirlwind three-day trip to Austin four years ago, right after he heard that he'd been hired. They took the house because it had lovely porches, the rent was cheap, and it let them take their time looking for a place to buy. Four years later they were still there, caught in the financial no-man's-land between an academic salary and a booming Austin real estate market.

As he moved along the street he fanned the flashlight under the cars, along the gravel driveways, calling the cat's name. In the parking lot of the Baptist church a couple sat in a dark car, talking.

When he got to Congress Avenue he stopped for a moment, staring down the long hill at the state capitol, all lit up a mile away. The wind blew a loose sheet of newspaper against the wall of the abandoned feedstore across the street. There was no one else out. It was too cold even for the street-walkers who used the motels a few blocks down.

It was the third of January, the week for ponderous editorials and special The Year In Pictures editions of all the slick periodicals; it was the time for taking stock. Ben was by nature an optimist, someone with both the knack and the inclination to cheer people up, but if someone had forced him to speak the truth, the truth was that things were not good.

Katy was finishing her teaching certification, but even with a second teacher's salary, they still weren't going to be able to touch the kinds of houses Katy had her heart set on. But it went beyond money; somewhere along the line some essential hope had been dimmed, if not extinguished. They were losing ground, in more ways than one, and they both knew it.

Turning to head home, a bit of motion caught his eye. On the far side of Congress Avenue a low-slung grey cat slipped silently over the curb.

"Dusty?" he called out.

The cat froze for a moment, head raised, and then ran, squeezing under the abandoned feed store. Ben hesitated. It probably wasn't Dusty—all grey cats looked alike anyway—but he had promised the children and it was a cold night. He didn't want to be responsible for the animal freezing to death.

He crossed the street, trotting ahead of a city bus wheezing up the hill. The two or three passengers looked, in the florescent light, like children of the damned. The feed store had been closed for more than nine months. A FOR SALE sign still hung in the window. It was amazing that the store had stayed open for as long as it had. Thirty years ago this had been the edge of town. People had pastured their horses where St. Ed's now stood, but Austin had exploded since then and the store had been reduced to an anachronism, a curious relic.

He had taken the kids in the store once or twice before it closed and it was a wonderful place, with chicks and rabbits for sale, screwworm medicine and liniment on the shelves, a big brass cash register and barrels full of everything under the sun.

He moved around the outside of the long stone building, whistling, calling the cat's name. He knelt at a place in the wall where the stonework had broken away and shone the light into a shallow, washed-out burrow, but there was nothing there. He stood up and shone the flashlight in through one of the dirty windowpanes. He was about to give up when he heard a long, distressed moan.

"Dusty?"

The sound had come from under the building and it sounded as if the cat was trapped. He called Dusty's name again and there was an answering cry, but this time it sounded fainter, further away. A dog barked, somewhere down the block.

He went around to the back of the building. A chain was wrapped through the handles of a set of battered double-doors, but the lock intended to secure it was busted. It took Ben only a few seconds to unravel the chain.

He stepped inside the old store. The place still smelled of sweet feed and there were still incubators and animal cages piled up against the wall. As he moved across the worn floorboards he heard scurrying in the rafters, probably rats. Carlights flared for a second at the front windows and then faded away.

The cat miaowed loudly, clearly in distress; it sounded like it was right under his feet. "Dusty? Hey, girl, hey, girl . . ."

The trick was how to get under there. He shone the light across the floor, into the dark corners. Then he saw the answer. Along the south wall, where they used to keep the bins of feed, was a small knotted tuft of rope jutting from a slightly raised section of the floor. It was a trapdoor.

He got down to one knee. It took three hard yanks to get the trap-door to budge; on the fourth he had it open. He lay the heavy, sled-like rectangle of wood against the wall and retrieved his flashlight.

He shone the light down into what looked like a root cellar, waving the beam over packed walls of dirt. The space was maybe eight feet deep at the center, but tapering quickly at either end. A smoky, burned-out light bulb hung from a frayed cord and there was a ladder with a couple of missing rungs.

"Hey, girl, come on! Come on!"

It would be like Dusty to play hard to get. He thought he heard a quick rustling, but he couldn't see her. What he did see was a fifty dollar bill, half-buried in the dust and rat droppings at the base of the ladder.

His first thought was that it couldn't be real, that it must be toy money. He sat there on his haunches, staring down at it. Two or three times in his life he'd found cash in the street, but never anything bigger than a ten. It had always made him feel lucky and guilty, in equal measure. Despite an easy-going demeanor, Ben was one of those people who always waited until the light said walk, as law-abiding as they come, someone whose entry in the Soap-Box Derby of Life had been packed with an extra load of super-ego.

He tested the top rung of the ladder with a foot. When he was sure that it would hold, he moved down carefully, one hand still gripping the floor above him. His heart pounded.

He picked up the fifty dollar bill, brushing off the dust. It was an old bill and smooth as velvet. It looked real enough.

He thought, Katy isn't going to believe this. He jammed the bill into his pocket, but as he turned to grab hold of the ladder he saw something else. Tucked back in the farthest recesses of the cellar was a milky-white sheet of plastic, draped around a large, casket-sized mass. He held the flashlight steadily on it for several seconds, the light reflecting off the rippled plastic, winking back at him.

He stepped forward, putting a knee against the sharp dirt incline, and tugged at the sheet. It crumpled to one side. Eight or nine red igloo coolers were lined up in two rows.

He caught hold of the handle of one of the coolers and pulled it toward him. It was heavier than he expected. He dragged it to the foot of the ladder.

The lid was taped shut, but the tape was old and dry. He sliced through it quickly with a fingernail. Pickles, he thought, it's probably nothing but old jam jars, but his hands were trembling as if he were an eleven-year-old boy.

He opened the lid. The cooler was filled to the top with stacks of fifty dollar bills. He took a quick, involuntary breath. The bills were in two rows, eight stacks per row, and the cooler itself was maybe a foot high. Each stack was wrapped in its own individual wrapper and taped shut.

He grabbed the corner of a second cooler, spun it toward him, then slid it down the rough dirt slope. His eyes stung from the molds and the dust. He opened the second cooler. It too was filled with fifties.

He knew it had to be dirty money. Either that or it was counterfeit; he wasn't an idiot. He knew he should leave, but he couldn't. It was the most extraordinary moment of his life and he wanted to savor it.

He bent down finally and undid the tape on one of the stacks. Each stack was divided into smaller, more manageable packets and secured by paper straps. Ben broke one of the paper straps and lifted out three bills, crisp and new. He fingered them gingerly, as if they were some sort of Japanese delicacy. The flashlight lay at his feet. It was starting to dim, the beam flickering along the dirt walls of the root cellar. He took out his wallet and put in all four of the fifties.

There was a loud thump above him, somewhere in the store. He didn't move for almost a minute. There was nothing more. He decided it must have been a door or a shutter, banging in the wind, but it was enough to spook him.

He slipped his wallet back in his pocket. Screw the cat, he was getting out of here. He retaped the stack of bills and shoved the coolers back into their original positions. He crawled up into the narrowest part of the cellar to retrieve the milky-white plastic. He tried to drape the sheet over the coolers so everything would look just the way he had found it, but it was tricky, working in such a tight, airless space. He did the best he could.

He batted the dirt from his trousers and picked up his flashlight. He climbed the rickety ladder and lowered the trapdoor softly back in place. Somewhere a siren rose and fell.

Stepping outside the building he quickly wrapped the chain around the handles of the double-doors. Across the street a light shone from a bathroom window, but there was no sign of anybody moving around inside. Directly behind the feed store was a small auto repair place, a dozen cars, some up on blocks, others with their hoods up, behind a high chain link fence.

When he got home the cat was there, crouched over a pan of warm milk in the kitchen. She had come up to the porch maybe five minutes after Ben had gone out looking for her.

"I'm sorry," Katy said.

"That's O.K.," he said. He set the flashlight on the table, unzipping his jacket. Abby knelt beside the cat, stroking it as it lapped hungrily at the milk. It looked as if it hadn't eaten in months.

"Are you all right?" Katy said.

"I'm fine. Why?"

"I don't know. You look upset."

"No, I'm fine. I wanted to say, when we were driving in, the van was acting up some. We should probably take it in tomorrow."

He saw the worry come over her face. "What do you think it is?"

"It's probably something small. But I think we need to be sure."

"I guess I can take it in after I take the kids to school."

"That would be great," Ben said.

He went in to take a bath. The smell of sweet feed was still on him. He leaned over the tub, testing the temperature of the water with his hand. He hadn't checked the other coolers, but if there were like the first two . . . There had to be several hundred thousand dollars in every one.

He took off his clothes. The bathroom filled with steam. He dug his wallet out of his trousers and opened it, riffling through the bills, just to be sure he hadn't hallucinated the whole thing. He had two hundred extra dollars in his pocket, all he had to do now was call the police and tell them what he had found, and he would be fine, it would be over. He heard his son, singing in his bedroom. He set his wallet back on the sink. So Merry Christmas, he thought, Merry Christmas.

Chapter Two

The next morning, waiting at the corner for the bus, Ben thumbed through his notes for his first lecture. The course on the Transcendentalists was a new one, entitled—he hoped not too pretentiously—"How Are We to Live?" Sunlight gleamed off the dirty windows of the feedstore across the street, the old building looking harmless as a clapboard front at Knott's Berry Farm.

The young Pakistani woman who worked at a gift store downtown sat on the bench, absorbed in her paper. Ben took the bus into campus most days. After four years he was one of the regulars and knew nearly all the faces. He'd turned it into a joke, one he'd repeated more than once: the only people who rode the buses in Austin were maids, patients from the mental hospital and assistant professors.

The bus was ten minutes late, which meant Ben missed his transfer at the Capitol and had to walk the rest of the way to the University, but nothing could dampen his buoyant mood. The weather was crisp, he had two hundred extra dollars in his pocket and the world was not quite the same.

When he walked into class at nine-thirty he was amazed to find all forty seats filled and people lined up against the wall. He knew better than to think it had to do with his wonderful reputation as a teacher. Two of the Americanists were away and a third had just gone on emergency medical leave which created a real crunch.

After going over the syllabus and answering questions, Ben read to them from *Walden*. Reading aloud to undergraduates was always a risky business, but if they couldn't respond to *Walden*, what were they going to respond to? His mother had given it to him for Christmas when he was fourteen and he had devoured it in two days. It had become the key book in his life.

His voice resonated like a preacher's. "I went to the woods because I wished to live deliberately, to front only the essential facts of life, and see if I could not learn what it had to teach, and not, when I came to die, discover that I had not lived. . . ." He raised his head, scanning the student faces. These words still had the power to move him, but what about them? They looked as frightened and bewildered as puppies at the pound.

After class Ben walked back to Parlin and stopped off at the mailroom (Ernestine Bryce had left him a second notice that he owed a dollar twenty-one for postage). By the time he got to his office a dozen kids were camped out in the hallway, waiting for him. He ushered them in, one by one, and listened to their stories about why they needed to get into his course. It was always like this at the beginning of the semester and Ben sometimes got himself into trouble by being kinder than he needed to be, but it all went fine until he got to the last in line, a swaggering wise guy in cowboy boots named Dan Sweeney.

Though shiny-faced and still carrying a layer of baby-fat, Sweeney was not exactly a kid; he was twenty-eight and had been knocking around the university for years. He needed one more course in American Lit to graduate, this course. When Ben told him what he'd told the others, that he had no control over registration, that it was a matter for the Undergraduate Advisor, Sweeney acted like he knew better, leaning back in his chair, his fingers locked behind his head.

"But I'll bet if you wrote a note, that would help," Sweeney said.

"That's not what they tell me," Ben said.

Sweeney grinned and hitched up his belt-buckle, big as any bull-rider's. "I know, but no harm in trying, right?"

Sweeney persisted. He'd heard what a great teacher Ben was and had been trying to get into his classes for the last two years. Emerson and Thoreau were his favorite authors and he'd gotten an A from Knapp in the Twain course last semester. If Ben wanted to sign him up as a conference student and just let him sit in, that would be all right with him. Exasperated, Ben finally wrote him a note just to get him out of the office.

As soon as the door was closed Ben tried to call Katy to see what the word was on the car, but only got the answering machine. He walked over to the Middle Eastern restaurant on Rio Grande. He ordered the chicken special, which he always did, and a glass of Chardonnay, which he never did, to celebrate his good fortune.

The dueling bouzoukis from *Never On Sunday* drifted from the speakers above the kitchen door and next to the window an intense young linguistics professor enthralled a table of women graduate students. When the wine came Ben raised his glass to the owner, a middle-aged Lebanese man with a wonderful smile, sitting at his usual table in the corner.

Waiting for his food, Ben checked his wallet, just to be sure the four fifties were still there. It still didn't feel quite real. Why would anyone have sealed up that amount of money under a feedstore and just leave it unprotected? Whoever they were, Ben was sure they would be back for it.

Part of him felt a little dirty for having taken any of it and yet another part of him regretted not having taken more, but taking more would only have been asking for it. From time to time there were stories in the Austin papers about the local drug busts, but Ben never read much more than the headlines. All he really knew was what he saw on television: cops kicking down tenement doors, young black men on the ground with their wrists handcuffed behind their backs.

At the next table they were talking of Richard Rorty, Derrida and the history of American pragmatism. Ben drained his wine glass. It would be insane for him to go back to the feedstore. He had a wonderful wife, two children that he loved, he wasn't going to risk that. But it was a hard thing to get out of your head, imagining what a difference money like that could make. They would buy a nice house, he could take a year's leave and get his book done, he wouldn't have to waste his time listening to dunderheads like Sweeney.

When his food arrived he ordered a second glass of wine. The chicken had never been better, garlicy and tender, served on a bed of yellow rice with a generous scoop of oliveh. He wolfed it down; he hadn't realized how hungry he was.

The bill came to a little under fifteen dollars. Ben pulled out one of the fifties and set it on the chocolate-colored plastic tray. When the soft-eyed young Lebanese waiter (Ben guessed that he was the owner's nephew) came to collect it he did a double-take.

"Is this O.K.?" Ben asked.

The slender waiter, usually so cheerful, was in a quandary. "Sure, of course," he said.

The waiter disappeared into the kitchen. Five minutes passed.

The linguistics professor and his admirers left sucking on pepper-mints. Ben sat with his fingertips on the edge of the table, trying to stay calm. He scrutinized the map of the Middle East on the wall, then glanced at his watch. The owner, sensing Ben's distress, got up and went back to the kitchen.

The wine had made Ben dizzy. What a fool he'd been to think he could get away with this. Until now he had not even considered the possibility that the money might be counterfeit. Or what if it was stolen? Somewhere he'd heard that restaurants have lists of serial numbers taped up next to their cash registers, numbers the police were looking for. He was on the verge of bolting when the owner came out with Ben's change.

"I'm so sorry," the owner said. He set the money on the table. "We have all these new people in the kitchen, we're a little confused today. I hope everything was all right?"

Ben picked his change off the tray and left a three dollar tip. His mouth was dry, his heart pounded. He gave the owner a reassuring pat on the forearm. "Better than ever," he said.

The news about the car was not good. When Ben got home that night Katy gave him the full report. Jeff, the manager at the Texaco station, said the gears were totally stripped. It might be possible to find a rebuilt transmission for seven hundred dollars, but the van already had so many miles on it they would probably be better off buying a new car.

"What does he mean, buy a new car?" Ben said. "How are we going to buy a new car?"

"People buy cars all the time," Katy said. "People who have a lot less than us." She stood at the stove, pouring brittle sticks of pasta into gently boiling water. "We could go to the Credit Union. I'm sure we could get a loan."

"And how would we pay that off?" She didn't answer, her face flushed above the steaming pot of water. He had a way sometimes, when he was frustrated, of being cutting, of making her feel stupid. "Let me call Jeff in the morning."

That night he tried to work on his lectures for Wednesday, but it was impossible to concentrate. Katy was scarcely speaking to him and it was his fault, for taking the tone he had, but she was nuts if she thought they could think for one minute about spending twenty thousand dollars on a new van.

He had never felt that Katy understood money. Her family wasn't rich, but they were comfortable. She had always had the feeling that you bought what you needed and somehow everything would work out.

It was not a faith that he shared. Ben's father had slaved away at a number of jobs—selling insurance, managing a small plastic draperies firm—and while they'd always had a respectable middle class life it had been an existence without any give to it. Ben had worked, all through high school and college, delivering papers, cleaning hotel rooms, shovelling peas in a canning factory, and it left him with the sense that if you took one false step the ground might open up and swallow you.

He shoved the stack of books away from him. A dog-earred copy of *The Imperial Self* tumbled to the floor. How in the hell could they afford a twenty-thousand dollar van? They didn't even have seven hundred dollars for a rebuilt transmission. What a joke: two blocks away there were thousands upon thousands of dollars sitting untouched in a root cellar, while there they were killing themselves over a few hundred.

He had no classes on Tuesday, but he went in anyway and called Jeff from his office. Jeff was singing a slightly happier tune to Ben than he had to Katy. The gears were shot, but he'd already found a rebuilt transmission and if Ben gave him the go-ahead he could have the car back to them in a day and a half. He looked the van over again and it wasn't in as bad shape as he'd originally thought. With any luck they could get another two, maybe even three more years out of it.

Ben walked over to the University Federal Credit Union, deposited the three remaining fifties and then went in to speak to one of the bank officers, an attractive young black woman with stylish silver earrings, about a loan. She had him fill out a series of forms, listing his previous employers and three personal references.

On the way back to his office he stopped at an umbrellaed stand for a couple of spring rolls. On the far side of Littlefield Fountain Nathaniel Harrison, frail as a reed and wearing rubber boots, rummaged through a concrete garbage receptacle. Nathaniel had been retired from the English Department for nearly ten years, but he was still a familiar figure around campus, making his rounds with his sack of crushed Coke cans over his shoulder. It wasn't as bad as it looked; Nathaniel was a fervent environmentalist, he wasn't doing it just for the money, but the sight of him always made Ben cringe. Nathaniel was like the Ghost of Christmas Future; it was the way academics at all but the most elite universities secretly feared they were going to end up.

That afternoon Ben found himself, in the middle of writing recommendations, taking out his wallet and counting his money. The fifties were gone now, but he still had sixteen bills—two twenties, two fives, and twelve ones. Sixteen bills pressed together were almost immeasurable thin, maybe as thick as the rind of an orange. How many could you get in an inch? Fifty? He guessed more. He leaned forward on his desk, doing the arithmetic on the back of a departmental newsletter.

If you could get a hundred fifty dollar bills in an inch—that would be pushing it but say you did—that would be five thousand dollars. Stack those fifties a foot high and you had sixty thousand dollars. Ben had counted sixteen stacks in the first cooler he'd opened. Multiply that times eight coolers and you would be looking at something over seven and a half million dollars.

For a week Ben tried to pretend that nothing had changed. He taught his classes and they got their van back and it ran like a dream. He put it all on his VISA, culled the dead bamboo in his back yard, took the cat to the vet and drove Matt and his friends to the UT basketball game against the Fellowship of Christian Athletes.

Yet every day, going to work and coming back, he was forced to pass the feedstore. The dirty windows stared at him like the clouded eyes of a genie, awaiting instructions. He went for long runs in the late afternoons, trying to wear himself out, trying to get it all out of his mind, but to no avail. He found it impossible to read or concentrate. He stood up his oldest friend at the University for lunch and when Katy sent him to the grocery store he came back with two of the four items she'd asked for.

There was more money in one of those coolers than he'd make in his entire academic career. But what was he going to do about it? Even if he managed to somehow get the coolers out from under the feedstore, what then? What was he going to do, hide them all in his tool shed? Keep all the money in boxes in his office? And what about Katy? It would be a secret he would have to keep from her forever.

The presence of the money worked its way into him like a slow-moving poison. His colleagues, people he would have judged, had he been in a normal mood, as ranging from the exasperating to the truly admirable to the truly brilliant, people with whom he'd been quite happy to serve on committees, joke in the hallways, gossip over lunch, now struck him as universally doomed, trapped, consumed by the pettiest of jealousies. As if to prove his case, one afternoon he ran into Richard Bates, the oldest of the Renaissance scholars, fresh from his annual trek over to the library to check out the university budget. Richard, his eyes puffy with cedar fever, was full of information about everyone's raises, who had gotten five hundred more and who had gotten five hundred less.

If only he hadn't had to pass the feedstore every day! The money was like an underground fire, fueling resentment, new and old. He saw now just how desperate his life was. He was forty-four years old, he didn't own a house, his car was falling apart, he had two kids and not a penny for their college education, a pittance in his pension. His problem was that he had never paid much attention to how the real world worked, as if being a good guy, doing your job, keeping everyone happy around you meant that things would work out in the end.

Everything came to a head on Wednesday night. A friend of Abby's, a tall girl with braces named Crissie, had been knocked down at school and had to be taken to the hospital. Another girl, an eighth grader, had tried to grab Crissie's Coke out of the Coke machine and when Crissie had refused to give it up the girl had hit her. Crissie had fallen and banged her head against the machine. Crissie's parents were talking of transferring schools.

"So is Crissie still in the hospital?" Ben swung his briefcase onto the living room couch. He picked up the mail and flipped quickly through it.

"No, she's at home," Katy said. "Ben, this is serious. We need to talk about this."

"Come on, these things happen."

"And last week someone set a fire in one of the bathrooms. And just before Christmas there was that big fight in the hallway."

"So what are we supposed to do? Pull Abby out of school?"

"I didn't say that." She flared quickly; she had put up with a week of his crankiness. "Don't put it all on me. You have just as many complaints as I do."

It was true. Carter was a magnet junior high, which mean it had an accelerated academic program that was used to attract bright students to a school in one of Austin's toughest neighborhoods. The goal was integration; the result was a two-tiered system that often seemed to reinforce resentment and distrust. All year long there had been incidents and, to make matters worse, the vaunted academic classes weren't as good as they'd been cracked up to be. In Abby's Honors English class, they had yet to write a paper or read a book.

"I didn't mean it like that," he said. "But what are our choices here? Are we going to pull her out and put her in a private school? And where are we going to get the money for that?"

"I can teach next year."

"I know."

"What do you mean, I know?"

"Katy, I've been a public school guy all my life . . ."

"Well, so have I."

"I know. I just can't see moving her. I'll go in, I'll talk to the principal. Abby's going to be fine. I promise."

That night as they lay in bed he reached across and put a hand on her hip.

"Are you O.K.?" he whispered.

"I'm O.K. Just tired." She was turned away from him, the covers pulled up around her chin.

He took his hand away. The branches of the live oak raked across the tin roof. If I do not do something, he thought, it will always be like this. Life will just go on getting smaller and more bitter. It was time to make a move.

The next day at work he called several self-storage firms in North Austin. The best deal was a place on Burnet that charged thirty-six dollars a month for a five by seven locker. The office was open until nine each night, when they closed the gates and let out the dogs.

At noon he walked over to Breed Hardware and bought a heavy-duty lock, one that opened with a key. As he was leaving he saw the chairman of his department looking over the wheelbarrows but Ben did not go over, just gave a wave from a distance.

That evening he brought Katy a bouquet of white daisies, a peace offering. After supper, while they were loading the dishwasher, he told her he needed to go into the office for a couple of hours. She made no objection. She looked lovely to him just then—her high cheekbones, her honest blue-gray eyes—suspicion was not part of her nature. All she asked was that he pick up a carton of milk on his way back; they would need it for the morning.

He walked out of the house a little before eight. He drove around the neighborhood a couple of times to calm his nerves. There was almost no traffic on Congress Avenue, just a couple of cars parked in front of Fran's Drive-In. He finally pulled into the alleyway behind the feedstore and turned off the ignition. He sat for five minutes, the flashlight in his lap. I still do not have to do this, he thought, I can still just start the car and drive home and everything will be just the way it's always been. A dog trotted up the alley, sniffed briefly at the tires of the van and then trotted off, tail high.

Ben got out of the car. The wound chain on the heavy wooden door was cold to the touch. He undid the chain and slid the door back just far enough for him to slid inside.

He snapped on the flashlight, shining the beam across the worn floorboards, the incubators and the stacked animal cages; nothing had been disturbed. He thought of his family: Abby lying on the bed, doing her homework, Katy working at her desk in the kitchen, Matt thumping around in his stocking feet in his bedroom, slam-dunking the nerf basketball on the miniature rim they'd rigged up on his closet door. They were only two blocks away, but it might as well have been half-way around the world.

The smell of sweet feed was oddly comforting. He opened the trap door and shone the flashlight into the root cellar. He hadn't dreamed it; it was all still there.

He made his way down the ladder. He pulled the plastic sheet to one side and dragged one of the coolers down the rough dirt slope. When he lifted it, the weight surprised him. It must have been at least fifty pounds. He worked the cooler up the ladder, pushing it ahead of him, balancing it for a second or two on each rung, and finally slid it onto the worn wooden floor. He rested on the ladder, his elbows splayed out on the floor like an exhausted swimmer at the edge of a pool. When he thought about it that afternoon he hadn't planned on taking more than one of the coolers, but now it seemed crazy not to take them all, he had already come so far.

It took him twenty minutes to wrestle the rest of them up from the root cellar. Two of the coolers, the ones at the back, were slick with mud where water had seeped through the cracks in the cellar wall, and the mud got on Ben's jacket.

Moonlight poured in through the windows. He lowered the trap-door and kicked it back into place. He straightened up, his hands in the small of his back, stretching. Now came the tricky part.

He carried the coolers out to the van, one by one, and stacked them behind the rear seat. Trying to stay calm, he kept repeating a home-made mantra: don't rush, don't panic, one step at a time, you are just a man going about his business. On every trip he was care-ful to close both the van door and the door to the feedstore, minimizing the chances of attracting the curiosity of any late-night dog-walker. Even though it was a cool night, he was drenched in sweat. With physical labor his fear began to ebb and it was replaced by a kind of giddiness, a kind of glee; he was getting away with it.

Seven down and one to go, he went inside for the last cooler. Moonlight made the warped wooden floorboards shimmer like an uneasy sea. He bent his knees, wrapped his fingers around the plaster handles of the cooler and lifted. He had to pause for a second, the muscles in his lower back starting to seize up.

The chain rattled outside the door. He froze. For several seconds there was nothing more. Maybe he'd just made it up, maybe it had just been the wind, but then he heard it again, the crawl of metal on metal, the sound like a low growl. Someone was unwrapping the chain from the door.

"Hey, fuckin' fuckhead, come on, get the lead out!" The voice was loud, drunken and slurred. Ben still hadn't taken a breath, his back muscles fluttering like moths.

The door banged as if someone had just slammed their shoulder into it and then it began to slide open, an arrow of streetlight racing across the floor. Ben silently set the cooler down, frantically scanning the store; there was no place to hide. His heart banged in his chest.

"So where'd everybody else go? Come on, get in here!"

"I'm not going in there." It was impossible to tell if the second voice was a man's or a woman's, it was so ruined and bull-frog deep. "Look, man, the door's already open. Somebody's in there."

"Nobody's in there. What the fuck are you talking about?"

"Then whose car is it, shithead? I'm not getting busted again."

Ben felt the wet hair on the back of his neck. He was standing in plain view; one glance through a window and they would see him. He moved swiftly and silently to the nearest wall and crouched low. The bare wood smelled of caramel and oats. He panted in low, shallow breaths, like a deer being run by hounds.

"What you so chicken for? You afraid you're going to piss in your pants again?"

"Hell with you."

There was a loud slap and then a scuffle, followed by the breaking of glass and the sharp yip of a dog.

"Look what you fucking did, man! What are we gonna do now? What are we gonna do?"

"I told you not to touch my fuckin' puppy-dog!"

A shadow moved across the narrow opening in the door and the dog whimpered again. Something scraped along the outer wall and then someone cleared their throat and spit lushly. Ben's worry now was that they would break into the van. He cursed himself for his greed. If he'd only been satisfied with one or two of the coolers, he would have been long gone by now.

"Where are you going, man?" The voice was alarmingly close. Whomever it was had planted themselves against the same wall as Ben; they were separated by two feet of wood and crumbling rock.

"I'm going back down to the store!" The second voice, the hoarse one, had moved off into the distance.

"What the hell are you going to the store for? You ain't got no money!"

The answer was garbled, incomprehensible. The man sitting on the opposite side of the wall from Ben have a low, shuddering belch. "Shit." He and Ben were so close Ben could hear his labored breathing, hear him scratch the back of his neck.

There was more shuffling, the sound of footsteps moving across gravel and then utter silence. Ben waited another two or three minutes before he had the nerve to move at all. He slipped to one of the side windows and peered out. The two men were nearly out of sight, still pushing and staggering against one another like buffoons, heading down the sidewalk towards the river. They must have been sixty yards away, it was too far to see much, except that one was big as a buffalo and the other small, the smaller one carrying a squirming puppy on his shoulder. Ben stood at the window until they disappeared from view.

He went to the back door and after a long few seconds, slid it slowly open another six inches. He stared into the dim alleyway, scanning the parking lot and the dark lawns. A huge live oak threw long shadows that twined like the arms of a Hindu god. Car lights appeared, moving slowly down the street, and swished past. Waiting any longer was probably more dangerous than going.

He looked over his shoulder. The last cooler still sat in the middle of the floor, forlorn as a lost lamb. He couldn't just leave it. Going back to retrieve it, it felt nearly twice as heavy as it had before. He waddled to the door, the pebbled plastic banging against his knees. He scanned the street and alleyway one last time, just to be sure, and then stepped sideways into the cool night air.

He swung the last container into the van and eased the tailgate shut. He went back to the feedstore, fingering the chain, not sure how it would be best to leave it. In the end he closed the doors tight again and wrapped the chain around the handles, just the way he'd found it.

As he drove down Congress Avenue his hands still shook. He was in an altered state, near delirium. Nothing had happened, he kept repeating over and over to himself, it was just a close call, even though it felt like so much more—a warning, an omen.

He cut over on Riverside and took the highway north. The capitol glowed, majestic against the night sky. He checked his watch; it was nearly eight-thirty. He felt a sudden surge of panic. The woman had said the office closed at nine. That was all he needed: seven million dollars in the back of his van and nowhere to put it.

He stepped on the gas, moving into the left lane, passing a shuddering cattle truck. He could see, through the metal slats, the helpless bovine eyes, the bodies pressed together, headed for slaughter. The engine hummed. Jeff was right; the car felt as if it was brandnew.

The highway divided East from West Austin, rich from poor, black from white. He passed the football stadium, huge as a canyon, lit up like a shrine, and passed the turn-off to Houston. He spotted a police car in the far right lane just in time, easing on the brake, checking his speedometer. He had to focus, he couldn't afford to let what had happened throw him or he was going to end up in a lot worse trouble. All he needed was to be pulled over, have a cop walk around the van, peering in the windows. He edged down under the speed limit. The police car slid off on the next exit and zoomed up the access road, turning on his siren.

Ben got off at Fifty-Third Street. Once he got to Burnet he picked his way through the stop and go traffic, passing the hodge-podge of taxidermists and palm-readers, cheap burger joints and RV dealers.

At a quarter to nine he drove through the gates of the North Austin Self Storage and parked in front of the office. When he came in, a motherly-looking woman with big hair and a pink sweater got up from behind her desk. Her name was Rose and she had a variety of forms for him to fill out.

Randy Travis sang softly on the radio. Rose explained about insurance, but Ben said he thought he could do without it. He gave her thirty-six dollars, cash, for the first month's rent, and signed the environmental statement. They did not send out bills, Rose said. If you didn't pay for sixty days, they would start sending out the auction notices. It wasn't an idle threat. Through the picture window behind her, Ben could see the jumble of repossessed roll-top desks, battered canoes, fraying wicker chairs.

She gave him a map. His locker would be in Building Seven, near the back of the lot. As he drove away from the office he saw her at the window, lowering the blinds.

There were at least twenty of the low concrete buildings, set out in rows like a military base. At the far end of the lot were parking spaces for RVs and boats.

Ben's building was one row in from the fence, well out of sight of the front office. He was able to drive his van right up to the metal door. He worked quickly, heaving the coolers into the locker like a man tossing bales of hay. It took him no more than five minutes. There was a steady hum of traffic on Burnet.

When he was done he walked to the corner of the concrete building and looked back towards the office just to be sure no one was coming.

He went back to the locker and examined the coolers one at a time. They were all filled with money, mostly fifties, some twenties, a few stacks of one hundreds. He undid one of the cellophaned packs; it was like undoing Girl Scout Cookies. The bills were banded so tightly together they looked as if they'd been pressed and they had a smell to them that was almost like chlorine. Each of the paper straps was stamped with a tiny scorpion, inside an inky circle. He took a thousand dollars, twenty fifty dollar bills. He could scarcely fold his wallet, but he didn't want to have to come back here every three days.

He shut the metal door and fastened it with the shiny new lock he'd bought that afternoon. He tried the key a couple of times and, when he was sure it worked, slipped it onto his key ring.

As he drove out of the lot he saw Rose, standing in the open door of her car. The office was dark now and she was talking to a slender boy in a hunting cap crouched by the high wire fence. Behind the fence three German Shepherds tussled and barked, excited as puppies, anxious to be let out.

He could not keep the money here forever, he knew that, he was going to have to find another place, but he couldn't think of that now. He was wired; he felt as if he'd just downed six cups of coffee. He remembered that Katy had asked him to pick up some milk.

When he got home the children were already in bed. Katy sat at her desk in the kitchen, some monstrous book on educational methods open in front of her. She wanted to know where he'd been. She'd called his office a couple of times.

He wiped the cold beads of condensation off the plastic container of milk and opened the refrigerator door. "I guess I must have been out in the hallway, talking to Ernie," he said. "You know how he is, once he gets going." It occurred to him that he had never really lied to her before; he was going to have to get used to it.

Chapter Three

He woke at five-thirty in the morning, knowing that he'd made the biggest mistake in his life. He stared up at the sloping ceiling. Katy slept soundly next to him. He had to undo this. But how? He tried to imagine himself moving all the coolers back, wrestling them down that rickety ladder, or driving out into the hill country and dumping them into the deepest river he could find.

He was in an utter panic. He'd come so close to being caught, and that in the first ten minutes. What in hell had made him think he could get away with this? What if one of those drunks had looked in the window? Ben didn't know that they hadn't. And if someone came asking, they would certainly be able to describe the van. They might even remember the license plate, the university parking sticker. What if the woman at the storage unit got curious? She had a key. What was to stop her from going to take a look?

For the next week Ben was in a state, making a hash of his lectures, accidentally locking himself out of his office, and when he came into the department on Thursday and saw two campus policemen joking with one of the secretaries he was sure they had come for him.

But no one did come for him. Life went on as it always did. The weather was lovely, with highs in the seventies, and at noon he would take his bag lunch and eat on the patio behind the Union, sitting at the wrought-iron tables, tossing bits of his sandwich to the pigeons and squirrels.

He deposited another two hundred dollars cash in the bank, making a point of using a new teller. Three hundred he kept in his wallet and the other five hundred he stashed in an envelope in the bottom drawer of his desk at school.

Katy's birthday was the last week in January. She kept saying that they should just celebrate at home, it was on a school night, after all, and it would be so much cheaper, but Ben insisted that they were going out.

They went to Castle Hill, a cheerful, upscale restaurant Ben had been to only once, back when he was being recruited. After the waitress, a diminutive young woman with a butterfly tattoo on her wrist, took their orders, she asked if anyone would be interested in an appetizer. Katy and the children all murmured no.

"Let's see what you have here," Ben said. He took his menu back from the waitress and opened it. "Why don't you bring us an order of the crab cakes and, let's see . . . the curried lamb empanadas with the coconut cilantro sauce." He exaggerated every syllable, making a joke out of it. After the waitress left, Katy shot him a look. Ben put up his hand. "Katy, it's going to be fine. It's your birthday."

So many times Ben had found himself on the verge of telling her everything and yet he always pulled up short. He was still trying to understand why. It always came back to the fact that telling her would risk having her say no and he didn't want anyone telling him no. He knew her. She was one of those law-abiding people, she would insist on his turning it all back. And what rational person wouldn't have had trouble with what he was doing? The odds of making it work were small, the dangers enormous. Katy was a fretter, a worrier, the pessimist of the two of them. She was not always the easiest person to have a frank discussion with. He had his own private business here; he was not about to let anyone take it away from him.

Abby was thrilled to be out on the town. A boothful of theatrical-looking people carried on at a table near the door and Abby was sure the dazzling blond in the silver dress was Nicolette Sheridan; Abby had read that she was in town to shoot a TV movie. Matt, who never had liked restaurants, was sweetly forbearing, looking very handsome and solemn as a Mennonite in his jacket and tie.

The food arrived and it was just as delicious as Ben remembered it. He had the pork loin, Katy the Thai salad, Matt some very fancy enchiladas and Abby the blackened catfish, but they all swapped back and forth, everyone getting a bite of everything. It was very noisy and hard to have a conversation, but when Jerry Jeff Walker came over to speak to the people at the next table, Abby's evening was made.

When the meal was over Ben got up and caught the waitress coming out of the kitchen. It took her just a second to find the bill. Ben glanced at it and handed her two fifties.

"Let me get you change," she said.

"No, no, you just keep it."

She was astonished. It was nearly a twenty dollar tip. Katy and the kids waited by the front door, unwrapping their mints. "Are you sure?"

"Absolutely. You have a good night."

When they got home Katy was banished to the living room while they put candles on the mousse cake that Ben had bought that afternoon at the Amandine bakery. Matt ran to turn off the lights and then they all marched in and sang Happy Birthday.

They cut the cake and Katy opened her present, the new biography of Lewis and Clark. Reading the inscription (Ben had compared her to Sacajewea, leading them all through the wilds of life), Katy reached across and pulled Ben's hand to her cheek. He was not ordinarily a big one for occasions. It was not one of his strong points, he was too Midwestern-casual, and she appreciated the effort. That night they made love for the first time in awhile.

To his surprise Ben found he actually got a kick out of having Sweeney in the classroom. Though he was the kind of student Ben needed to keep in check, he was also the one to call on to liven up a discussion.

He was something of a hero to the younger male students in the class. About once a week he came in looking seriously rumpled and wearing sunglasses at nine-thirty in the morning, a sure sign of hard living. He entertained the back of the room with his wise-cracks, flirted with the girls and yet, more than anyone else on the roster, had a genuine intellectual curiosity. After class he would wait around so he could walk Ben back to Parlin, wanting to know what Ben thought about Kerouac or Kesey, Martin Amis or Raymond Carver. One afternoon he showed up at Ben's office with an old copy of *Raritan* that he'd found at Half-Price books, containing the first article Ben had ever published.

He may have been a reader, but no one would have called Sweeney refined. When Ellen Pyle, a bright, delicately-complexioned transfer student from Bryn Mawr, objected that there was no place for women in *Walden*, Sweeney couldn't resist.

"Hey, come on, we're not talking about country club memberships on the Main Line here."

Ellen colored, but she didn't back down. "I wasn't talking about country clubs. It just seems to me that anytime anything having remotely to do with women or the encumbrances of domesticity comes up—the notion that you might to work to pass something on to your children, say—Thoreau goes on the attack."

"So, what, you want him to date?" Sweeney said.

"Mr. Sweeney!" Ben said. "That's enough."

"You want me to say it?" Ellen shot back. "O.K., I'll say it. I think he's a misogynist!"

"Oh, man." Sweeney shook his head wearily. "Where am I supposed to start. The guy was into chastity. Better him than me, but I say, more power to him. I'm serious. He was trying, if you'll excuse the term, trying to clear all the clap-trap out of his life." The remark was greeted by a chorus of groans and jeers. "Seriously. He was trying to get things down to what really mattered. I wish I could do that. I'm not joking."

Two class periods later, Sweeney, as if to clear up any possible misunderstanding, brought his girlfriend to class, a stunningly sexy and world-weary blonde in her mid-forties who looked like Marianne Faithful. It created a sensation among his claque in the back of the room.

What was Ben going to do with all that money? At first he was too paralyzed to do anything. It seemed insoluble. Someone, sometime, was going to notice that the money was gone and he knew he could not leave it at the storage unit forever.

The first thing he did was what all academics do when faced with an impossible problem: research. He made several forays to the library, but the books he was able to find about money laundering offered little help. They were all focussed on drug cartels, international banking, high-finance razzle-dazzle. He felt as if he was drowning in an alphabet soup of CTRs, CMIRs, cyberpayments, and NBFIs. There were things he found out that he was happy to know; banks, for example, were required to report any cash transactions over ten thousand dollars, but he wasn't about to deposit ten thousand dollars, or five, or two. He knew instinctively that the key was not acting too quickly, not attracting anyone's attention.

On the first of February Ben drove up to the storage unit to pay the next month's rent. Rose was by herself in the office, smoking cigarettes and watching *Murder She Wrote*. As she wrote out his receipt Ben made the mistake of asking how she was. Her husband had had a stroke during the fall and now it seemed as if he'd almost given up, he wasn't taking his medicine like he should and refusing to go to therapy. At least she had her grandchildren. They were her salvation, cute as they could be and just full of the dickens. One of them was going to be in the school play and Rose was making his lion costume.

She snubbed out her cigarette, narrowing her eyes against the rising smoke, and handed Ben his receipt. Her bee-hive hairdo was a marvel of construction: delicate as cotton candy and yet solid as a helmet. "So do you have kids?"

He hesitated; he was not looking to make friends. "Two," he said.

"How old?" Outside, a pickup rumbled through the gate, pulling a boat along behind.

"Thirteen and eleven," Ben said.

"Oh, I envy you. Those are the best years. I hope you realize what you've got."

"I do," he said. He folded his receipt neatly in two and pushed away from the counter. "Rose, it was great talking to you."

Outside the night air was cool and there was no on else on the lot except for the man in the maroon A and M hat and his son unhitching their boat. It was nearly eight-thirty. Ben had told Katy he was just returning some books to the library.

He drove the van back to Building Seven and turned into the narrow lane. He grabbed his briefcase, got out of the van and took his key from his wallet. Instinctively he looked over his shoulder, even though he knew he was well out of sight of the office. It took him a moment to undo the lock, fingers clumsy from the cold (either that, or it was nerves). He yanked open the metal door. All eight coolers were still there, looming like polar bears in their dark cell.

He stepped inside and pulled the door shut behind him. For several seconds he was plunged into utter darkness. He fished for the overhead cord, caught it, and snapped on the single naked bulb.

He opened the coolers, one, two, three. . . . The money was just as he had left it, packed in as snugly as saltines in the cellophane wrappers. He stopped and took a deep breath, collecting himself. The overhead light still swayed on its cord, shadows rocking up and down the walls like a silent cradle. A roach scuttled out from under one of the coolers and tumbled down through the planked floor.

Ben began to cry. He didn't know why. Maybe it was out of relief that the money was still there, maybe it was out of sadness for what he was doing to himself. He slammed the lid down on the last cooler and leaned back against the wall, squeezing his face with a hand. So fuck me, he thought, so fuck me. High up in the corner was a spider web full of roly-polys.

He picked up his briefcase and unzipped it, taking out the over-sized manila envelope. The first time he'd taken a thousand dollars. This time he took two thousand.

It had only been five months since they'd bought Matt his last pair of basketball shoes. but he was growing by leaps and bounds. On the court he and his team-mates looked like puppy-dogs, a tangle of huge, floppy feet and skinny limbs.

The shoes that Matt yearned for were the new Michael Jordan Nikes, but they cost more than a hundred dollars and Matt was a conscientious kid; it worried him, expecting his parents to spend all that money.

Ben took him to Rooster Andrews on Saturday. The sporting goods store smelled of leather and Ben lead Matt past the bins of soccer balls and rows of burnt orange jackets. The clerk was busy with someone else, so they had a few minutes to scrutinize the wall of footwear. There seemed to be more kinds of basketball shoes than there were flavors of ice-cream. They came in every color, some had straps, others had blinking lights in the heel or air pumps sewn into the tongue, but when the apologetic clerk finally came over, Ben said, "I think he'd like to try on a pair of those Michael Jordans."

Matt's mouth became a perfect o of astonishment.

"Let's just see how they feel," Ben said.

The clerk, a husky college kid who looked as if he'd be long off the tee, disappeared into the back room and was back a moment later with a red and white box of nine and a halfs. Matt sat in a low chair and the clerk laced the shoes up for him, squeezing the toes to make sure there was still room to grow. The great UT All-Americans from the Forties and Fifties stared down from their grainy black and white posters on the walls.

"Get up and walk around and see what you think," the clerk said. A six-year old boy danced down the aisle with a football under his arm while his mother looked through the team jerseys. Matt rose and walked slowly in front of the long mirrors as if he was walking on eggshells. His face shone.

"How do they feel?" Ben said.

"They feel great."

Ben stared at his son. With his skinny shoulders and huge, clear blue eyes he suddenly looked fragile as a four day old calf. The shoes glistened as if they'd been basted in frosting. Damn it, Ben thought, what was the point of having seven million dollars sitting in a locker if you couldn't buy your kid a hundred dollar pair of sneakers?

"We'll take them," Ben said.

With tax it came to a little over one hundred and fifteen dollars. Ben paid at the front with three fifties. Because of the amount of the purchase the clerk never blinked twice. Matt wore the shoes out of the store.

When they got home Katy was in the front yard, raking up the dead branches that had fallen during the big windstorm the night before. Matt was out of the sliding door before Ben could even put the van in park.

"Hey, Mom, look what Dad got me!" He stood in the driveway, his smile a mile wide. "Michael Jordans."

Katy, in sweat pants and green turtle-neck, leaned her rake against the tree. "I see."

"Aren't they great?"

"They are great." Ben knew the tone. He grabbed the plastic bag containing Matt's old pair of shoes and got out of the van.

"I'm going to call Cameron," Matt said. He bounded up the steps and let the door slam behind him.

Ben moved slowly across the lawn. He bent down and picked up a sodden branch, snapping it in two before jamming it in the plastic trashcan.

"So how much were they?" Katy asked. She pulled the blue bandanna out of her hair and worked at the knot.

It would not do to lie. "A little over a hundred."

"Ben. . . ."

"The kid never asks for anything."

"I know that, but I thought we'd already discussed this."

Ben dropped his head for a second. The winter lawn might as well have been straw, patchy and brown, and the neighbor's Doberman had made his daily donation at the curb.

"Sometimes you just need to do things," Ben said.

"Ben, I know, but there are some things we just can't afford."

"But maybe we can."

"What do you mean?"

He stared at her. Even on a cool day, the top of her turtleneck was soaked in sweat. Why not tell her now? What was he so god-damned afraid of? He trusted her with his life, with his children, why not this?

The door slammed. They both looked up. Matt leapt down the stairs, the basketball under his arm. He waved to them both.

"Cameron's coming over!"

"Great!" Ben shouted back.

They watched Matt dribble across the street, losing the ball for a second as he tried to put it between his legs. He recovered, racing across the church parking lot. The white shoes flashed over grey asphalt. Look at him, Ben thought. He knew he had done the right thing. Matt stutter-stepped, then took two long strides and leapt as high as he could, laying the ball off the backboard of the basket at the far end of the lot. This was a boy who felt, right now, as if he could jump over the moon.

Ben reached out and took his wife's hand. "Katy, it's going to be O.K., I promise. I promise."

Ben had been a child of admirable candor. When he knocked a baseball through the window of the parochial school he walked up to the front door (it was an overcast March day and there were still dirty banks of snow on the Wisconsin playground) and told the nuns that he'd been the one who'd done it. When he hit a concrete median in a rainstorm one night and threw the wheels of the family car out of alignment, he owned up to his father the first thing in the morning.

He'd always been a little on the sensitive side and his family moved so many times it seemed as if he was always the new kid in town. He read books, tromped in the woods with his home-made bow and arrow and organized pick-up baseball games for the other boys whose fathers had neglected to sign them up for Little League. Once a bully came by his house looking for a fight and Ben, galvanized by terror, had wrestled the whale-sized newspaper boy to the ground, but once he'd gotten on top, he promptly surrendered.

He was a late bloomer. His friends came from his church youth group, not from high school. He never drank a beer until he was eighteen and never kissed a girl until his graduation party when everybody was pretty much kissing everybody.

He met Annette Molinaro his sophomore year at the University of Michigan. She was from San Francisco and a brilliant student of Chinese, small with long brown hair that came nearly to her waist, and a little bossy. It was the first relationship for both of them. On their second date she took him to an Impeach Nixon rally. They studied together, three hours every evening (Ben's grades improved markedly during their courtship) and smoked a moderate amount of dope.

After graduation she went to China for a year to teach English, a choice that left Ben mystified and hurt. Why would she ever want to be apart? He spent twelve lonely months in New York, working for the Welfare Department, going down to the Village on the weekend to see musicals about transvestite gorillas and writing Annette two anxious letters a week. When she got back they were married on a mountaintop above Sausalito.

She got a job with the Ford Foundation and it was there that she met Chang Wei, a young Chinese refugee. Chang was a former Red Guard and a gymnast who had made his break for freedom during the final round of the high bar competition at an international meet in Hong Kong. He had applied for political asylum and was writing a book about his experiences. Annette helped him obtain a grant for the book and then began to work as his translator.

Chang became a friend. He started to come over for supper with them several times a week. He was gentle, polite and still struggling with his English. Ben took him down to Riverside to play touch football. Chang was muscled and quick, but huddles took forever, Ben trying to explain to him what a down and out was, and a buttonhook. In the end, Ben would just outline the plays in the dirt with a stick.

Ben was so naive then. He didn't see what was coming. Chang was something of a celebrity in New York (except, of course, for that handful of Upper West Side radicals who still could describe themselves as Maoists) and there were dinners with James Michener and Martin Scorsese, the heads of foundations and human rights organizations. More often than not, Annette would go along with him to act as his interpreter.

Ben was busy himself. His first play was being produced in a church basement in Soho and some days he would leave the house at eight in the morning, go directly from work to rehearsal and return home after midnight. Chang stopped coming to the house for dinner.

Then one Saturday morning Annette burst into tears and fled the apartment. When she came back two hours later, they sat down together in the kitchen. The air smelled of Comet Cleanser.

"So what is it?" he said.

"Nothing," she said. She shook her head. She'd had her hair cut and it was Jean Seberg short. "Nothing, really."

He reached across the rickety oak table to touch her hand. "Come on."

"I don't know. Some things maybe it's better not to talk about."

"That's not true. Not if you're married. I can handle it."

"You think?" She looked up at him with glistening brown eyes. Somewhere down on Broadway a street musician was playing very bad saxophone.

"I know I can."

She was silent for a long time. "We've been sleeping together. Chang and I."

It turned out that Ben was the one who'd been lying. He'd said he could handle it and he couldn't, not at all. It had never occurred to him that something like this was even possible. They talked and talked, for days, for weeks. She was an honest person. When he asked her a direct question she gave him a direct answer and that did not make things any better. She didn't want to end the marriage, but she wasn't ready to dump Chang either.

They met once, the three of them. Chang's difficulties with English made him seem somewhat simpler than he was, but he didn't flinch from what he'd done. He'd stood up to Mao; after that everything was a piece of cake. He was sorry to hurt his friend Ben, but he felt what he felt. They were all quite civil. Only later did Ben lose it entirely. "He's using you, you know that! He's just trying to get an American passport, it's the oldest scam in the book!"

Ben moved out finally. He was too ashamed to tell his parents, managing to conceal from them what had happened until the following Christmas. The only person he told the whole story to was Jonathan, Ben's closest friend and a young actor. It turned out to be a mistake. Jonathan, though he was the most supportive guy in the world, had never been able to resist a good tale and this was an irresistible one: cuckolded by an ex-Red Guard. Someone at a party made a crack and Ben realized to his horror that Jonathan had spilled the beans. Ben and Jonathan had a massive falling out and didn't speak for six months.

Ben learned his lesson: he learned to keep things to himself. For nearly three years he went emotionally underground. For a long time he didn't date and when he did, there was always something to make it impossible. Maybe what had happened between him and Annette had been the irreparable wound, or less melodramatically, maybe it had just made him, a naturally cautious man, more cautious. It wasn't until he met Katy, whose integrity shone like a beacon, that he felt he'd met a person he could utterly trust.

Over the years he'd come to hate frankness: the blabbers, the afternoon talk shows, the share your pain kind of guys. Emily Dickinson had it right; the truth needed to be told slant. No one could take it straight on: not the colleague whose life was sustained by the illusion that it was merely a cruel trick of fate that he was here in Texas, surrounded by, as he put it, ham and eggers, instead of being tenured at Yale, not the woman down the street married to the blowhard who consoled herself with the belief that he was so wonderful with the children.

Of course Ben should have told Katy about the money. He should have owned up, but he couldn't. The Nineties were not an era that held the truth in high regard (witness any congressional hearing or the French lit crit spin doctors, the advocates of deliberate slipperiness) but that wasn't it. The problem with Ben really wasn't a problem of the times. It was just the North Dakota in him. He was becoming more and more like his uncles, his mother's brothers, growing increasingly silent as the years passed, living alone in brick farmhouses after everyone had left, keeping their sorrows to themselves, knowing that talk seldom made anything better.

Chapter Four

He developed a simple set of rules. He never tried to cash a fifty for any purchase under twenty dollars; he'd learned his lesson at the Middle-Eastern restaurant. Once he'd broken a fifty at a place he never tried it at that place again. He avoided breaking large bills in the neighborhood or in places that he and Katy frequented.

Despite the rules, he gradually found ways to work the money into their life: buying sixty-five dollars worth of groceries with a one hundred dollar bill and pocketing the change, paying for his teeth cleaning in cash and bringing back the receipt and filing it with insurance, taking Abby and three of her friends to the movies and, while they were buying popcorn, paying for the tickets with one of his secreted fifties. Buying books was good. Any hard-cover book cost twenty-five to thirty-five dollars, which meant no cashier ever thought twice about cashing a fifty.

In a ledger in his office, he kept a record of all his transactions, as scrupulous as Thoreau.

AMT. CASHED	PURCHASE	
150.00	115.22	basketball shoes
100.00	65.17	groceries
100.00	62.50	Bookstop
100.00	60.00	Dr. Norman
50.00	25.00	movies
100.00	100.00	Castle Hill
50.00	36.00	Half-Price Books
50.00	22.50	b. cake

50.00	31.00	Appolinaire's
750.00	486.39	

Add to that the four hundred dollars he'd deposited in the bank and there was more than eleven hundred dollars he'd brought into his life in a single month. Yet it's effect was unnoticeable. When Ben sat down to do the bills, his bank balance, because of the hit they'd taken on the rebuilt transmission, was actually two hundred and forty-five dollars less than it had been at the end of December.

Ben stood in front of the open door of the cooler, trying to find a chilled twelve dollar of wine, when the bell sounded at the front of the liquor store. He glanced over his shoulder; two nice-looking men in rayon shirts had just come in, Mexicans or Colombians he would have guessed, and the clerk pushed up from his stool to greet them.

Ben was not a man who knew wines. His method was to get into a respectable price range and then pick a classy label. Not that he needed to impress anyone tonight; he and Katy were going over to their friends the Stricklands for fajitas and a game of hearts. He pulled a Fetzer Zinfandel from the top rack and headed for the front of the store.

He wasn't sure what made him pull up short; maybe it was the slightly queer look on the clerk's face or maybe it was the way one of the men stared intently out into the parking lot as if he were standing guard. For a second Ben thought he'd stumbled onto the start of a robbery, but it wasn't a robbery; just the opposite. The second of the two men, the taller one, was being perfectly cordial, almost courtly.

"It's just a question," he said. "All we want to know is whether anybody's been throwing around a lot of money in the neighborhood. Throwing big parties. Buying fancy cars."

"Not that I know of," the clerk said. The clerk's eyes were wide open, like an about-to-be-gigged frog.

"You're sure?"

"I'm sure."

It was as if Ben was invisible. He stood maybe ten feet away, clutching his wet bottle of Zinfandel, partially shielded by a cardboard cutout of the Bacardi girl. Both interrogators wore pants with no belts and their shoes were freshly shined. This was the moment Ben knew would come; for months he'd known it would come.

"So who would know?" the talker of the two asked.

"I don't really know."

The man who'd been watching the parking lot looked back quickly, irritated, and spied Ben for the first time. His friend was unperturbed. "I'll tell you what," he said. He pulled out his wallet and removed a hundred dollar bill. "Here's a little something," he said. "Just to keep your eyes open." As the man reached across the counter with the bill, Ben saw, between the man's thumb and forefinger, the inky black tatoo of a scorpion.

For the next two days Ben was in the blackest of moods, roller-coastering between raw terror and the wallow of self-disgust. What could he possibly have been thinking? That no one would notice that seven million dollars was missing? He'd been living in a dream world.

He couldn't sleep at night, tossing and turning, finally going out on the living room couch so he didn't disturb Katy. At four in the morning he found himself sitting with a glass of water in his hand, watching the headlights of a car crawl down the block, swing around the corner and slowly dissolve into darkness.

Days were equally grim. In the mailroom one of his colleagues gave him a quick double-take. "Whoa. What's wrong, man? You look like your dog died."

What was he going to do? It wasn't as if he could just give the money back; these people would kill him. Could he just let it sit in the storage unit and let it rot? Or drive into the country and leave all eight coolers in the middle of a cornfield? What a sensation that would be. There would be police, reporters. . . . And what if someone happened to spot him?

The other option was to call the police. He'd always rejected the thought before, but it wasn't too late. What crime had he actually committed? Maybe none. He'd been a little slow in reporting what he'd found, but anyone could understand that. He'd spent a little more than a thousand dollars and he could find a way to give it back; if it meant saving the lives of his family he sure as hell would find a way. He'd been lucky to see those two guys in the liquor store; it had been a wake-up call. This was a chance to get out before things got ugly. Was he going to spend the next thirty years running and hiding? He wasn't a criminal. He didn't have the nerves for it and he didn't have the training.

After the Qualifying Exam meeting on Tuesday he went to his office. He flopped the phone book open to the City Section and ran his finger down the page until he found the number of the Police Department.

Three times he picked up the receiver and sat with it in his hand, unable to dial. He'd never really been in the wrong before, his entire life. What if they arrested him? What if it came out in the papers? He would be the laughing-stock of the university; it could end up costing him his job. He had no business doing this until he talked to Katy.

The fourth time he picked up the receiver he finally punched in the number. It rang three times and a woman with a strong West Texas accent answered.

"Austin Police Department."

"Yes. Hello. I . . . uh . . . I wondered if I could speak to one of the officers."

"In regard to what?" She sounded as if it had been a long day.

"I found something that I think might have been stolen."

"A car?"

"No, not a car."

"Excuse me, I'm going to have to put you on hold."

With that she left him hanging in the air. He could feel something bubbling, high in his throat. He leaned forward in his chair and rubbed his temples with his fingers. Nobody gave a damn. He was on his own.

A knock on the door made him start. "Professor Lindberg?" The knock sounded him again. "Professor Lindberg, are you in there?" It was Marcie from the Graduate Office; he had promised her his course description for the fall.

"I'll be right with you," he said. He set the receiver back on the phone, gently, the way you might set a fallen baby bird back in its nest.

The next day, when he thought about what he'd nearly done, he wondered what had come over him. He felt vaguely ashamed. How could he have let himself get worked up in such a state? What a break it had been, the woman on the switchboard putting him on hold. What a narrow escape! She could have put him through to some grand-standing cop out to make a name for himself and Ben could have ended up with his face plastered all over the morning *american Statesman*, his life in ruins. He needed to calm down, to truly think this through, not just go crazy.

It was a good thing he hadn't given the switchboard operator his name. On the other hand, if anyone in the world had Caller I.D.

you'd figure it would be the police. He wasn't going to think about it. You'd have to be totally paranoid to believe that the cops would go through every phone call they got in a day to check out who it was from.

The February weather continued to be sunny and gorgeous. After one day and then two, the urgency he'd felt began to ebb, like the fading of an old toothache. No Colombian bad guys with machine guns showed up at his door. Every day he took the bus into work and every day he came back. In the evenings he helped his kids with their homework and watched the Seinfeld reruns at nine-thirty with Matt. Ordinary life closed in around him, comforting as a balm over a wound.

He got a call from Sammy Bishop, the manager of the softball team, saying that their first practice was on Sunday. It always caught Ben off-guard, starting the spring softball season in February, but then this was Texas.

He had played on the team for four years. It was a squad loosely sponsored by *Texas Progressive*, a muck-raking and constantly impoverished left-wing publication that had been around since the fifties. A little over half the players had some affiliation with the magazine. The slick-fielding shortstop was a former editor, the midwife who'd once brought a tape recorder to the dugout so they could play the Sandinista national anthem before the game was a board member and there were a couple of laid-back lawyers and actors who were always willing to pitch in during fund-raisers. Ben had found his own political instincts growing increasingly cranky and complicated as he'd gotten older, but these were people he felt comfortable with and he loved softball.

On Sunday Ben was one of the first ones out. They threw some behind the bleachers, warming up stiff arms, joking around, trading stories, and when it was time to hit Ben was the first one to the plate.

His first swings felt slow and leaden. He kept hitting the ball into the dirt and in off the hands, despite the fact that Sammy's soft tosses looked big as melons, but finally he got into a groove. He hit three or four shots in a row, the last one hard enough that Alex misjudged it in right field, coming in only to have it soar ten feet over his head and rattle off the fence on one bounce. Ben flipped his bat away and went to retrieve his glove.

He trotted out to the outfield where Alex and Don Marcus were gabbing about some dope-dealing client of Alex's who'd just been arrested.

"It's stupid," Alex said. "You'd think these FBI guys would have something better to do with their time. Charlie's just this old Travis Heights hippie who maybe sells ten ounces of marijuana a week and running his money through these gun and knife shows. If they're going to bust him they might as well bust half of South Austin."

Tracy, one of the new women Sammy had recruited, laced a hard liner over second. Don scampered over to see if he could make a shoe-string catch, but the ball skipped under his glove. Everyone hooted and Sammy waved for Don to come in and take his cuts.

Ben jogged out to retrieve the ball. In the distance white steam curled out of the Power Station towers. He underhanded the ball into Alex, who whirled and lobbed it in the direction of the mound, the ball bumping and rolling across the rough dirt infield.

"I don't understand," Ben said. "When you say he was running this money through these gun and knife shows, what do you mean?"

"It's simple. It's the oldest scam in the world," Alex said. Tracy hit a scorcher down the right field line. She'd played softball for the U.T. varsity and even though her politics were suspect (she worked in marketing), she looked as if she was just what the team needed. "Say you're a small-time dope dealer. You've got all this cash, right? And you've got no way to account for it with Uncle Sam. So you go to a gun show, you buy a gun for eight hundred dollars, cash, you walk down the aisle and sell it to another guy for six hundred and you get yourself a receipt."

"I'm sorry, Alex, I'm a little slow here." Don whirled three bats behind his head as he walked to the plate and all the fielders moved around to the left.

"If the IRS ever asks you, you tell them the gun was part of your grandfather's private collection." Alex ran his hand over his salt and pepper beard and then pounded his glove. "It's so simple a three year old could get away with it. Except, of course, unless you're Charlie and make the mistake of blabbing to somebody and then, when they call you in, lose all your boxes of receipts."

Ben stopped leaving his wallet on the dresser at night. He didn't want Katy coming on a wad of fifties in those early morning scrambles for lunch money. With each week that passed Ben had become more cautious, more able to imagine the million nightmarish scenarios through which he might be discovered: Rose, say, calling the

house after a monster rainstorm had damaged some of the roofs of
the storage units and getting Katy on the phone, or a suspicious
bookstore clerk, a slip of the tongue, some cleaning guy at the University opening a drawer that he shouldn't.

Yet there was no sign that Katy was suspicious. There had been
the incident in the front yard after he bought Matt's basketball
shoes, but nothing else really. It was almost too easy. He was the one
who paid the bills and Katy was not what anyone would call a fas-
tidious balancer of the check-book. What he was banking on was an
unspoken reservoir of trust and hadn't he earned it? Through seventeen years of marriage he had been an utterly faithful husband.
As far as he could tell, she hadn't noticed any difference in their lives.

The difference came when Katy started her practice teaching the
second week of February, fourth grade at an elementary school in
East Austin. It was not easy for any of them. Katy was, as a friend
once labelled her, a genius of domestic life. She was the most com-
petent human being Ben had ever met and, at home, a person of
strong opinions, no push-over, yet she'd always had a weird lack of
self-confidence about work.

She didn't really want to go back to work—she wasn't sure how
it would affect Matt and Abby, she wasn't sure she would be any
good as a teacher, she was older now, she'd been away for too long—
but she felt as if there wasn't any choice. For them to be able to buy
a house, to have the kind of life they wanted to have, they needed
two incomes. And besides, now, when they were at faculty parties
and people asked her what she did, she would have an answer. She
would finish her certification in the spring and apply for paying jobs
in the fall.

The consequences of her being gone all day were immediate. She
had to be at Ortiz Elementary by seven-fifteen, which meant getting
up before six. Ben had to take both children to school and at night
Katy was up until eleven-thirty making lesson plans. He was now
the one doing the dishes and sorting the laundry. On Wednesday
night when she had her educational methods class at the University
Ben would take Matt and Abby to Mr. Gatti's for pizza.

What a sham it was! It was eating Ben alive. They had all the
money they would ever need, Ben just had to find a way for them to
use it; someone smarter or bolder would have figured it out by now.
He continued to spend hours in the library, his head aswirl with tales
of bank examiners and the Russian mafia. What he was looking for
was a simple scheme. What it boiled down to was he had to either

find a way to get into a cash intensive business like a casino, a massage parlor or an amusement arcade or he had to get up enough nerve to get on a plane to the Bahamas with bagfuls of money. He still could not imagine how he would do either.

On Tuesday night Katy was working late, preparing a unit on the Indians of Texas, and Ben watched the news alone—there was another report on the MOPAC rapist and a report on cedar fever—but when it was over he shambled into the kitchen, looking for company.

"You about ready to go to bed?" he said.

"Not quite yet. You go ahead." She smiled at him, curled up in the big chair by the desk. It had never been a problem, Ben being attracted to her. People always said she looked a little like Audrey Hepburn. She would always deflect that—no, she was just a simple country girl, she would counter—and though she was stronger-looking than Audrey Hepburn, there was something to what people said.

"You sure?" Ben said. "You look tired."

"I just have to get this done. I won't be long."

He went upstairs and brushed his teeth and got into bed. He tossed and turned, but only found himself getting angrier and angrier. When did they ever go to bed together anymore? She was just too stubborn, too obsessive. Maybe he was being a big baby, but every night was like this. He rolled over, scrunching up his pillow. A siren wailed in the distance.

He must have fallen asleep, because when he woke it felt like the middle of the night. He reached across, patting the cold bedspread, and then realized that Katy wasn't there. He turned and saw the line of light under the door; she was still down in the kitchen. He got out of bed and peered at the digital clock. It was twelve-fifteen.

He padded down the stairs in his over-sized Milwaukee Brewers t-shirt. Katy sat hunched over the desk now, making a huge chart out of construction paper.

"Katy, come on, this is nuts. It's nearly twelve-thirty."

As she swung around, magic marker in hand, he could see the map of Texas she'd made with the names of all the Indian tribes in bright colors—Comanche and Apache, Karankawa and Caddo.

"It's almost done," Katy said.

"God damn it!" Ben said. "This is for a bunch of fourth-graders!"

She turned away from him and snapped the top back on the magic marker. Ben waited, not sure what she was going to do and then he realized that she was crying.

"I'm sorry," Ben said. Somewhere the cat scratched at an outside screen, waiting to be let in. Ben stood motionless for several seconds, feeling like a hairy beast in his underwear, and then came down the stairs. The floor was cold on his bare feet. He put his hand on her shoulder and she slid out from under his touch.

"What is wrong, Ben?"

"We're both just tired."

"It's more than that. Ever since we got back from Christmas you've seemed so angry."

"I'm not angry."

"Is it my teaching, is that it?"

"No."

"Then what is it? I feel as if you're somewhere else. I feel as if, sometimes, you just looking at me as if I'm crazy."

He ran his tongue across his teeth, like a man who has just swallowed a bitter pill. "No, you're not the one who's crazy, I promise."

On Wednesday night, when Katy was at the University and the kids were in bed, Ben sat in front of the television, eating a piece of cake and watching an old John Wayne Western. When the commercials came on he leaned over to switch channels, but his finger froze on the dial. The ad was for the Travis County Knife and Gun Show, all day Saturday and Sunday at the Coliseum.

On Sunday afternoon Ben announced to Katy that he was going to the Hike and Bike Trail and take a run. Instead he drove to his office, got eight one hundred dollar bills out of the envelope in the bottom drawer of his desk and drove back to the Coliseum.

The parking lot was jammed. Ben had to drive around for three or four minutes before he found a place and when he got out of the van an old country couple was packing a brand-new rifle into the trunk of the car next to him.

Tickets were three dollars and the signs plastered around the box-office windows were ominous—NO LIVE AMMO—NO CONCEALED WEAPONS. Inside, the space was cavernous and echoey as a roller rink. Ben wandered up and down the aisles, getting the lay of the land, telling himself that this was just an experiment, a foray.

There was every kind of gun and everything associated with guns—grips, scopes, holsters, ammo clips—but there were also crossbows and peppergas cannisters, blowguns and paintball equipment. It had the down-at-the-heels feel of a carnival on an Indian reservation. The chubby eleven year old son of one of the exhibitors sat in a metal chair stuffing his face with nachos while the loud-speakers blared out the old country song, "I Fought the Law and the Law Won." At a bookstand of survivalist literature a scar-faced man wearing two floppy stocking hats, one set atop the other like stacked ice-cream cones, perused a pamphlet entitled, BIG SISTER IS WATCHING YOU.

It struck Ben how many of the people there were maimed or crippled in some way; a man in camouflage gear sitting in a wheelchair, spitting snuff into a metal cup, a huge Chicano skinhead in a Dallas Cowboy jacket hobbling past on crutches.

His heart dropped when he saw, at several tables, men filling out forms. It wasn't as simple as Alex had described it. Guns had to be registered, there were waiting periods and checks run by local police departments, the last thing Ben needed.

Set against the west wall, away from the other booths, was a sagging white banner that announced Western Specialties. Antique guns were laid out on coyote skins. Ben wandered from table to table, fingering the tags. He ran his hand over the polished stock of a long rifle that looked as if it could have belonged to Daniel Boone.

"Beautiful gun, isn't it? Go ahead, pick it up." The old man behind the table had the manner of a British colonial officer and a hat decorated with rattlesnake rattles. He picked the gun up and laid it in Ben's hands. Ben turned it over. He hadn't held a gun since he'd gone squirrel-hunting when he was fifteen.

"It's an old cavalry gun. Reproduction of an Eighteen Seventy-three Winchester. It's a great shooting gun. You can still hit a steel silhouette at three hundred yards with it. Let me show you this. . . ." The old man reached across and slid back a thin metal panel on the top of the barrel. "That's the dust shield. When they were out riding they needed it to keep the grit out of the works."

"So how much is it?"

"Eight hundred dollars."

"Now let me ask you. I'm new to all this. Say I wanted to buy this gun, there would be a certain amount of paperwork. . . ."

Ben thought he was being subtle, but the man in the rattlesnake hat was a mile ahead of him. "Well, with that one there would be. But let me show you something else." He took the rifle from Ben and laid it carefully back on the coyote skin. He gestured to the revolvers at the far end of the table.

"Now these over here are part of my private collection, which means nobody has to fill out any Brady Bill forms, there's no background check. You pay me, you can walk right out of here with your gun. There's a lot of good honest people in this country, they just don't like the government messing in their business."

He took a small, shiny revolver that had been propped up by an owl's pelvis and offered it for inspection, handle first. The weight of the gun surprised Ben.

"Colt Thunderer with a bird's head grip. Three and a half inch barrel, it's a fine piece for conceal and carry. In the Old West they used to call them belly guns."

"So how much is it?"

"I can give it to you for five hundred and fifty dollars. I'll pay the tax."

Ben stared at the gun in his hand, so small it looked like a toy. If he bought it, he was then faced with the task of selling it. Alex had said all he had to do was walk down the aisle and find a buyer, but what if he wasn't able to, where could he keep it? He couldn't imagine taking it home. What if one of the kids found it?

"O.K., for you, I'll knock it down to five twenty-five."

Ben glanced up at the old man. He thought Ben's hesitation was just part of his bargaining technique. He gave a wry little smile as if to say, you're too slick for me, and the smile caught Ben off-guard, dispelling his fear for just long enough.

"O.K.," Ben found himself saying, "five twenty-five. You take cash?"

"Absolutely."

Ben handed the gun back to the man in the rattlesnake hat and reached for his wallet. He took a sidelong glance, just to be sure than no one was watching, and then counted out five hundreds and a fifty. The man in the rattlesnake hat went to his cashbox and gave Ben two twenties and a five. He wrote a receipt, wrapped the gun in a soft grey cloth and set it quietly in a small cardboard box. He slipped the box into a plastic bag and handed the bag to Ben.

"It's been a pleasure doing business with you," he said.

"It's been a pleasure doing business with you," Ben said and they shook hands. Ben could feel the blood racing through his temples. He had taken four or five steps before he heard someone call out behind him.

"Hey, professor!"

Ben turned. Sweeney, looking quite delighted, stumbled out from between two racks of t-shirts.

"Hey, professor, how you doin'?" Sweeney set a t-shirt emblazoned with the picture of a Golden Retriever back on its hanger and sauntered over, his thumbs in the pockets of his jeans. "Geez, you never know who you're going to run into at these places, do you?"

"I guess not," Ben said. Sweeney could not hide how pleased he was.

"So what you doin' here?"

"Nothing much. It's just interesting to look."

"Looks like you've been doing more than looking." Sweeney tapped Ben's bag lightly with his finger. Ben felt his face color; he shouldn't have tried to lie; he wasn't any good at it. Sweeney's big smile faded, turned curious and speculative.

"Listen, Dan, it's good to see you, but I'm afraid I've got to run."

"You serious? I was just on my way out myself," Sweeney said. "I'll walk you out."

They made their way silently past the security guards, out into the sunlight. A woman was selling wooden popguns out of the back of her truck. Across the street Ben could see a team of rowers out on Town Lake, perfectly synchronized, knifing through the water. Ben felt sick to his stomach, but he couldn't afford to panic.

"So I guess we're doing old Margaret Fuller next week, huh?" Sweeney said.

"That's right."

"I'll tell you, I've been having a great time in there. It's probably one of the best courses I've ever had at the University. No bull."

"That's always nice to hear." The plastic sack with the gun inside swung at Ben's side. Ben gestured with his thumb. "I guess I'm parked over here."

"Listen, I've been meaning to ask you about something, if you had a minute."

"Sure."

Sweeney rubbed his nose with his knuckle. "I was wondering if you'd like to go over to The Green Mesquite, let me buy you a beer, we could talk about it. I haven't had anything to eat all day."

"I should be getting home."

Sweeney ruminated for a moment, toeing a spot of tar on the cement, then looked up sharply. "It won't take long. I just need your advice about something."

Ordinarily Ben wouldn't have let himself be bullied, but he was in a weak position; this was not a moment when he wanted to piss Sweeney off. "Sure. Why not? For a few minutes."

Sweeney grinned. "Great. I'll meet you over there."

Ben went to his van, fuming, and slipped the gun under his front seat. It didn't look as if he was going to be selling it today. He drove over to The Green Mesquite, berating himself for letting Sweeney badger him into this. Sweeney was just a student and Ben knew how to handle students; he needed to remind himself of that.

Sweeney was waiting in the small parking lot as Ben drove in, leaning against the portable sign that announced TWO MEAT PLATE 5.79. He looked happy as a lark. Inside they found a booth near the front and Ben ordered a Coke while Sweeney ordered a Shiner Bach and a brisket platter—barbeque, beans, coleslaw, creamy potato salad, the works. Sweeney ate with relish; Ben noticed for the first time how small his hands were.

What Sweeney wanted advice about was graduate school. He loved books and it seemed to him that being a professor would be a great life, but he wanted to know what the chances would be for someone like himself, realistically. His overall GPA wasn't great—he'd flunked out as a freshman and come close a couple of other times back when he was young and foolish—but he did have a straight 4.0 in his upper division English classes.

Sweeney ordered a second Shiner and shook the ketchup bottle of barbque sauce over his brisket. The brown sauce sputtered out in short flatulent bursts. Ben nursed his Coke.

Ben gave him the advice he gave to everyone: don't do it unless you can get into a first-rate program. The profession was too tight. There were some areas where they were still hiring—Rhetoric and Composition, Third World—but the old dream of getting out of graduate school and going to a big research university where you would teach a two-two load and write your books was slipping away for all but the most select elite.

Sweeney seemed to take it like a man. The waitress came by with his beer. A band had begun to warm up in the sunny beer garden. He wiped off the mouth of his bottle.

"That bad, huh?" Sweeney said.

"That bad."

"Hope it's not so bad you're thinking about shooting yourself."

"What do you mean?"

"I was joking." Sweeney took a swig of his beer. "So what kind of gun did you get?" In the next booth two old men in cheap Sunday suits leaned over their cobbler.

"A Colt Thunderer."

"Are you kidding me? The little one with the short barrel? Man, that is a pretty little gun. I don't believe this. I was thinking about buying that myself. So what does it shoot?"

"What do you mean?" The fan moved slowly overhead. At the counter a huge man in suspenders pointed out a spot of barbeque sauce on his shirt to the cashier.

"What caliber. Forty-fives, forty-four forty. . . ."

"I don't remember."

Sweeney picked at the label on his bottle, sensing Ben's discomfort. If he thought Ben was a fool, he kept it to himself. "If you don't mind my asking, what did you pay for it?"

Ben hesitated. Sweeney beamed. It occurred to Ben that maybe the beer had loosened him up, made him a little more aggressive.

"A little over five hundred."

"Not bad," Sweeney said. A waitress cruised by carrying two huge platters of ribs. "What would you say if I offered you six for it?"

"I just bought it."

"I know you just bought it. What about six-fifty?"

The music coming out of the beer garden wasn't bad. They were playing some old Bill Monroe song with furious mandolins. Through the screen door Ben could see an old couple dancing, the flash of a red skirt. Sweeney leaned to one side so he could wrestle his wallet free. He counted out seven one hundred dollar bills and set them on the green checkered tablecloth.

Chapter Five

He did not sell Sweeney the gun. Sitting with Sweeney's seven hundred dollars on the green checkered tablecloth in front of him, he balked, though he knew that balking alone was not enough to save him.

In class on Monday Ben could scarcely bring himself to look at Sweeney. Ben considered calling him up after the bell, telling him that he would appreciate Sweeney's not mentioning their encounter at the Coliseum, but decided against it. He didn't want to add any more spice to an already spicy situation.

The cat was probably already out of the bag anyway. What student could resist telling a story about their pistol-packing professor? Ben fully expected the story to be all over the department in a matter of hours. That afternoon Ben drove to Lake Buchanan and threw the Colt Thunderer over the dam.

All day Tuesday he kept waiting for someone to come up to him and say something, yet no one did. On Wednesday when Ben walked into class Sweeney was reading an article in *The Daily Texan* out loud to his claque in the back. Ben walked to the podium, waiting for the first smirk, the first knowing snicker, some sign that Sweeney had spilled the beans, but there was none.

On Thursday Sweeney came in to discuss his term paper. The topic was a good one: Going Native, Thoreau and the Indians. Ben suggested that he read the captivity tales in Michael Slotkin's *Regeneration Through Violence* and Robert Sayre's book.

As Sweeney dutifully scribbled down all the references, there was a timid knock on the door. Ben leaned across and opened the door, staring up into the kindly face of Sam Steinbach, the department's senior Americanist.

"I'm sorry," Sam said. "I see you're busy."

"No, that's fine," Ben said. "We're just about done anyway."

"All I need is thirty seconds," Sam said.

"Sure." Ben rose from his chair, gesturing to Sweeney to stay put. "Don't go anywhere. I'll be right back." Ben followed Steinbach into the hallway, pulling the door shut behind him. "Everything all right?"

"Everything's fine." Sam was a sweet man, with the sad eyes of a beagle and the furtive manners of a police informer. He was the world's leading authority of William Dean Howells and he'd been through the academic wars. "You know we have this candidate coming in tomorrow."

"Yes. I was planning on going to his talk."

"Margaret and I were intending to have a small dinner party for him but a couple of people have bailed on us. Charles read his world and says hell will have to freeze over before he even speaks to the man and Jane has the flu. I know this is awfully last minute, but I was hoping that you and your wife might come."

"We'd be delighted to," Ben said. "Let me just check at home to be sure it's all right and I'll call you."

"I appreciate this. Margaret and I both like Kathy so much and she's so gracious at these things. . . ."

"Katy," Ben said.

"Katy! That's right! I'm sorry." Sam looked both ways just to be sure no graduate students were within earshot. "It's not as if I'm so crazy about the man's work myself. I mean, class, race, gender, well, whoop de do. But we all need to be civilized about these things." He clapped Ben heartily on the shoulder. "Thank God there are still a few people who write in English around here. How's the work coming?"

"Great guns," Ben said. If he let him, Sam would go on all afternoon and Ben was starting to get nervous about leaving Sweeney unattended in his office. He took a step away. "I'll call you tonight."

When Ben pushed open the door, Sweeney was sitting just as Ben had left him, with his backpack between his ankles, but there was something different about him, something a little Sunday Schoolboy smarmy about his smile.

"So where were we?" Ben asked.

"I think we're done," Sweeney said. "At least I hope we are, because I've got enough reading here to last me till Christmas." Ben stared at him. There was definitely something off; he could hear it in Sweeney's voice.

"I've got something for you," Sweeney said. He dug an orange flyer out of his backpack and handed it to Ben. It was the announcement of a club opening downtown in two weeks. "It would be great if you could come. It's going to be cool. It's a little place me and my friends have been putting together."

"I'd love to," Ben said. "But I'm afraid we're going to be out of town."

Sweeney grinned. "I guess those are the breaks."

As soon as Sweeney left, Ben closed the door and went to his desk. He yanked open the bottom drawer and with trembling hands rifled through the stacks of student papers and battered manuscript boxes. He lifted out the manila envelope concealed in the back and undid the metal clasp.

He poured the contents onto his desk, seventeen hundred dollars, all if fifties. He counted it again, just to be sure, then put it all back in the tawny envelope. He lay the envelope in the drawer and carefully re-buried in under a mountain of paper.

He sat for a moment, covering his eyes with his hands. He could hear students laughing in the hallway, passing between classes. It was crazy to think that Sweeney would have had the nerve to go through his desk. Then what had he seen on Sweeney's face? Maybe Ben was just losing it, making things up out of thin air.

He opened his eyes and scanned the room. His gaze drifted and then snagged. There it was: the ledger, sitting in clear view atop some old course schedules on the bookshelf. He leaned forward and snatched it.

It shouldn't have been there. Ben had always kept it in the corner file cabinet, behind the teaching evaluation folders. Every time he made an entry he was scrupulous about putting the ledger back. How could he be slipping up like this?

He flipped quickly though it. There were three full pages of entries now. He turned to the last set of columns, letting his eyes run down the neat rows of figures.

AMT. CASHED	PURCHASE	
100.00	75.40	Run-Tex
50.00	18.12	Chevron
50.00	37.57	Randall's

100.00	83.85	Fitting Stool
100.00	70.34	Circuit City
50.00	29.25	Wal-Mart
	50.00	34.66 Office Depot
100.00	82.00	HEB
550.00	525.00	Gun Show

They drove to Mississippi for spring break and spent a week on the farm with Katy's mother, her brother and his family. Everyone took care of themselves. Abby and Matt had their cousins, Katy had her mother and Ben worked and read until the late afternoon when he rounded up the children and the cane poles and drove them to the Twin Ponds where they fished for bream until the sun went down.

It was a wonderful week, but when they got back to Austin obligation descended like a hammer. Katy still had four weeks of practice teaching and Ben was inundated with classes, the reading of term papers and the ferrying of children.

The dread he felt was constant, like a low grade fever. He was faced with an impossible task; he wanted the money to make a difference in their lives, yet he had to do it in such a way that Katy didn't notice that difference. The storage unit was not safe enough. Not only was there the risk of being spotted, but each time he went he was forced to tell Katy another lie. Someone was going to discover the money was gone, sooner or later, and when they did, they would come looking for him, come looking with a vengeance.

One night Katy shook him out of a deep sleep. He rolled onto his side, thinking the problem was that he had been snoring, but she shook him again. "Ben, there is someone outside," she said.

"What?"

"There's someone outside on the lawn."

He pushed up on his elbows, still groggy. "What time is it?"

"Almost midnight."

His heart was pounding. He didn't move and, after a second, he could hear voices too, and a soft thudding sound, close to the house.

"Would you go see?"

"Yeah," Ben said.

He rolled out of bed and felt along the top of his dresser until he found his glasses. He went to the window and peered out. He didn't see anyone, just the long shadows of the trees stretching across the dry lawn, but because the bedroom was up under the pitched roof, his field of vision was restricted. He went to the closet. As he pulled out his metal softball bat it made a soft ping against the wooden door frame.

"What are you doing?" Katy said.

"Nothing," he said. "I'm just going to go see."

He crept down the stairs in his bare feet, dressed only in his underwear, and moved past Abby's bedroom, through the dining room, into the front hall. He heard the patter of running feet; it almost sounded as if there was someone up on the porch. If they killed him it was one thing, just as long as they left his family alone. It occurred to him to call the police, but there wasn't that much time.

He went to the front door. He held the bat at his side and turned the knob slowly, careful not to make a sound, and eased the door open. Long white streamers floated in the live oak tree and there were also streamers wrapped around the bushes on the side lawn.

"Look out! He's coming!"

The warning cry was young and feminine. Suddenly Ben saw them; three or four twelve year old girls standing on the dark lawn with their rolls of toilet paper, a couple more leaning against parked cars at the curb. Another girl burst out of the bushes to Ben's left and then they all ran, not stopping until they were halfway down the block.

Ben stood in the half-open doorway watching them, skittish as deer under the streetlight, unsure whether he was coming after them or not. He thought he recognized one of them from Matt's class. After a few seconds they began to drift on down the street.

Ben leaned the metal bat against the desk. He stood there for a couple of minutes, just breathing, in and out, trying to get back to normal, and then bent down and picked up a roll of toilet paper from the porch and began to reel it in.

Night after night he lay in bed, trying to come up with a solution. The things he found himself considering bordered on absurdity: purchasing herds of cattle in Mexico, buying lottery tickets by the thousands, opening a chain of copy shops. He cursed himself for his ignorance. What did he know about the way the world worked? Nothing. He felt like a wasp, trapped between two panes of glass, battering endlessly and in vain. Then one evening, taking a shower, the solution came to him, so obvious he couldn't believe he hadn't thought of it before. He called Jonathan the next afternoon from school.

He had met Jonathan in New York, nearly twenty years ago, and their friendship had survived through good times and bad. Jonathan had been an actor then and quite a good one, small, dark, and flamboyant, with huge eyes and mobile features, the Al Pacino of Off-Off-Broadway he used to call himself, but after banging around for ten years he went to work in a producer's office and eventually became a producer himself.

His first big legitimate success came when he brought in some of the money to revive *Showboat*. Katy and Ben had taken the kids to New York and Jonathan had gotten them orchestra seats and took them backstage afterwards to meet the stars. It was the most glamorous night in the kids' lives, and perhaps in Katy and Ben's.

Jonathan had since gone on to produce a number of shows on his own—some had been successes, others not—but he was always looking for money. Also in his favor, given what Ben intended to propose, was that Jonathan, charming and as generous as he was, was not above bending the rules when it suited him.

"Hey, my man!" Jonathan's voice blasted through the phone; Ben had to hold the receiver a little away from his ear.

"Great, Jonathan, how you doin'?"

"Great, man! So how's Texas? Those big gushers still coming in down there?" As far as Jonathan was concerned, Texas might as well have been in the Gobi desert. "Your family O.K.?"

"Yeah, we're doing fine. So how are things up in the Apple?"

"Oh, you don't want to know. My love-life's as big a mess as ever, but I'll get through it. The good news is I'm trying to raise money for our pal David's play and I think we've just lined up John Tillinger to direct."

"Listen, Jonathan, there's a reason I called. There's a guy I know down here. He's got a lot of money."

"Sounds like a guy I'd like to meet." There was a series of bangs and rustlings on the other end of the line. "Hey, sweetheart, you're going out, could you get me a Danish and some coffee . . . You're a doll. . . . So what about this friend of yours?"

"I think he might be interested in investing."

"So give me his name."

"There's just one catch. I don't know if it would be a problem or not. I think it's in cash."

Jonathan brayed with laughter. "That's too wonderful! So what, he wants me to launder his drug money for him?"

"Jonathan, it's not what you think."

"So where did you meet this guy?"

"Some party. He seems like a perfectly respectable guy. He's got a couple of kids, a nice wife, a big house in the hills."

"So what is he, one of those S and L guys?"

"I don't know, Jonathan, I don't know."

"Of course you don't know, you big lug, but *I* know. If I were you I would not be hanging around this guy."

"I'm sorry. I shouldn't have called."

"Hey, what are you talking about? I've been missing you guys. When are you coming up to the city? I want to see those kids of yours!"

Sweeney had become a model of decorum—a bit more serious than before, a bit quieter, but quick to take on the role of Ben's defender in any classroom debate. On their walks back to Parlin after class Sweeney gradually began to open up about himself. He'd grown up just outside Houston and his father had been a charmer, a drinker, a fast-talker who'd made a lot of money and then lost it all a half-dozen times. He'd been in the lawn-maintenance business, run a topless bar and an air-conditioning company. "If you can go broke in the air-conditioning business in Houston," Sweeney said, "what hope can there be?" One week he would beat Sweeney with a razor-strap after catching him trying to make plum wine in his closet and the next week he would pull Sweeney out of school so they could go fly-fishing in New Mexico. His father left the family for good when Sweeney was seventeen and two years later was shot to death outside a casino in Atlantic City.

The more they talked, the clearer it got to Ben that, even though Sweeney was twenty-eight, he was still very much a student. Behind all the strut and flash was an essential naivete; Sweeney still believed there were answers to the Big Questions.

One morning they stood in front of the statue of a Civil War general, talking about life in the Eighteen-Forties as students poured out of the double-doors of Parlin. "So do you think things were better then?" Sweeney asked.

"It's a complicated question," Ben said.

"I know it's complicated, but what do you think?"

"I think it was better. I think there was more hope then. I think there was a real enthusiasm about democracy. You understand when I say this, I'm aware that slavery still existed, that the Indians were being decimated."

"Yeah, yeah, I know . . ." The sea of students parted around them. In the Calhoun walkway the department's senior medievalist snuck a quick smoke between classes.

"But on the other hand there was this magnificent and unexplored country out there. If things weren't working out in one place you could always pick up and go." A frisbee hovered above the green lawn. "Maybe it was just that the country was younger then."

"What do you mean?"

"You know how it is when you're young. You feel like you can take on anything, you're so full of juice. But later on things get more complicated. You realize that you don't have as many choices as you thought you had."

Their eyes met for a second and then Sweeney looked away. A Buildings and Grounds truck eased its way down the sidewalk with a crew of men with rakes in the back.

"But you do," Sweeney said. "Still have choices. Only I guess sometimes you don't realize it."

Sometimes when Katy finally came to bed she would tell Ben stories about what her days were like: reciting the pledge of allegiance in a noisy gym, the kids fussing in the hallway over who was going to be line leader (Katy had learned early on that teachers were judged on how orderly their lines were). Half the battle was crowd management; most of the day seemed to be spent telling kids to keep their hands to themselves. The kids Katy was seeing had so much other than school to deal with: a drug-addicted mother, a father in prison, eviction notices, welfare checks that didn't arrive. The joke was that all the children were on Ridilin and all the teachers on Prosac.

Ben had not foreseen the effects of prolonged deceit. Keeping the money secret was a little like keeping a mistress; deceptions compounded in unexpected ways. Every day that passed only made the possibility of honesty more remote.

The way things were now he couldn't help but become increasingly angry at Katy, as unfair as that was. She'd become any obstacle, an adversary. He'd become even more convinced that if he did tell her she would make him turn the money in. Even if she did go along, she would waffle, there would be qualms, her insecurities would make it impossible. Or she'd say something to her sister. Didn't she tell everything to her sister? No, this was a one-person operation.

One afternoon Ben came upon a gathering on men in suits in a state of high hilarity in front of the departmental office. Several of

them he knew—the chairman and a couple of the deans whose faces
Ben recognized from their pictures in *The Daily Texan*—and one he
didn't—a handsome, smallish man in his mid-sixties whose stories
were keeping the others in stitches. The older man had a spark and
an ease, with an open collar and the ruddy, wind-burned complex-
ion of someone who spent a lot of time out of doors.

The chairman waved Ben over and introduced him, but Ben did-
n't quite catch the older man's name. Late in the afternoon Ben
asked one of the secretaries what was going on. She said there had
been a big lunch with a potential donor, someone who was actually
considering giving the department a new building.

Why was Ben the last man on earth to understand? Money talks
and it was talking to him, night and day. The possibilities were dazzling, almost infinite. All he needed was to keep his head on his
shoulders. All his life, he saw now, he'd been living in a fog of book-
ish idealism. He'd never come to terms with the real world. He'd
never done the most basic thing a man was supposed to do (a phrase
he could have never dared use around his own department); he had-
n't provided for his family, not well enough. This was not, when he
really thought about it, the first time he'd ever lied to Katy. The first
lie had been telling her all those years that everything was going to
be O.K., when he didn't have a clue.

Yet he needed her more than ever. For the past week he hadn't
been able to go to sleep unless he was touching her hand or shoulder. He kept telling her that he loved her, too many times, like some
anxious nineteen year old. He had always been the easy-going one
with the kids, the one they would turn to after Katy laid down the
law, but now he was increasingly short-tempered.

How could he keep such a thing secret? There were too many ways
to be tripped up. One Saturday morning he walked into the kitchen
to find Katy in front of the washing machine, emptying out the
pockets of a pair of his trousers.

"Here," she said. "You may want these."

Without examining what she had, she poured it all in his hands: a
pen, a half-dozen quarters and the crumpled-up receipt for Burnet
Self-Storage.

The last weekend in March Patrick O'Bannon, a robust Australian
poet, came to give a reading. Ben was one of several faculty members who went to dinner with him after his Dylan Thomas-like per-
formance and, to Ben's dismay, the one who was somehow roped

into showing O'Bannon Austin's nightlife. O'Bannon was a blues fanatic and when someone mentioned at dinner that the fabled Mississippi bluesman Son Jones was playing at *Cinders*, O'Bannon's big blue eyes went wide with yearning.

Cinders had been around for a decade, succeeding in spite of its dubious location, sandwiched between abandoned warehouses and the Union Pacific tracks. In the past two or three years a couple of smaller clubs and a dismal all-night coffee shop had taken root around it, but it had lost little of its back-alley appeal.

It was a Friday night and Ben and O'Bannon had to park more than a block away, along a pot-holed street that ran along the tracks. The club was raucous and smoky, but Ben spotted three guys from the History Department he knew. All three were going through divorces and huddled around a tiny table with a visiting English economist, a lovely, long-necked woman with Pre-Raphaelite looks and a capacity for beer. It took O'Bannon no more than ten minutes to become fast friends with all of them.

Ben stayed for one set. Son Jones had an implacable manner, a raspy voice and lyrics as down and dirty as any middle-aged suburban white man could want. The audience went wild. O'Bannon stood and whistled and cheered as if he was at a rugby match, put his hand on the shoulder of the English economist, whispering something in her ear that made her laugh.

Ben saw that he was no longer needed. When he told O'Bannon at midnight that he was taking off, it was not a problem; the Irish poet was happy to find his own way home.

Stepping out into the cool night air, Ben realized how weary he was. He'd been up since six. People were still arriving; a black couple hurried between cars, the man fussing at his wife for making them late. She was fifty, a little heavy, in a black dress that shimmered like fish scales and she wobbled a bit, trying to cross the gravel in high heels.

Ben made his way along the pitted street. The moon above the Austin Power Plant was full, gleaming along the railroad tracks. His jacket smelled of smoke; he knew that Katy would make him take it to the cleaners when he got home.

The gutting sound of a motorcycle made him look up. A broad-shouldered kid with no helmet wheeled his Harley over the curb on one of the other clubs. Outside the low concrete building, arguing with a group of musicians, stood Sweeney. Above the door the neon sign read: THE RAILYARD.

Ben stared. If this was the club that Sweeney had been talking about opening with his friends, they were in serious trouble. There were only a half dozen cars parked out front and one of them belonged to the disgruntled drummer loading his traps into the back seat. The cinder block building was painted purple and the biggest yucca plant Ben had ever seen obscured one of the barred windows.

The pale, spiky-haired musicians seemed melancholy, but Sweeney was filled with Rotarian vigor; it was impossible to tell if Sweeney was trying to talk them into or out of something.

It took Sweeney nearly a minute before he realized he was being watched. He turned, squinting at Ben, taking a few seconds more. He cupped his hands to his eyes, just to be sure.

"Professor?"

"Hey. How you doin'?"

Ben could hear the steely sound of Son Jones's guitar coming from *Cinders*, starting up the second set. Sweeney slipped something into the shirt pocket of one of the musicians, excusing himself, and sauntered over.

"I was wondering if you were ever going to show up!" Sweeney clapped him on the shoulder, his breath sweet with alcohol.

"Actually I was just around the corner."

"You mean over at *Cinders*? That Son Jones is fucking great, isn't he?" Sweeney was in too good a mood to be offended. Ben reached into his pocket for his car keys. "Listen, why don't you come in, let me show you around?"

"Maybe some other time."

"It would only take a minute. Come on. What are you going to do, go home and correct papers? It's Friday night!" He took Ben by the elbow.

The inside of the club was a revelation. The walls were covered with the work of local artists, most of it bright and whimsical, Southwestern funk. Lamps had been made of Mexican whorehouse dolls and each glass-covered table had its own rock and roll collage. A lot of care had gone into it, though only two or three couples sat at tables and the bar was deserted.

Ben stared at a hubcap and chicken wire construction that loomed over the jukebox. "It's great," he said.

"Isn't it? My girlfriend, Rebecca, the one who came to class? She talked all her artist friends into donating stuff." Sweeney leaned across the counter and shouted to the bartender drying glasses at the far end of the bar. "Toby, I want you to meet somebody!"

The bartender, tall, mild and movie star handsome, set a glass on the overhead rack and came over to say hello.

"This is my English professor," Sweeney said. "The guy who changed my life. This is Toby." The bartender reached across and shook Ben's hand. "Why don't you give us a couple of those Shiner Bachs?" Elbows up on the bar, Sweeney turned to Ben. "You hungry? We got some great Mexican food. . . ."

"No, I'm fine," Ben said.

Toby got them their beers and they went to a table in the corner. The floor was slippery with sawdust and Maria Muldauer crooned softly on the jukebox. Sweeney crossed his boots in front of him and leaned back.

"Man, you keep surprising me!" he said.

"How do you mean?"

"I don't know. It's just that you turn out to be a wilder guy than I thought."

Ben took an unhappy swig of his beer. He tried to tell himself that he was under no obligation to stay, but it wasn't true. There was an obligation even if the terms hadn't been spelled out, an obligation contracted the afternoon Sweeney had spotted him at the Coliseum.

"So it's going O.K.?"

"You mean this? Oh, yeah, it's going fine. We've got some great bands lined up. It's going to take a little time for word to get around, but we knew that, going in. It's a hell of a lot of fun. And that's the point, right?"

Sweeney dug a chip deep into a bowl of salsa and managed to spill half of it before it got to his mouth. Sweeney was probably drunk.

"I've been meaning to come in," Sweeney said. "I've had this idea kicking around in my head."

"You mean about graduate school?"

"No, not about graduate school." Sweeney squashed some of the spilled salsa as if it was a bug and then licked it off his thumb. He hunched forward. "It's just a thought. You know how things come to you sometimes. We've got a really good deal going here. Really good."

"Yeah."

"Well, if you were looking for someplace to put some extra cash to work for you, it might be good for both of us."

"I don't know what you're saying," Ben said. A single microphone stood gleaming on the bare, black stage.

"I'm just saying it's a nice opportunity," Sweeney said.

"You're asking me to invest in your club?" Ben said. Sweeney picked mournfully at the label of his beer bottle. "But I'm your teacher."

"I know that."

"I think it would be better if it just stayed that way."

Chapter Six

Sweeney had made an offer. The question was, what was it? Unless Ben had misread him, it had almost sounded as if Sweeney had offered to launder money through his club, but how could Sweeney have known? Either he was a mind-reader or he'd gotten a peek at the ledger in Ben's office after all. It was all a little too perfect. Maybe it had only been a casual remark, a shot in the dark, maybe Sweeney had just been a little drunk and talking big, but it was unnerving.

The club was just the kind of cash intensive business Ben was looking for. But could he trust Sweeney? He had not forgotten the seven hundred dollars Sweeney had laid on the table at The Green Mesquite that afternoon. No, he did not trust Sweeney. Not enough.

On the tenth of April they got a letter from their landlords. The Bells, an academic couple who'd moved to Santa Barbara, had decided to put their house on the market. It was a gracious and apologetic letter, thanking Ben and Katy for taking such good care of their home for the past four years. They wanted to give Ben and Katy enough time to look for a new place, unless, of course, they wanted to buy the house themselves. They were listing the house at two hundred and sixty thousand dollars.

"God damn California liberals," Ben said. He sat at the kitchen table, staring at the hand-written letter. It was ten in the evening and the children were in bed. "They're dreaming if they think they can get two-sixty."

Katy opened the dishwasher, letting the steam escape before she pulled out the rack. "So what are we going to do?" she said.

The cat scratched at the back door. Ben got up and dug a cupful of catfood out of the blue bag.

"What are we going to tell them, Ben?"

He looked at her as if she was crazy; she was really hoping they might buy the place. "What is there to tell them? It looks like we're looking for a new house."

Two days later the real estate agent, a tall and high-strung West Austin divorcee named Darcy Kennedy came by to get a key. She needed to know when the best time would be for her to show the house. She would always call before she came, she said, and the Bells had agreed to lower the rent by a hundred a month to make up for any inconvenience, as long as they agreed to keep the house presentable for prospective buyers. When she left she drove a metal FOR SALE sign in the front yard.

Abby was up in arms. She didn't see how anyone had the right to look in her room when she wasn't there. She was ready to leave Austin, go back and live in Mississippi with her cousins. Matt, the quieter of the two, just listened, but that evening, when Ben went into his room to say goodnight, he asked Ben what school he would be going to in the fall.

On Saturday Darcy Kennedy called again. She had a couple with her from Palo Alto who were just in Austin for the weekend and she wondered if it would be all right to bring them by. Katy sprang into action; she couldn't help herself. She rousted Matt from the couch in the living room where he'd been watching cartoons in his pajamas, put away the breakfast dishes and asked Ben if he would clear off his desk.

"Hey, it's not as if the Queen of England was coming to visit," Ben said.

"Maybe not," Katy said, "but we don't want the place to look like a pigsty."

At a bit past ten in the morning Darcy Kennedy's towncar pulled up in front of the house. The couple's name was Reeves and they were in their early thirties. He was a computer executive with a firm handshake and a no-nonsense manner and his wife, in her red blazer, looked like a runner.

Katy offered them coffee. They all said no, they were fine. Scanning the kitchen, Mrs. Reeves did not look happy. She kept glancing at the pencil markings on the doorframe where Ben and Katy had recorded the children's heights throughout the years. Mrs. Reeves looked like the kind of woman who would have everything stripped down to the original wood within a week.

"So is there much crime in the neighborhood?" Mrs. Reeves said.

"No, not really," Ben said. "Just a few drifters."

When Darcy Kennedy took the couple upstairs Ben went to the study and tried to pay some bills, but he was too angry to concentrate. He could hear toilets flushing over head, closets opening and closing. When he looked out the window and saw the neighbor's Doberman crapping on the front yard, he was overcome with fondness for the animal; he just hoped Mrs. Reeves saw him too.

The door opened softly behind him. Ben turned to face Katy. "So what do you think?" she said.

"They're not going to buy this house," Ben said. "Not in a million years."

Two days later Darcy Kennedy called to say that the house had been sold.

When Ellen Pyle, in a spirited classroom discussion about the nature of friendship in the early nineteenth century, said that she thought Emerson and Thoreau were gay, Sweeney hit the roof.

"Just hold your horses for a minute here, sister," Sweeney said. "Where do you get that?"

"I'm not saying it's a bad thing," Ellen said. She sat a couple of rows in front of him and had to twist around to face him. "But come on. Emerson has Thoreau come live in his house for two years, they go for long walks every day, Emerson gives him the land to build his cabin on, Thoreau gets this big crush on Emerson's wife. . . ."

"Oh, my God," Sweeney groaned.

Ben stood at the front of the room, arms folded, keeping mum. Ellen and Sweeney had been going at it for most of the semester and it had not been a bad thing for class discussion.

The offer Sweeney had made that night at the club had not come up again. If anything, Sweeney had seemed a bit abashed ever since, as if he knew he'd overstepped. Perhaps to make up for it, his midterm had been the best in class.

"So are you saying they were actually doing it?" Sweeney said. That drew a couple of snickers from Sweeney's sophomore admirers.

Irritated now, Ellen pushed up the sleeve of her London School of Economics t-shirt. "I don't know what they were doing. It was a very repressed time."

"Oh, I see. They weren't psychologically aware enough. I mean, Jesus God. Maybe we're the ones who are too uptight. Aren't we the ones who need to turn everything into some sniggery sit-com joke? Did it ever occur to you that for some people friendship might actually be more important that sex? Having someone you can tell your deepest secrets to, knowing that they'll cover your back."

"Mr. Sweeney, I believe you've made your point," Ben said. In the back row a girl was surreptitiously trying to apply her lip-gloss. "Anyone else?"

Their lease ran until July One and Katy started looking immediately. She had a friend who handled rentals all over the city and who began taking Katy to see places in the evenings. The prices people were asking were a revelation. For years Ben and Katy had groused about paying the Bells twelve hundred a month for a three bedroom house in a non-neighborhood, but now it looked as if that was a steal. Renting anything comparable was going to cost them eighteen hundred to two thousand a month unless they were willing to rent a place within spitting distance of the highway.

Some nights Katy cried. She saw their lives spiralling downward; even if she did teach in the fall, how could they afford that kind of money? She didn't see a solution. Ben kept telling her that everything was going to work out, they shouldn't rush into things, but his reassurances only made her angry. How do you know that, she would say, how do you know it's going to work out? How could he tell her? He had enough money to buy the governor's mansion, three times over.

Getting off the bus, Ben hustled across the street, but even at a distance he could see the Closed sign in the window of the cleaners. He cursed softly under his breath, the pink receipt in his hand. It was the second time in a week he'd promised Katy he'd pick up the laundry and the second time he'd failed.

He thought he saw a light burning in the back. Maybe he was in luck. He went to the door and knocked loudly, then cupped his hand to his eyes and peered in, straining to see past the racks of clothes wrapped in ghostly cellophane.

"Hey, mister, you have a dollar you could spare?"

Ben turned. A homeless old woman, dressed as fantastically as a creature out of Doctor Seuss, huddled against the low wall at the corner of the building, her wire shopping cart at her side, jammed with all her worldly possessions. She could have been anywhere from forty to sixty, with tiny, hard eyes and dirt-streaked cheeks. She wore scuffed, mismatched men's shoes with sagging candy-cane striped socks and various layers of tattered shirts and blouses.

Ben knew the reigning progressive opinion was that it did no good to give money to pan-handlers, that nine chances out of ten it was going to go for alcohol or drugs, but Ben wasn't a big one for just turning his back on people.

"Sure," he said finally. Scratching her face, she scrutinized him as he took out his wallet. Her teeth were as variously colored as kernels of Indian corn. A UPS truck rumbled past on Congress Avenue; it was just a little past six. He handed her a dollar bill. "Here you go."

She took the bill, folding it once and then twice. "Thief!" she hissed at him.

He stared at her, dumfounded. "What?"

"You're the one, aren't you? The one who took it."

For a second he thought he was going to faint, everything tipping as if he was in a steeply banking plane. She had to be talking about something else. How could she possibly know? She was just a mad old woman. As she pulled up her knees to tuck the dollar bill in one of her many pockets, Ben could see the skin on her shins, slick as a frog's and pocked by open sores.

"So where are you hiding it?" Her voice rose to a raspy screech. A half dozen grackles winged their way towards the river. Across the street the windows of the abandoned feedstore flashed like semaphores in the setting sun.

"I don't know what you're talking about."

"Oh, yes, you do." Her face was red and inflamed as a boil, a soiled scarf knotted around her neck. She put a hand on the low wall behind her and struggled to her feet. "What are you looking at me for? Don't you look at me!" She bumped the cart over the low curb, nearly upending it, then rattled it across the parking lot. "You people think you can get away with murder, don't you? Well, you're wrong! You're wrong!" She fled down the sidewalk, the cart, with its one squeaking wheel, careening before her like a runaway carriage.

Katy was dismayed to discover that he hadn't made it to the dry cleaners in time. She turned off the faucet and dried her hands on a kitchen towel, the freshly washed lettuce sitting in a colander on the counter.

"Oh, my God, Ben," she said.

"I know, I'm sorry. I'll walk over first thing in the morning, O.K. I'm sorry!"

The unexpected emotion of his response caught her off-guard. She gave him a quick look. Cokie Roberts interviewed David Sedaris on the radio and a pot of water for pasta boiled softly on the stove.

"Are you all right?" she said. "You look ill."

"I'm fine."

"Did something happen?"

"No." He fingered a piece of sliced onion on the counter, avoiding her gaze.

"Why don't you go lie down?" she said. "Supper will be ready in a few minutes."

He went upstairs and lay down on the bed. His head was swarming. Was it possible? That someone had seen him take it? It all came welling back, that night in January, the rattling of the chair at the door, the drunken voices outside. He remembered the terror he'd felt, the constriction in his throat, and he remembered the elation he'd felt later, when he thought he'd lucked out, squeezed through undetected, but maybe he hadn't squeezed through, maybe there had been someone peering through one of the grimy windows as he stood over the trapdoor, holding the last of the coolers, or maybe they'd been bedded down under the trees outside, watching as he drove away.

But it didn't make any sense. If she or anyone else knew the money was there, why wouldn't they have taken it themselves? No, the woman was crazy. Crazy people are always accusing people of things, their lives riddled by infinite, addled grievance. This was just the thanks he got for giving her a dollar.

But she had called him a thief. What else could she have meant? His mistake was letting her walk away. He should have pressed her for more, but he'd been too stunned to do anything.

After dinner he got into the car and drove slowly through the neighborhood. Several people were out with their dogs, a father pushed his child in a blue stroller and an older man worked on his rock wall. On Congress Avenue he saw a couple of bearded drifters with dirty bedrolls headed down towards the bridge, but there was not a trace of the old woman.

Katy had found a place in Tarrytown she wanted Ben to look at. For the first time in months she was excited. It was a nice neighborhood, she said, and a good school district. Abby could go to Austin High where she already had several friends. The landlord was asking fourteen hundred, but he'd said over the phone that the price was negotiable.

They drove over on a Saturday afternoon. Ben was not really himself. Every night for a solid week he'd been going out at night, looking for the old woman with the shopping cart, cruising the HEB parking lots, the neighborhood dumpsters, checking out Stacey Park and the woods below the School for the Deaf, and he'd come up with nothing. He hadn't been able to sleep, unable to get her out of his mind. He'd gone over it a million times, from a million angles. If she'd seen something (and he was not at all sure that she had), how would that change things? four months had already passed. She hadn't gone to the police and he doubted that she would. If she did, who would believe her?

Maybe she was a pal of the two drunks. He remembered one of them saying, "Where'd everybody else go?" Maybe she was the everybody else. Maybe she'd come dragging along later, stood in the shadow of the gnarled live oak tree, watching him load the last cooler into the van. But even if she had, what was he supposed to do, bring the money back? No, not because of some senile old loon. Yet for all of his attempts to banish her from his consciousness she stayed with him night and day.

The West Austin neighborhood was lovely, with big oaks and green-shuttered brick houses that could have been lifted straight out of New England. Everything seemed greener and more shaded than South Austin; it felt as if the temperature had suddenly dropped ten degrees. There had to be a catch, Ben thought, and then he saw what the catch was.

The house looked like a rotting barge: low, ranch-style, and in need of a paint job. As they drove up the landlord was hauling a huge limb out of a patchy front yard that hadn't been cut for months. The landlord's name was Stanley Heller, a man with thinning hair and nerves of a rabbit.

He led them on a hurried tour of the house. There was no furniture except for a set of bedsprings sagging against the wall in the back bedroom. Several of the light switches were broken and the small, fenced-in back yard was littered with dog turds. The previous tenant had apparently left in a hurry. Heller's wife wanted fourteen hundred, but he was willing to give it to them for twelve as long as he didn't have to paint. He smiled at Katy; it was clear that she had charmed him.

Ben could feel Katy waiting for him to say yes. "We'll let you know," Ben said. "Would it be all right if we called you tomorrow sometime?"

"That would be fine," Heller said.

After the landlord drove off Katy and Ben sat in the car, talking. "I could fix this place up," she said. "I could make it nice."

"It just seems so dark to me," he said. "There's no light."

A woman pushed a double stroller down the street with two Prince Edward terriers on leashes at her side. "We're not going to find anyplace better," she said.

"You don't know that."

"But I do know. You haven't been looking at the places I've been looking at."

He stared at the patchy lawn, littered with sticks. This was what their life would be without that money. He looked back at her quickly. She began to cry.

A pony-tailed workman, his nose and mouth covered by a rippled white mask, leaned over a set of sawhorses, spray-painting a screen door purple. He was so absorbed in his task that he didn't hear Ben drive into the gravel parking lot, only looking up after Ben got out and slammed the van door.

"Is Sweeney here?" Ben said.

The pony-tailed worker lifted the mask, moving it up on his forehead where it sat like a white horn. "I think he's inside."

When Ben entered the club Sweeney was sitting alone at a corner table, his back turned. The only other person in the place was a waitress, filling salt shakers at the bar and watching the Jenny Jones Show (two black teen-agers screamed and jabbed fingers at one another while the audience roared). The waitress got up, reaching for a menu.

"That's all right," Ben said. "I'm just here to see my friend."

Sweeney lifted his head, looking back over his shoulder. "Hey."

"Hey. You got a minute?"

"I've got all the time in the world."

It was a sight to warm a teacher's heart: a dog-eared copy of *Walden*, a library edition of *Young Man Thoreau* and an array of three by five cards fanned out across the table. Sweeney had been studying, an empty beer bottle at his left elbow.

Ben pulled up a chair. Sweeney cleared away the three by five cards. He looked concerned. "Everything O.K.?"

"Oh, yeah," Ben said. The waitress had disappeared into the kitchen. "When I was here a few weeks ago you made me a proposal."

Sweeney stared blankly. "Yeah."

"I wonder if you could just go over for me what that proposal was."

Sweeney, thoughtful now, rubbed at a spot behind his right ear. "I think all I said was that if you had some money to invest I could help you out."

"The way I remember it, you said cash."

Sweeney frowned. "Maybe so. I don't remember."

"What I need to know is whether or not the offer is still open."

Sweeney let go a small puff of surprise. "I don't know. I'd have to talk to my partners." The rumbling was indistinct at first, but it drew closer and then was pierced by the familiar whistle of a train. It sounded as if it was coming right at them.

"I'd rather you didn't," Ben said. He had to raise his voice to make himself heard. "I'd rather you didn't talk to anyone."

"You're not trying to set me up, are you?"

"No."

Sweeney rested his thumbnail against his teeth, considering. The roar obliterated everything. Ben glanced at the window; he could see the freight cars flashing by, the alternating slats of dark and light. We do not ride upon the railroad, Thoreau had said, the railroad rides upon us.

Sweeney said something, but Ben couldn't make out what it was. "I'm sorry," Ben said.

Sweeney repeated what he'd said and this time Ben was able to read his lips: "I'll have to think about it."

The semester was almost over. On Wednesday Ben had everyone do their teaching evaluations and spent the remainder of the hour answering questions about the exam. Sweeney caught up with him in the hallway after class.

"I wondered if you would have time to have lunch tomorrow," Sweeney said. Ben glanced quickly at Ellen Pyle, waiting in the doorway to have a word with him.

"I suppose we could do that."

"Why don't I pick you up?" Sweeney hefted his backpack onto his shoulder. "Say in front of the Littlefield Fountain about twelve?"

On Thursday Ben was at the fountain at the stroke of noon. Several scantily-clad coeds sunned on the wall above the splashing water and long lines had already formed at the Saigon Egg-roll stand.

Ben waited for nearly fifteen minutes, scanning every car that came by, half-hoping that Sweeney wouldn't show up. He felt a little as if he was jumping off a pier in the dark, but what else could he do? He'd exhausted every other possibility and he couldn't put it off any longer.

Ben had been over what he was about to do a million times. At least with Sweeney there was a certain rapport, a reservoir of respect, and he'd already proven that he was capable of loyalty—he hadn't blabbed to the other students about the gun business. Ben felt more than a little guilty about taking advantage of that. Strictly speaking he was contributing to the corruption of a student, though it seemed highly likely that Sweeney had been corrupted before.

As the bells tolled for a quarter after, a dusty red Bronco took a squealing U-turn in front of the church, scattering pedestrians, and pulled to the curb. Sweeney leaned across to roll down the window.

"Sorry I'm late."

They drove to a fish place on Airport that Sweeney claimed had great Po'Boys. A giant plastic shark loomed above the glass counter and a sallow Cajun took their order. Drinks, the old man explained, they'd have to get for themselves from the machine in the corner. Sweeney, loaded with quarters, got a big Red for himself and a Coke for Ben.

The only other customers were two truck drivers waiting for take-out and Ben and Sweeney had their pick of a dozen empty tables. At first Sweeney seemed nervous and distracted. His major preoccupation seemed to be the plight of the Rockets in the playoffs. He was a big Olajawon fan, but Sweeney was concerned that they seemed to have surrounded him once again with a team of CBA castoffs. As Sweeney talked on and on Ben realized that Sweeney was just trying to size him up, trying to get comfortable.

"So what changed your mind?" Sweeney said finally.

"About what?"

"About investing your money."

"Does it matter?"

"It might." Sweeney took a swig of his Big Red. He nodded toward the counter. "I think our order is ready."

The Po'Boys were all that Sweeney had promised and they were nearly buried under mountains of fries. Sweeney methodically doused everything in catsup. Ben could only watch, too tense to eat. Sweeney took a big crunching bite, then wiped a little mayonnaise from the corner of his mouth with a napkin.

"It feels sort of weird, doesn't it?" Sweeney said.

"What do you mean?" Ben said.

"Our doing this. I know, I was the one who brought it up. I just want to be sure that you know what you're getting into."

"I think I do."

Sweeney stopped chewing for a moment. "Listen, I don't want to get you into trouble and I don't want to get myself into trouble either. And where this money is coming from, I don't care, as long as you're not selling kiddie porn. But if we do this, it's just between us. I don't want anybody hearing about it."

"I understand."

"So how much do you want to invest?"

Ben didn't know; he pulled a number out of the air. "What if we started with six hundred a week."

"Cash."

"Cash," Ben said. Sweeney gave a low, soft whistle; Ben didn't know if that meant the figure was low or if it was high. "So what would you say my return on that might be?"

"Five hundred sound about right?"

"That would be fine. And you would give me a check."

"Yeah, I'd give you a check. We could list you as one of the partners, or as a vendor, whatever you say." The white aproned Cajun knelt behind the display case, arranging slabs of redfish on banks of crushed ice.

"And no one will get into trouble," Ben said.

"That's the way it's supposed to work." Sweeney put a fist to his chest as if he had gas. He looked sorrowful and young all of a sudden.

"What's wrong?" Ben said.

"I don't know. I just loved your class so much."

"And does this have to change that?"

"Not really. I guess there's just more to life than what you read in books."

Chapter Seven

He was only part way there. The task now was coming up with a story for Katy. He was going to be getting a check for five hundred dollars once a week and he needed a way to explain that.

He had an aunt who'd died a couple of years before, leaving behind an eight hundred acre farm in North Dakota and the estate had yet to be settled. That seemed like a credible enough explanation for a windfall, but Ben could just see Katy getting on the phone with Ben's sisters or one of his eight cousins in North Dakota and blowing that one out of the water in about ten seconds. The same was true of any story he concocted about a grant or a book contract dropping out of the blue; it would be too easy to check out; his colleagues would get wind of it; there were too many ways to be tripped up.

He kept coming back to one possibility. In the mid-eighties Ben had worked on a series for public television on American Writers and the West. He had written several of the scripts, one on the paleontologists Cope and Marsh and their adventures in Wyoming, another on Walter Van Tilberg Clark. Two years later he received a check for sixty-two hundred for the sale of foreign rights and, three years after that, a second check arrived for twenty-seven hundred dollars. Those two checks were the closest thing to a bonanza Ben had ever experienced. It wasn't altogether out of the realm of possibility that he might receive a third check. All he had to do was get Katy to believe it.

On Friday he and Katy went to see *Dr. Zhivago* at the Paramount. It had been thirty years since Ben had seen it and he had forgotten how astonishingly beautiful it was. It was a movie that could make you fall in love with the cold again—Omar Sharif and Julie Christie's tryst in an icicled ruin, a candle glowing inside a frosted pane, horses pounding through the blowing snow. Ben found himself moved more than he expected by the story of the respectable doctor torn between two women, destroyed by his secret life.

Walking out of the theatre into the moist Texas night was like walking into a sauna; summer was so close. They went up the street to a small coffee shop for a cappuccino. It was an Austin version of Little Italy, a jazz and cheesecake type of place, and the light fixtures so arty they could have been mistaken for aboriginal artifacts, baskets from the Upper Sepic.

Ben blew across his cup, wiping up some of excess foam with his finger. "I have some wonderful news," he said.

"What's that?" Katy said. A couple in bicycle helmets and black Velcro pants leaned across the marble-topped counter, laughing, forehead to forehead.

"You remember the old PBS series I worked for?"

She brightened instantly. "You got another check?"

"Yeah." He stared down at the stone table. He had still not gotten used to lying to her.

"That's funny," Katy said. "I didn't see it in the mail."

Ben glanced quickly at her. "It came to the department. They must not have had the right address. It's been bouncing around for awhile."

"That's great. How much was it?"

"It's a nice amount of money." A Spanish guitar thrummed mournfully through the sound system. "But I've been thinking about this. It seems like every time we get a little boost we buy a couple of things and then we're right back where we started." She snapped off a bit of biscotti and set it on her tongue; he could see that she thought he was somehow blaming her. "I'd like to do something else this time."

"Like what?"

"I'd like to invest this," he said. She brushed a strand of auburn hair from her eyes. "There's some people from school, they've started a new club."

"A club? what do you mean, a club?"

"A music club."

She was incredulous. "You're joking."

"I'm not joking. This place is going to be very successful."

"We don't have enough money to rent a decent house and we're putting money into a night club?"

"Katy, it's not what it sounds like. . . ."

"Isn't it?"

"Just once in my life I'd like to see if we could get ahead. . . ." He wasn't aware of raising his voice, but one of the bicyclists looked back at them.

"You've been to this place?"

"A couple of times, yes."

"And where is it?"

"It's just behind *Cinders*, the old blues club." His stomach churned with self-contempt and late-night caffeine.

"Do I have a vote in this?"

"It's going to be fine, I promise you. I've already set it up so we'll be getting weekly checks, we'll be the first ones to be paid off. Trust me, Katy, there is no way we can lose." He knew he sounded like a fool, but there was no other choice. He had to just bull his way through.

"You mean you've already agreed?"

"Yes," he said. She was stunned.

"So how much was it?"

"I told you. . . ."

"I want to know exactly."

"A little over five thousand dollars."

"Jesus, Ben." He reached out for her hand, but she pulled away. She picked up a packet of NutraSweet as if she was about to open it and then just tossed it at the napkin holder. "I think it's time for us to go home."

The young woman sitting in his office was an appallingly bad liar. She'd missed nineteen out of thirty classes, she knew she was in trouble and was willing to try anything. She'd had to go to L.A. because her company had received a music award, she said, and while she was out there her rental car had exploded on the Santa Monica Freeway and then when she got back to Austin her ex-boyfriend had been hit by a baseball bat in a brawl and had been in a coma for two weeks.

"So I just wanted to know if I could do an extra paper or something to make up for the classes I've missed," she said. She was attractive in a B movie kind of way—huge eyes, full lips, skin-tight jeans and lots of red hair and vivid makeup—and she was used to getting by on that.

"It's too late," Ben said softly. He had a hard time being hard and the word had gotten around, only making things harder still. "The semester's over."

"You mean even if I do really well on the exam. . . ."

"I'm sorry. The syllabus says six absences in grounds for failing the course." Ben swivelled in his chair. In the drawer of his desk was an envelope with twelve fifties in it. Sweeney was supposed to have been at his office at two; it was now nearly three and there was no sign of him. "I've cut people breaks before, but this isn't even close."

She began to cry. Ben looked away. He hated this office, the puce-green walls, the stacks of yellowing papers. He was supposed to go through another twenty years of this? She got out a tissue and wiped at her eyes; her mascara had started to run. There was a sharp knock at the door.

Ben got up and opened it. Sweeney stood there looking like Jimmy Buffett in a Hawaiian shirt and a new tan.

"Sorry I'm late," Sweeney said. It took him a beat before he realized that Ben had someone with him. "Oh, I'm sorry. . . ."

"I was just leaving," the girl said. She rose, unsteady on her high heels, and gathered up her books. "I'm going to go speak to the Undergraduate Advisor," she said.

"That's your privilege," Ben said. Sweeney gave her the once-over as she swept by. "Mr. Sweeney." Ben gestured him to a chair. Sweeney stepped inside as the door closed behind him.

"She didn't seem too happy."

"She wasn't. You look like you got a little sun."

"I went out to the lake with my girlfriend this weekend. You ever been on one of those jet-skis? Man, you could kill yourself on one of those things, I'm telling you. So when are they going to get you a window in this place?"

"I'm not sure."

Sweeney sat with his boot across his knee, confident and relaxed. Ben could smell the coconut oil five feet away. There was the slightest hitch of hesitation, each waiting for the other to make the first move; they both knew it was a moment.

"You got something for me?" Sweeney said.

"I do," Ben said.

Ben opened his desk drawer and handed the envelope to Sweeney.

Sweeney opened it, flicking quickly through the money without bothering to count it.

"Great," Sweeney said. He leaned to one side so he could pry his wallet out of his back pocket. He slid the stack of bills into the wallet, tapping it all in place, and took out a check. "This is for you."

He handed the check to Ben. It was made out for five hundred dollars, signed by Sweeney, with the *Railyard* address stamped in the upper left hand corner.

"I've got something else for you too," Sweeney said. He leaned over and unzipped his backpack. He pulled out a thick, cream-colored and slightly bent envelope and offered it, arm's length.

"What's this?"

"Open it and see."

Ben took the envelope and worked his forefinger under the flap, tearing it open. It was an invitation to graduation. The air conditioner kicked in, shuddering in the wall.

"I was hoping my uncle could come up, but he's not feeling so well, so I thought, why not invite my teacher? I was hoping maybe I could take you and your wife out to dinner. You'd get to meet my girlfriend Rebecca. It took me nearly a decade to get out of this place, I'd kind of like to celebrate it." Ben stared down at the gothic script. Sweeney was too smart not to notice his hesitation. "Unless it would make you uncomfortable."

"No, it wouldn't make me uncomfortable at all. I'll just have to ask."

The last thing Ben wanted was Sweeney anywhere near Katy. Things were tough enough at home the way it was.

The storm had not blown over. The night they came home from *Dr. Zhivago* they were up until two, arguing. It was incomprehensible to her that he would put five thousand dollars into a music club without talking to her about it. She did not understand. What was this, some kind of mid-life crisis?

It wasn't as if he'd gone out and bought a Jaguar, he said. This was going to create a steady income for them. There was going to be five hundred a week coming in; they were finally going to be able to afford the kind of house Katy had always wanted.

Ben had miscalculated how big a deal it was going to be. Perhaps because of what he wasn't telling her, five thousand seemed like chicken feed to him; it didn't to her. For a solid week anger hung over the house like the deep blue of an impending norther. Whether they talked about it or didn't talk about it, it was still there. All sorts of other things got dragged in, old wounds re-opened. Katy felt betrayed and shaken; this was so unlike him she felt as if she needed to re-think everything.

The children did not miss what was going on. One afternoon, driving Abby to her softball practice, she asked Ben, "Are you and Mom going to get a divorce?"

"Of course not, honey," he said. "What makes you think that?"

"I don't know. It just seems like you're mad at each other all the time."

"That's not really true, Abby. We disagree sometimes, but everybody does that . . . Hey, we love each other. And we love you." Abby, unpersuaded, did not look at him, pounding the pocket of her baseball glove.

His one consolation was going by the bank to be sure that Sweeney's check had cleared. The bank teller slid the feathery bank statement across the counter to him. The available balance was one thousand one hundred and eighty-three. One week before it had been six hundred eighty-three. In a few days there would be five hundred more and five hundred more after that. The cavalry was coming, to rescue them all. Katy would see. It was a matter of time, but she *would* see.

The university was emptying out. They were just half-way through the exam period and the library was already tomb-like, it was possible to find parking spaces again and the lines at restaurants had vanished. Everything was relaxed. Coming out of the copy room one morning Ben ran into Dick Dennison wheeling his bike into his office.

"Hey, just the man I was looking for." Dick grinned, unbuckling his plastic helmet. He had reason to be in a good mood. Dick was on leave for the coming year, with a semester in France and a semester in Boston. "Listen, you got a minute?"

"Sure."

Ben followed him into his office. The narrow room was jammed with packing boxes; there must have been at least twenty of them, piled high enough to block the lower half of the window.

"Jesus," Ben said.

"I know," Dick said. "I've got everything I own in here. I'm supposed to fly to Paris on Wednesday and I've been working like a dog to get ready."

He rested the bicycle carefully against the mountain of books. Dick was one of the creative writing faculty and a lover of experimental French fiction (his most recent enthusiasm was a novel written without the use of the letter e). Fit, in his mid-forties and still single, Dick was always off for somewhere—Haiti, Africa, India—in search of the telling detail and there were times it was hard not to be envious.

"I need to ask you a favor, man," Dick said.

"You name it."

"They're giving me all this grief upstairs about my office. They've got all these visiting faculty coming in next fall and no place to put them, but I'll be damned if I'm going to have some crazy Irishman in here burning holes in my carpet, so I told Carol you were going to be using my office."

"You told her what?"

"I told her we'd talked about it and that it was all worked out, that you needed a quiet place to get your book done. I had to say something."

Ben stared at him and then gave a low laugh. "Dick, it's fine. Don't worry about it."

"I really appreciate this. Here, I can give you the key right now." He worked his key off his key ring and handed it to Ben. "And feel free to use it. It's not exactly a bad idea. You know how hard it is to get anything done in your office, people knocking on the door every five minutes. Here, nobody'll even know you're around."

Ben scanned the book shelves, the copies of *The Paris Review* and Gordon Lish's *Quarterly* neatly lined up in rows, the Samuel Beckett poster on the wall, considering the possibilities.

"If you want, you can even have the phone turned off," Dick said. "You'll have your own little hideaway."

"Who knows?" Ben said.

Dick gave him a soul handshake. "My man. I'll send you a postcard from the Eiffel Tower."

When Sweeney came to Ben's office the following Wednesday something was off. He seemed distracted, even vaguely hostile. Ben had never known him not to want to talk, but he didn't want to talk today. They made the exchange, cash for check, and Sweeney was ready to go.

"You all right?" Ben asked.

"I'm fine."

Ben gestured to the pile of blue books on his desk. "I haven't read your exam yet, but I'm looking forward to it."

"Whatever," Sweeney said. His tan was peeling and he kept rubbing his forehead. Ben folded his check in two and put it in his shirt pocket.

"Listen, I've been meaning to call you about your invitation, but these friends of ours were supposed to be coming in for the weekend and we just haven't heard from them, yes or no." It was not the deftest of lies.

"I understand," Sweeney said. So that was it; Sweeney's voice gave it all away.

"I'll tell you what. They're really more friends of Katy's, maybe I could let her entertain them for the afternoon and you and I and your girlfriend could go out to celebrate."

"I'd really like it if your wife would come."

Ben said nothing for several seconds. "Let me talk to her," he said. "We'll see if we can work something out. And I'll call you. I promise."

It kept gnawing at him, Abby thinking they might be getting a divorce. After seventeen years of marriage Ben and Katy had weathered so much more than their children could ever know.

They had met in New York at a loft party given by an Italian sculptor whose artistic reputation rested on giant kinetic chickens. Ben was twenty-six, Katy twenty-five. He was still recovering from the shattering of his first marriage and just quit his job as a caseworker at the Welfare Department to pursue playwriting full-time. She had just come to New York after breaking off a relationship with a Seattle lawyer and was working for a publisher.

At the beginning she just wanted to be friends. She loved the fact that he was such a great listener—most of the men she'd been out with in her first six months in New York had done nothing but talk about themselves, for hours on end—but Ben's grooming was not the best. It was summer, it was hot, and she was finicky. Years later she would entertain company with the story (it had grown wildly exaggerated, he thought) of the first time she saw his apartment—the chicken bones under the hi-fi, the roach that crawled across the bowl of salad at the most inopportune moment.

Her therapist, an ex-priest and ex-novelist, was a problem. Ben was convinced she was secretly in love with him. She baby-sat for his children. She felt he had saved her life. For the first time she viewed the world psychologically, she said, even though every time she quoted him he sounded like an idiot.

Ben persevered. He began to shower twice a day, trimmed his beard, lost ten pounds and called in an exterminator. All his friends found her charming; what they couldn't see was how hard-headed she was in private. He was very much in love with her. She was physically radiant, a country girl in the big city, riding her bike fearlessly to work every morning through the mid-town traffic, hauling Ben off to incomprehensible loft performances and to the screening of her brother's documentaries on Mississippi blues at the Museum of Natural History.

There was the inevitable trading of romantic histories. Despite her impeccable Southern manners, Katy didn't pull any punches— her stories of college boyfriends, slimy photography instructors and, most of all, the egomaniacal lawyer she's wasted four years on were enough to make anybody wince. Ben, Mr. Bohemian Playwright, turned out to be the reticent one. It caught Katy by surprise. On the surface he was so easy, so non-judgmental, but she soon learned there were buttons he didn't like to have pushed and one was the button of his first marriage.

What won her in the end, he was convinced, was the theatre. His short plays were being produced all over town, in tiny sub-basements in the Village, churches on the East Side, settlement houses in Harlem. More often than not the productions went unreviewed and the audiences seldom topped fifty, but they were good plays, anyone sitting out in those ratty folding chairs knew, and afterward, after the hat had been passed, Katy and Ben would go out for a beer and a hamburger with the actors.

They would push a few tables together and order a pitcher or two and eat french fries off one another's plates and laugh and tell jokes. It felt like family and Ben was everyone's hero. The excitement was infectious. They were actors, after all, and it was their job to be convincing; what they seemed most convinced about was that Ben was a genius and that great things lay just around the corner, for all of them.

The year after they were married Abby was born. Looking back, those seemed like such innocent times. They had absolutely no money, but such hope. Their friends were mostly other young parents they met at the sandbox at One Hundred and Third and Riverside, and their idea of a big day out was pushing the kids in strollers through the Bronx Zoo.

But it also seemed as if there were always signs that something wonderful was about to happen: a knock-out reading at New Dramatists, an encouraging note from Joe Papp, his buddy Jonathan taking the scripts around to his producer friends.

The problem was they couldn't live on signs. What looked like Ben's big break turned into a debacle when a production of his play at The Manhattan Theatre Club was savaged by John Simon. He went to work for a PBS series to make a little money and auditioned as a writer for a daytime soap. Katy got pregnant again. She was a trooper, but she talked more and more about moving out of the city; all their friends with kids seemed to be leaving.

One March night they had a huge, confidence-rattling fight, the first real fight in their marriage. It wasn't about money, but it was, he saw that now, looking back; it was about all those implicit promises that come with marriage. He had been a full-time playwright for five years. No one could say he hadn't given it a shot. It was great to be uncompromising if you were a genius, but what if you were merely B+? It was his hanging onto his dreams that was making them all miserable.

He applied to graduate school at Columbia. It took him six years to get his Ph.D., six years of unrelenting poverty, even with Katy working and both their parents pitching in. The kids got too big to both fit in the maid's room, so Abby slept on a couch behind a screen in the living room. At times it felt as if it would never end, as if they were forever doomed to live in the same two bedroom apartment with the paint cracking off the ceiling and the broken tile in the shower.

When he flew to Austin for an interview he was not optimistic. They were looking at three people and all indications were that he was third on the list. Two days later, after he returned to New York the call came offering him the job.

It felt like a miracle. He had a tenure-track job at a major university and anyone they'd ever met who'd ever lived in Austin loved the place. Matt, just eight years old, wanted to know if he'd get to see real cowboys. When they had their big party to celebrate Jonathan came over with a cassette of the old Joey Bishop movie, "Four For Texas."

On Friday, after a long editing session with one of his graduate students, Ben took the bus home. An elderly black man in blue overalls sat on a mower, cutting the grass in front of the abandoned feedstore. The mower spat gravel as it bumped over the uneven ground. It was the first sign of activity at the store in months. Ben stood and stared for nearly a minute.

He crossed Congress Avenue, hustling the last few feet to avoid a careening bread truck. The weather was strange. For days Austin had been under a health alert, the skies obscured by smoke from the hundreds of fires burning in Mexico. Most of the fires had been set by small farmers, clearing their fields for spring planting, and they'd been unable to control them in a countryside parched by a El Nino-fed drought. After a week it had become increasingly oppressive, ominous as a Biblical warning, and early in the morning the smoke hung close to the ground, clinging to the houses, thick as a London fog.

He waved to the klatsch of hippie mothers gathered on the porch of one of the corner bungalows. One of the women, nose-ringed, in a diaphanous dress, waved back. Barefoot children chased one another with wooden swords, emitting blood-curdling yells.

Ben was halfway down the next block before he saw Sweeney's dusty red Bronco at the curb in front of his house. His first thought was that there had been a disaster, that they had been found out. He walked faster, beginning to run, but then he saw them standing in the front yard, Katy and Sweeney. She was in sweatpants and t-shirt, leaning against a spade. She'd been planting roses and Sweeney held one of the stubby, clipped bushes on his hip, making himself useful.

Katy was laughing. Matt and his friend Cameron played catch in the street, throwing a rubber football with a long plastic tail that whistled as it arced above the telephone lines. Katy saw Ben first, Sweeney turning a second later.

"Hey," Sweeney said.

"Hey."

Ben was furious and yet he couldn't let on. Katy wiped the sweat from her forehead, leaving just a trace of peat above her eyebrow. How much had Sweeney told her?

"I hope you don't mind," Sweeney said. "I hadn't heard from you all and I was just driving by, I thought I'd stop in and see if you were coming to my graduation party."

"I think it would be fine," Katy said. "I don't think we're doing anything tomorrow." Ben could tell from her tone that Sweeney had charmed her. The football whined somewhere in the soot-ridden air above them and Ben's throat felt suddenly raw.

"That would be great," Sweeney said. He looked away for a second, taking everything in: the house, the nine year old van, the neighborhood. He didn't seem to mind that he'd been lied to; it just made things that much more interesting. "I guess you haven't had a chance to talk about it."

"We've been pretty busy," Ben said.

Sweeney grinned. "So I guess what they say about these absentminded professors is right, huh?"

Cameron took a running start, flinging the football as far as he could. The ball careened off the telephone pole and bounded across the lawn.

"Take this for a minute, would you?" Sweeney said.

He handed the potted rosebush to Ben and trotted over to retrieve the football. Ben had tried to call Sweeney twice that afternoon and missed him, but that would do him no good now. Sweeney waved to Matt to start running.

"Go deep, go deep. . . ." Matt sprinted and then hesitated. "Come on, we're going for seven here!"

Sweeney threw a long, picture-perfect spiral that screamed like an incoming missile. Matt made a stumbling one-handed catch and came up grinning, the ball held aloft. Sweeney applauded.

"There you go!" Sweeney raised both hands in the air, signalling touchdown. He looked back at Katy and Ben. "That's quite a little athlete you've got there." He rubbed his palms on his jeans. "Your wife was telling me she's from Mississippi. It's funny how these things work. My grandfather used to raise cotton right across the river from Vicksburg. It just shows you, it's a smaller world than you think."

Sweeney gazed steadily at Ben. The look was even, not hostile, but not conciliatory either. Ben remembered the first time they had met in his office, how Sweeney wouldn't leave until he got permission to take Ben's class; he was the kind of guy who didn't like to take no for an answer.

"Listen, I don't want to keep you from supper," Sweeney said. The sun glowed dully in the smoke-filled skies. "But I'll see you all tomorrow."

Ben and Katy met Sweeney and his girlfriend just past one o'clock at the Littlefield Fountain. They made quite a sight together: Sweeney stalwart as a doughboy in his cap and gown, Rebecca tall and imperious and at least fifteen years older than he was, with her

Marianne Faithful bangs and an oat-colored dress slit provocatively up the side.

The hill was covered with black-gowned seniors posing for pictures with their families and Sweeney insisted on pictures too, first of Rebecca and himself, then of Ben and himself, and finally a shot of all of them together with the tower in the background, taken by a helpful Asian graduate student. If Ben still carried any residual anger over Sweeney's unannounced visit to his house, Sweeney wasn't noticing; he acted as if they were the oldest of pals.

Afterwards they all piled into Sweeney's Bronco and drove the fifteen miles out to the most expensive restaurant in the county, a place frequented largely by personal injury lawyers and lobbyists. The wind had turned and the skies were blue for the first time in ten days. Sweeney made it clear that he was picking up the tab; nobody was pulling nickel on his big day.

They sat outside under the live oak trees; all the tables were decorated with bouquets of baby's breath and yellow roses. The Texas sun gleamed off the windshields of the Jaguars and Mercedes lining the gravel road.

Sweeney ordered champagne and told funny stories about Ben as a teacher—how his hair popped up when he got excited, how he would go, "Hmm, hmm, interesting," when a student said something idiotic.

The restaurant's specialty was wild game; Katy ordered a hot and crispy pheasant with mango aioli and Rebecca asked for the ostrich. The breeze blew a napkin off the next table and a white-shirted young waiter had to run to retrieve it.

By the second glass of champagne Rebecca was well on her way to telling Ben her life story in her low whiskey voice. She was British and had been married and divorced four times, most recently from the son of one of Dallas's wealthiest families. She had a teen-age daughter, away at boarding school in Massachusetts. She was a woman who knew books and movies; she'd first come to the States to work on a John Schlesinger film. She was charming but hard, with the habit of relaying the most astonishingly intimate details in the most off-handed way.

Ben listened, but his real attention was on the conversation between Katy and Sweeney across the table. He was in torment. Katy had yet to make the connection between Sweeney and the music club Ben had invested his purported residual check in and Ben hadn't told her, hoping to somehow slide by. It may have been a mistake, but what choice did he have? It was a no-win situation. If he told Katy and she started asking questions, Sweeney would go through the roof; if he didn't tell her and it came out anyway, she would feel betrayed.

So far, so good. Katy was delighted by the restaurant and she found Sweeney hilarious. He teased her about her accent and she teased him right back, Ben couldn't quite hear about what, but she soon had him roaring. Sweeney seemed to be able to bring something out in her, a sense of play, that Ben hadn't seen in her in a long time.

By the time the food arrived Ben was a little stunned by the sun and the champagne. The other three were still going strong, trying to remember the words to "Proud Mary." Ben sat back and sawed away at his exotic meat.

Sweeney did a five minute take-off on the commencement speaker that was worthy of Billy Crystal, they talked about their favorite high school teachers and then opened graduation presents. Sweeney was the only one who had room for dessert. The others ordered coffee and while they were waiting Rebecca leaned forward on her elbows.

"So what will you be doing this summer?" she said.

Katy looked over at Ben for help. "We're not sure yet. One thing we know, we're looking for a place."

"Really?" Rebecca said. Ben looked down, frowning, brushing some crumbs off the white tablecloth.

"Our landlord has decided to sell."

A pall fell momentarily over the conversation. A boat-tailed grackle strutted across the lawn, then flew up suddenly as a waiter came down the stairs with Sweeney's hot fudge sundae.

"I'm sure you'll find something. I was looking at the paper the other day and some wonderful places have just come on the market," Rebecca said.

"I don't think we can afford to buy right now," Katy said.

Ben gave her a quick dirty look. She didn't have to tell them that. Sweeney seemed dumfounded; something didn't make sense here.

"So we're looking," Katy said.

"Well, then," Rebecca said. "I think you should come stay at my place."

Katy shook her head, embarrassed. "No, we couldn't."

"I'm not just being polite," Rebecca said. "I've been looking for someone. I'm moving to Santa Fe in July for at least a year."

The waiter set the brimming sundae in front of Sweeney. Sweeney flicked his napkin and then tucked it under his collar like a six year old tucking in his bib. A single strand of hot fudge rolled down the fluted glass like a glistening tear.

"I'm telling you, it would be perfect," Sweeney said. He was looking only at Katy now, not at Ben. He plucked the cherry off the top of the sundae and popped it in his mouth, sucking it clean. "It's got a pool, the whole works. You're not going to believe it."

That night Ben went into the bathroom while Katy was in the shower. June bugs batted against the narrow window and the mirror was clouded with steam.

"Is that you, Ben?"

"Yeah." He could just barely see her through the plastic shower curtain, her image blurred and out-of-focus as she rinsed her hair. "So did you have a good time this afternoon?" He spoke up to make himself heard over the rush of the water.

"Yes, I thought it was great," she said. "It was very generous of them."

"I thought you should know," he said. "Sweeney is one of the guys who's put money into the club."

The water went off, the pipes shuddering for a second. Katy pulled back the shower curtain and faced him, her wet hair slicked back. her bare shoulders glistening.

"Why didn't you tell me before?"

He took the towel from the back of the chair and handed it to her. "I meant to. I suppose I didn't want to put a damper on this afternoon."

She wiped her face dry with the towel. "What's done is done," she said. He knew from her tone that she was still a long way from forgiving him. "I thought they were both very charming."

The following Wednesday when Sweeney came to Ben's office for their weekly exchange, Sweeney was in an ebullient mood. He still couldn't get over the fact that he'd graduated and when he said he wanted to go to lunch, Ben didn't have the heart to say no.

The first summer session didn't start for another week and the campus had the languorous quality of a northwoods Bible retreat. A librarian sat under the trees in front of the Union, feeding bits of his sandwich to a squirrel and skateboarders clattered in an out of the empty stone fountain.

"I'm telling you, man, I'm going to miss this place," Sweeney said. "Lots of memories, lots of memories . . ."

They crossed over to the Drag, Sweeney waving to a sorority girl at the cash machine, exchanging cheery hellos with the woman running the Korean egg roll stand. It felt a little like walking down the street with the mayor.

Sweeney had just launched into a complicated story about his freshman year, something about the Aggies stealing Bevo off the roof of the Coop, when Ben saw the wire shopping cart with the one warped wheel. It sat on the sidewalk in front of a recently vacate store and it was just as he remembered it—stuffed with milk cartons and pillows, soiled overcoats and plastic dishes. As they moved closer he could see the old woman too, huddled in the recessed entryway. She still wore her scuffed, mismatched men's shoes and her sagging candy-cane socks, but as a final madcap touch she'd added several strands of Mardi Gras beads over her layers of tattered blouses.

She saw him a second after he saw her. The wise thing would have been to just walk on by, but Ben was confused—after all, hadn't he been the one looking for her, for nearly two months? He hesitated and the hesitation was enough to set her off.

"What are you looking at me for?" Her voice sounded as if someone had just run a cheese grater down her vocal cords. "You've got no right, looking at me!" Sweeney, who'd walked on, turned back at the commotion, but the old woman's fury was aimed totally at Ben. "I know what you did! I know!"

"What's the problem here?" Sweeney said. "You picking on my buddy?"

She recoiled as if she'd been slapped, grabbing at her beads. Above her head and behind dirty glass a sign proclaimed, in huge letters: EVERYTHING MUST GO 50% OFF!

"Don't you touch me!" the old woman screamed. Sweeney stepped away, both palms in the air. Three or four people, one of them the Assistant Dean of Liberal Arts, had stopped on the sidewalk to stare.

"Nobody's touching you," Sweeney said.

She gaped at him for a second to be sure and then lurched to her feet. She grabbed her shopping cart and fled down the street, the bad wheel squealing as she went. Laughing, Sweeney turned back to Ben.

"So what did you do to her?"

"I didn't do anything," Ben said.

Sweeney's smile faded. "You don't *know* her, do you?" he asked.

"No," Ben said.

Sweeney stared down the sidewalk as the old woman disappeared under the umbrellas of the Renaissance Fair. He turned and stared at Ben again, assessing. He put a hand on Ben's elbow. "Hey, let's go get ourselves a cheese steak."

Chapter Eight

As soon as he entered the locker he knew something was different; he just couldn't put his finger on what it was. He swung his maroon briefcase down on the planked floor as the heavy door latched shut behind him. He yanked on the overhead cord, snapping on the single bare bulb.

All eight coolers were still there, in two rows, with one of the coolers set sideways on top of another. Was that the way he'd left them? He couldn't remember. He flipped the coolers open one by one; as far as he could tell nothing had been removed. There was only one stack that had been broken into—the stack he'd been taking fifties from all along—and even that was down by no more than an inch.

He took a moment, scanning the narrow, tomb-like room. On a hot May afternoon—it had been all the way up to ninety by noon—the locker was still cool, smelling of mildew and other people's rotting furniture.

He hated coming here. He did not like being reminded of just how precarious his position was, how all his hopes, all his promises to Katy, all the money now flowing into his bank account, rested on his ability to keep this airless room secret from the world.

A wasp bumped lazily against the naked bulb. He heard voices murmuring outside. He froze for several seconds, waiting until the voices had passed on. He shut the tops of the coolers, all but one. He was jumpy and cross; he hadn't been sleeping well for more than a month.

He took two or three deep breaths, trying to calm himself, then unzipped his briefcase and removed a large manila envelope. He got to one knee, counted out sixty fifties and slipped them into the en-velope. He had it all worked out: six hundred a week would go to Sweeney, with an extra six hundred for his own walking around money. It meant that Ben would not have to come back for another month. The key was not being seen here too often, not giving any-one a reason to start asking questions.

He closed the metal clasp on the envelope and slipped it back into his briefcase. He flipped the top of the cooler down, leaning hard on it to be sure it was closed tight. As he rose to his feet something caught his eye in the far corner of the storage locker. He moved a couple of steps closer to be sure; three or four cigarette butts lay scattered on the floor and there were three or four more that had fallen through the planks to the concrete below.

He just stared for a moment, dizzy suddenly, blood pounding through his temples. He bent down and shredded one of the butts between his fingers. It was impossible to tell how fresh it was. Maybe the butts had been there all along, when he first rented the place, and he just hadn't noticed. But how could he not have noticed? He'd been back here five or six times, surely he would have noticed.

He looked up at the rafters, back at the latched door, trying to fig-ure it out. There was no sign of a break-in. Who could have been in here? The woman in the office? One of the night watchmen? He rubbed the back of his thumb slowly across his mouth, uninten-tionally getting a little tobacco on his tongue. He grimaced, trying to wipe the acrid taste away.

He tried to imagine someone sitting in the dark, smoking, sur-rounded by seven and a half million dollars. How could they not take any? Maybe they had. If they had a way in they would surely return. Ben could come back in a week and find the locker totally empty.

He went to the first cooler and opened it. At the top of the open stack of fifties there were still a few loose bills, but beneath those bills the money was all divided into neat packets by green paper straps. On the straps were the stamps of the inky black scorpions, their tails curled and ready to strike. He gathered the packets by the handful, stashing them into his briefcase. The loose bills he just jammed in his pockets with trembling fingers. He wasn't calculating now; instinct drove him, instinct and fear. He shook the briefcase by the handles to make more room, then tore the cellophane off a sec-ond stack of fifties, filling the briefcase with as much as it could hold.

He rested his forehead against the door for a second before opening it, trying to compose himself. He leaned against the latch and stepped out into the heat. Rows of low concrete buildings baked in mid-afternoon sun; there was no one else around. The grass along the chain-link fence was parched and yellow, desperately needed rain.

He opened the rear of the van and swung the briefcase inside. He spied the roll of duct tape under the seat; he retrieved it and slammed the trunk shut.

He stepped back up into the locker and pulled the door closed behind him. He wrapped each of the coolers in duct tape, three times around, length-wise and width wise. He was in some kind of state. He got six of the eight coolers wrapped before he ran out of tape. Maybe it was a futile gesture, but if they were going to get his money, he was at least going to make it hard for them.

He drove down to school and locked his briefcase in the bottom drawer of his file cabinet. The campus was empty; it was the quietest time of the year, between graduation and summer school. The only people he saw as he was leaving were two maintenance men sitting in a truck in front of the Old Music Building, listening to the radio.

The next morning Ben came in early and counted the money; he had eighty-seven thousand eight hundred and fifty dollars in cash. He entered the money neatly in his ledger. He felt ashamed and shaken by his behavior the previous afternoon. He knew that he'd over-reacted, that it probably had all been in his imagination. Still, it was all he could do to resist the temptation to go back to the storage unit to be sure the rest of the money was still there.

He stacked the money neatly in several Kinko's boxes, put the boxes in his briefcase and took a cab out to a bank in Westlake (Katy had the van for the day). He amazed himself how relaxed he was, talking with the bank officer, filling out the forms for the safety deposit box.

They took him to a small room where they left him alone. Everyone was so respectful, so discrete, it reminded him of the moment the doctor and nurse leave you to make a urine sample. He packed the eighty-seven thousand eight hundred and fifty dollars neatly in the box—it turned out to be just the right size—and locked it.

Outside, waiting for the cab, he worked the key to the safety deposit box onto his key ring. He felt as if he'd done well. All the same, he knew he had a task in front of him. He was going to have to move all the money out of the storage unit and move it all soon.

. . .

Using the map that Rebecca had drawn them, they drove up into the hills, following gravel roads that divided and divided again, cutting under limestone cliffs that shone in the afternoon sun. They drove along a high ridge, passing radio towers, rolling over ancient cattle gaps. There were only two or three houses they could actually see from the road and even though they were only minutes away from the suburban palaces of the computer royalty, it still felt wild and remote.

They parked along the road and when they got out four deer scampered into the brush sixty feet ahead of them. They walked up the steep hill, Ben taking Katy's hand so she wouldn't fall. Cedar and honey-suckle crowded the caliche driveway so they couldn't see the house until they were nearly on it, but when it finally came into view Katy let out a small, involuntary gasp.

It was a fortress; the mammoth white stucco walls and terracotta tile roof reminded Ben of a Mexican hacienda or a French villa. Around the corner of the house Ben could see the shimmering blue water of a pool and, beyond the pool, the distant brown hills.

They knocked at the heavy carved door and waited. After a moment there was a scurry and the hoarse barking of a dog. A moment after that a Mexican maid with heavy Mayan features opened the door.

"We're here to see Rebecca?" Ben said.

The maid nodded and smiled; Ben suspected that she didn't speak English. Even as the maid gestured them to come in, Rebecca was sweeping down the stairs in a peach-colored silk blouse and a remarkably short tan skirt. She gave Ben and Katy each a quick kiss on the cheek.

"I'm sorry, my darlings, I was just on the phone," Rebecca said.

"So you've met Zoila?"

When the maid smiled again, nodding hello, Ben could see her gold tooth. Rebecca spoke quickly to her in Spanish and Zoila slipped away to the kitchen.

Rebecca took Katy by the arm. "It's so wonderful of you to come all this way. Please, let me give you the tour."

As huge as the house had seemed from the outside, on the inside it had the slightly stuffed quality of an English cottage. Pillows and cushions were everywhere in the living room, but the most remarkable thing about the room was the photographs; there seemed to be hundreds of them, many in expensive silver frames, lined up on every table and ledge. There was a photograph of Rebecca arm in arm with Clint Eastwood and Ronald Reagan, photos of her in Hawaii, skiing in Switzerland, on safari in Africa, posing under the arch of two giant elephant tusks with an ex-husband (it was clear that she had been breathtakingly beautiful when she was young).

She ushered them out of the living room into a small walled garden with a fountain. A couple of large, delicately colored fish drifted in the small pool and a turtle surfaced for a second and then disappeared in a wink.

As Rebecca led them up the stairs to the second floor, Ben glanced over her shoulder and saw a little boy staring at them through the bannister. He had huge brown eyes, brown skin and a tiny red car clutched in his right hand. As soon as Ben spotted him, he darted away.

This was Roberto, Rebecca said. He was Zoila's son and had just turned four. Rebecca wouldn't be able to take the two of them with her to Santa Fe and she hoped that wouldn't be a problem. They would stay with the house, if it was all right with Katy and Ben. Zoila was not an accomplished cook yet, but she was learning, and she cleaned, did laundry, made beds and had a wonderful disposition.

Ben listened, quietly appalled. How could they possibly have a maid? The people in Ethnic and Third World would kill him if they found out. As they marched down the hallway he tried to catch Katy's eye, but she wasn't looking at him.

All the bedrooms were on the second floor and there were six of them. The bedroom on the left Rebecca wanted to use to store all the stuff she wasn't going to be able to take with her and the one next to it was Zoila and Roberto's room (glancing inside, Ben could see an ironing board, still set up, some stacked shoe boxes, and old radio). The other four, of course, would all be theirs, to use as they wished. Maybe it was just Rebecca's manner, but she sounded as if everything had already been decided, as if she'd already made them a gift of the house.

"Ben, come look." Katy stood in the doorway of Rebecca's daughter's room. Ben stared over her shoulder at the canopied bed and the softly blowing white curtains, the rows of miniature horses lined up on the French provincial furniture.

"Abby would love this," Katy said.

"I know," Ben said.

They went back downstairs and Rebecca excused herself for a moment, stepping into the kitchen to speak to Zoila. Three Jack

Russell terriers jumped up on the chairs, barked furiously and then ran out again. Ben leaned over, scrutinizing an autographed color photo of Mick Jagger hanging next to the cabinet of English crockery. A huge parrot swung upside down, eyeing them warily, biting at the wires of his cage.

Rebecca took them outside. The view was spectacular; the pool seemed to hang at the very edge of the cliff. As Rebecca led Katy through the rose garden Ben stood at the fence, staring down at the blue ribbon of the Colorado miles below. This all felt a little too good to be true.

After a couple of minutes Zoila came out with a full tray of goodies. Ben smiled warmly at her, as if to say that he was not really party to this. They sat by the pool and Rebecca poured Katy and Ben tea. She talked about her trials at the Texas Film Commission, how politically difficult it had been for her since the election of the Republican governor. It was going to be good for her to get away from it all for awhile, she said.

"Hey, you guys, how you doin'?"

Ben looked back over his shoulder. Sweeney swung through the kitchen door and strode down the walk. Rebecca rose to greet him. He took her hand for a second, kissing her on the check, then turned and gave Ben a soft sock on the shoulder. Katy sat with her teacup, smiling up at him.

"It's nice to see you," Katy said.

"Not as nice as it is to see you." Sweeney leaned across and gave Katy a peck on the cheek. "Didn't I tell you? Isn't it great?" It struck Ben that Sweeney was awfully cheerful for someone whose girlfriend was leaving town.

"It's wonderful," Katy said.

The automatic pool cleaner writhed across the bright blue water. Sweeney dragged a plastic chair over to join them.

"Zoila!" Rebecca's voice was suddenly imperious, almost harsh; it took Ben by surprise. "Una taza por Senor Sweeney, por favor!"

"Can you believe we're sitting out here having tea?" Sweeney said. "Pretty damn civilized if you ask me!"

Zoila came down the walk with another cup. Behind her, Roberto stood in the kitchen door, watching them as he tried to sit on one of the Jack Russell terriers.

"So what do you think?" Sweeney said. He leaned forward and took one of Oreos off the plate, twisting the two halves of the cookie apart. Halfmoons of sweat curved under his armpits.

"I don't know. It's utterly amazing," Ben said. "I just don't know if it's for us. I wonder if it would a little too isolated for the kids."

"Not really," Rebecca said. "The people across the road have three teen-age daughters. And the schools are excellent."

Katy said nothing, stirring her tea. An antique rocking horse stared at them through the glass windows of the poolhouse, ears back, nostrils flaring.

"I'll bet your kids would love it," Sweeney said. "Having all their friends out to swim. And at night you should see the deer."

"I just don't know if we can afford something this grand," Ben said.

"All I'm looking for is someone who would take good care of the place," Rebecca said. "If you could pay Zoila, which is four hundred a month, and pick up the utilities, that would be it." Sweeney grinned, bits of black Oreo between his teeth.

Ben was still for a moment. He could feel everyone watching him; none of them understood how he could possibly consider saying no. Water guzzled down one of the pool drains.

"I'm telling you, you can't beat a deal like that," Sweeney said.

Ben glanced warily at Katy. "So what do you think?"

Her face shone. "I think it would be great."

Chapter Nine

Ben and Katy stood on the hill beyond the outfield fence watching Abby's softball game. It was dusk—nearly eight—and it was still hot, traffic whooshing by on First Street. Suburbans were parked everywhere on the grass like great beasts at rest and even now, in the fourth inning, a mother and her daughter in a green jersey hurried toward the field. On the far side of the access road the slope leading up to the railroad tracks looked strangely denuded, cleared of underbrush to discourage homeless squatters; the remains of their camps were still there, bulldozed into great heaps for the city to take away, piles of broken crating and cardboard, the tailends of soiled blankets.

Katy was quiet. They had already had one fight, the night before and it seemed as if they were about to have another. Katy had fallen in love with Rebecca's house immediately and had been astonished and then furious at how strongly Ben had been against their taking it.

A great shout went up as a girl with a red pony-tail hit a fly ball that the spindly left-fielder misjudged. As the red-headed girl sped around to third her teammates rose to cheer.

Ben watched as Abby strode to the plate, glancing over her shoulder to laugh at something her coach said. Girls' sports seemed to Ben to be infinitely better than boys'; the girls actually managed to have fun. Ben had once heard a parent at one of Matt's Little League games talking, without irony, about how their son was going to make it to the majors and support them in their old age.

"I'm sorry about last night," Ben said.

"I'm sorry too," Katy said. "I guess I just didn't understand."

Ben stared across the field. Abby took the first pitch for a ball. She stepped away to let the catcher throw the ball back, then took her stance again, just the way Ben had taught her: bat held high, elbow up, back leg slightly bent.

"I don't see how we could find a better deal," Katy said. "How much could the utilities be? Three hundred a month? If you're worried about it, I'm sure Rebecca would show us last summer's bills. Plus Zoila, that's seven hundred at the most. That's four hundred less than we're paying now."

"I know. But it's such an ostentatious house."

"But it's so beautiful, Ben. I just think it would be a great adventure."

Abby fouled the second pitch back off the screen. How many hours of batting practice had he and Abby put in together? First in New York in Riverside Park with a red plastic bat that was nearly as big as she was and later in their backyard in Austin with wiffle balls. She'd gotten good enough that she would hit one out of three onto the roof and in the spring when Ben cleaned the gutters he would find three or four of the white plastic balls up there, nestled in among the twigs and rotting leaving like the eggs of some giant condor.

"I just think it would be better for us to get into a real neighborhood, someplace permanent," Ben said. "What if Rebecca decides she doesn't like Santa Fe and wants to come back in six months?"

Abby hit a line drive over the second baseman and, by the time the right fielder arced a lollypop throw back in, Abby was safely on second. Katy, exasperated now, wasn't even watching.

"She told us a year, Ben."

"I know what she told us. I just don't think it's the most practical thing. We'd be so far from town and Abby's going to be driving in a few months, I'm not so sure I want her on those roads at night."

"That's ridiculous. You know that's not it."

"Then what is it?"

"I don't know. Something else. Something you're not saying."

He stared out at his daughter, so beautiful, standing at second base, waving to her team-mates. He wanted his old life back. "I don't know," he said. "Maybe I just don't like the idea of being up there with all those rich people."

On Sunday Ben had a softball game of his own, but he didn't go. Instead he tossed his mitt into the front seat of the van and drove to the self-storage unit on Burnet.

The lights on the lot shone bright and pitiless, as if they were glaring down on a prison yard. As Ben pulled through the front gate a father and his burly son wrestled a yellow pull-out couch off the back of a mud-spattered truck, too absorbed in their task to even look up. Ben drove down to Building Seven, backing around so that the van was nearly flush to the wall.

He worked quickly. He was able to get four of the coolers in the far back, two in the back seat, one on the floor, one in the front on the passenger seat. Somehow it seemed as if they took more room than before, as if they had somehow swollen after the long months of darkness. He covered them as best he was able with a couple of threadbare bedspreads he'd snuck out of the linen closet. The whole operation took him less than fifteen minutes.

He drove back to the front office. He was pleased to discover that Rose wasn't there. In her place was a pimply teen-ager in a Baylor Bears hat who could scarcely be roused from the Sunday Sports section. When Ben announced that he was checking out, the boy swung his feet down from the desk.

The kid turned out to be slow as molasses. It took him three or four minutes to find the right ledger and then he couldn't find a pen. Ben drummed his fingers on the counter. Through the window he could see his van parked outside, packed to the gills, the flimsy bedspreads draped over everything. The boy finally found a ballpoint that would work and wrote out a final receipt that Ben crumpled and tossed as soon as he was out the door.

Traffic was light. It was a little after nine. Katy, thinking he was at his game, wouldn't be expecting him for at least another hour. Even though he knew it was foolish, he kept checking his rear view mirror, just to be sure he wasn't being followed. Every sense seemed to be magnified, quickened. The coolers squeaked, rubbing together as the van swayed around a curve, and once or twice Ben could have sworn he heard a rustling as if there was someone huddling under the bedspreads in the back.

It turned out not to be just his imagination. Pulling up to a red light on Guadalupe he felt something on his collar, then something tickling his neck. He swatted quickly at it, batting a sleek roach against the windshield. Trying to right itself, the wriggling insect slid off the dashboard.

"Damn!" Ben said. He tried to jam the van into Park so he could step across and stomp it, but he wasn't quick enough. The roach scuttled to safety under the seats.

A car honked behind him. The light had changed to green. Ben wrenched the van back into Drive and eased into the intersection. He rubbed the back of his neck, disgusted; the roach must have been lurking in one of the coolers. There were no doubt others, living undisturbed for months; he was going to have to check.

He turned left on Twenty-First Street. On a Sunday night there was no guard at the traffic booth and the campus seemed deserted. He came around on the Inner Campus Drive and parked across from the north doors of Parlin Hall.

Getting out of the van, the heat slapped him in the face like a great moist towel. This was the hard part, the next few minutes, but there was no helping that, he just had to get through it as quickly and efficiently as he could.

He slid open the side door of the van and pulled out the first of the coolers, setting it on the sidewalk as he locked the car. His heart pounded. Far off he could hear a band playing, the slurred sound carrying on the heavy night air.

He carried the cooler across the road, setting it down again while he fumbled through his tangle of keys. If someone saw him right now, what could they possibly think he was doing? A professor getting back late from a picnic? He opened the outer door, holding it open with a foot and reaching back to catch the handle of the cooler. He slid it toward him, then lifted it, and pivoted into the dark building.

He edged his way up the stairs. There were light switches, but he didn't want to use them. He didn't want any campus policemen coming to investigate why one of the buildings was suddenly lit up late at night.

He moved on down the dark hallway, the only source of illumination the dull flickering Exit light at the far end. He passed the ghostly displays for the Oxford Summer Program, a bust of Shakespeare, a painted jester's mask. He passed the window outside the departmental office, filled with snapshots of his colleagues, one clowning, jamming his umbrella in the jaws of a stone lion in Beijing, another posing with a sheep in the Scottish highlands, another leaning against a wall in Southern France. He really didn't need any light; he knew this place by heart.

He backed into the door handle at the end of the hallway, shoving it open. There was a second door at the bottom of the stairs and as he maneuvered his way through it he knocked the cooler accidentally, nearly dropping it; he felt a sharp twinge in his back. He duck-walked down the hallways to Dick's office, opened it and shoved the cooler inside.

It took nearly forty minutes to move all the eight coolers, much longer than he had anticipated. It was slow work, not just the trek down the long hallways, but the constant locking and unlocking of the van, the building, Dick's office.

His only bad moment came when a lone cyclist came out of nowhere, whizzing silently past as Ben stood frozen by the open door of the van, but the cyclist was gone in a moment, swooshing around the Architecture Building like a darting bat. The only other people Ben saw were a couple holding hands under the trees in front of the Humanities Research Center and they drifted off after a minute or two for a more private spot.

Standing finally in Dick's office with all eight coolers stacked in front of him, Ben was amazed at how much space they took. Between the eight coolers and all of Dick's packing boxes there was barely room to get to the desk.

Maybe it was craziness bringing it all here, but from the moment he'd seen the cigarette butts on the floor of the storage unit, he'd known he had to do something and had to do it fast.

Dick's office would serve, at least until he found someplace better. It had its advantages. Dick was going to be away for fifteen months. Aside from the evening cleaning crews, Ben was the only one with a key. The monthly trips up to Burnet had become too risky anyway, bound to attract attention if they hadn't already. Here, Ben would have daily access to the money.

In a way it was perfect. Surely the last place anyone would come looking for seven million dollars was in an assistant professor's office. Ben knew from experience he had nothing to worry about from the cleaning crews; they were in and out in fifteen seconds. The chances of theft were minimal. In the four years he'd been in Austin there had been only two break-ins in the department, both over the holidays, and in both cases the thieves had been interested only in computers.

It took Ben another half hour to rearrange everything, barricading the eight coolers against the far wall, burying them under an avalanche of rugs and boxes of avant-garde fiction. It looked pretty convincing when he was done, not much different than the office of any other pack-rat academic away in Europe. Who would have guessed that there was enough under there to pay the entire department's salaries for years.

He checked his watch. It was nearly ten-thirty. Katy was going to be wondering where he was. As he left the office he jiggled the door-knob a couple of times to be sure it was unlocked. He tucked in his shirt, moving quickly toward the Exit sign.

There was a soft cough from the far end of the hallway. Ben stopped dead in his tracks. He strained to hear; for several seconds there was only the steady blowing of the air conditioning, but then it was broken by a jangling of keys.

"Hello?" Ben said.

There was a sharp click and the overhead florescent lights flick-ered on. Nancy Rankin, junior medievalist, stood in the doorway of her office, looking frightened as a deer.

"Hey, Nancy."

"Hey."

"What are you doing?"

"I just came in to use my printer," she said.

He and Nancy had come to the University the same year. She was single, smart, from a working class family in Ohio and was finishing a mammoth book on linguistics and critical theory. She often worked late in the night and was the author, Ben suspected, of many of the subversive one-liners scrawled anonymously across the posters advertising scholarly talks.

The question was, how long had she been standing there? She couldn't have been there while he was lugging the coolers down the hallway. She couldn't have been sitting in her office in the dark, un-less she had been sleeping. No. She must have just come in; that was why he'd heard the keys. But what if she'd passed Dick's office? What if she'd heard him sliding the boxes around?

"How about you?"

"Oh, I just came in to get something," he said.

Suddenly he was aware of how he must have looked to her in his sneakers and tattered Milwaukee Brewers t-shirt. She was still half hidden in the doorway.

"We'll have to have lunch this week," he said. "It's been too long."

Locusts sang in the honey-suckle as Ben trudged up the caliche driveway. A sprinkler sent soft arcs of water over the flower beds next to the massive house and Ben had to step through a snarl of hoses to knock at the carved wooden door.

After several seconds Zoila opened the door. She seemed de-lighted to see him. "How are you?" Ben said.

"Fine," Zoila said softly. She gestured him to follow her.

As they moved through the house the Jack Russell terriers swirled around his feet, barking, and then disappeared. Roberto stood in the kitchen, eating a peach, wearing only a heavy diaper.

"Hey, Roberto!" Ben said. The little boy was not about to be won over so easily. When Ben tried to give him a high five Roberto turned and ran into the laundry room.

Rebecca was in the pool. As Ben came down the walk she waved to him. "Ben! Do you want to swim? I'm sure Zoila can find you a suit."

"No, no, I'm fine."

He took a chair and sat by the edge of the pool. Rebecca was totally at ease in the water. She swam facing him, doing the sidestroke with no more apparent effort than a woman stretching out on the silkiest of couches. It was hard not to notice her tanned, lithe body; Ben had the definite sense that he was being invited to notice. She chatted away, asking about Katy and the children. Ben leaned forward in his chair, stolid as a farmer.

She finished her laps, pulling herself out of the water, and grabbed a towel off one of the plastic lounge chairs. "Would you like anything to drink? Iced tea? Coke?"

"A Coke would be great," Ben said.

"Zoila? Zoila!" The maid materialized at the kitchen door. "A Coke for Mr. Lindberg, por favor!"

Rebecca sat down carefully in the chair next to him, draping her towel over her shoulders. "So you've come around."

"Yes, I seem to have come around," Ben said.

It was a done deal. They were taking the house, despite all of Ben's misgivings. He had been outvoted. Katy had dug in her heels and Abby had taken her side. What fifteen year old was going to say no to a place with a pool? Ben was not in a good position to offer much resistance. After all the ruckus about the mythical residual check he owed Katy one.

Zoila brought him a Coke and Rebecca watched him drink it, drying her arms. "So will you be teaching this summer?" she said.

"No. Just writing my book."

"It sounds like a wonderful life. You must be very content." He glanced quickly at her. Was she teasing him? She didn't seem to be. "Your wife is so lovely and Sweeney says your kids are terrific."

"Things are pretty good," he said.

She stood up, tossing her towel aside, and leaned across for a terrycloth robe that lay at the edge of the pool. The blue of the water was so intense it almost seemed unreal, something only a painter could come up with. "And where did you go to graduate school? Not here."

"No. Columbia."

"Oh, really?" She brightened, as if this was the most delightful thing she'd ever heard. "I used to know people there, years ago."

"Such as?"

"Lionel Trilling."

Ben laughed. "Yes, I've heard of him."

Rebecca slipped into the robe, knotting the belt loosely at her waist. "I'm not saying that I knew him well. I met him three or four times at parties. I was very young, but he was very nice to me. I love his books. They must seem very old-fashioned now."

"I love his books too," Ben said.

"*Sincerity And Authenticity*. It's wonderful, isn't it?"

"Yes, it is." He sipped the last of his Coke.

"And so which are you?"

"I beg your pardon?"

"Sincere or authentic."

"I may be a little too old to be either," Ben said.

The answer seemed to please her. "That's a relief."

Ben rattled the ice in his empty glass. Wind rustled through the stand of bamboo. Sitting next to the water, the day almost felt cool. She gazed steadily at him; he could see the curiosity in her eyes.

"Maybe I should show you around," she said.

"Of course."

He put his glass down on the glass table and she took him on a tour of the backyard, showing him the switch on the side of the poolhouse for the hot tub, the cut-off valve for the gas. He had forgotten how spectacular the view was from up here; even on a hazy day he could make out the dome of the capitol, miles away.

The dogs she would take with her, she said. The parrot she might leave, if that was all right. If he squawked too much they should put his cage in the sink in the laundry room, it always quieted him down.

"This is very generous of you," Ben said. "Everyone is very excited."

"I'm delighted you're taking the house," she said. "I'm just in love with your wife. You know I've never done this before. I spoke to my friend Didi . . . I'm sure you'll meet her, she lives down at the far end of the canyon. Anyway, they rent their house every summer when they go to Maine. Her only suggestion was that I should get a deposit, just in case."

"Of course," Ben said. Awkwardness hung in the air. "How much would you like?"

A tawny cat clawed up on the fence and bounded across the lawn. Rebecca went down on one knee. "Come here, Puss, come here." The cat stared for a moment and then approached warily. Rebecca scooped the cat up in her arms and began to scratch her behind the ears. "That's a good cat. What Didi suggested was the equivalent of one month's rent. Of course I'm not charging rent, but what Didi usually asks for is four thousand dollars."

"Four thousand," Ben said.

The cat rolled over in her arms. Rebecca ran a long finger slowly through the soft fur. "Look at her, she's nothing but an old tart." She knelt down and let the cat flow out of her arms. "If it's too much, please tell me," she said. "I've never been very good at these money things."

"I'll talk to Katy. It's just that in the summer the university doesn't pay us, but I'm sure we can work something out."

"I'm sure. The important thing is that you'll be in the house. Oh, there's one other thing I want to show you."

She took him around to the side of the house where a canoe hung in a rough shed. She showed him the scarred metal locker where she kept the paddles and four yellow life preservers. There were some wonderful places to take the children canoeing, she said, all within a couple of hours drive. She had a book she could show him.

"Please," she said. "I don't want you to worry about the money. Whatever you decide is reasonable."

"I understand. We'll talk it over."

"Oh, and I should mention. . . ." The locusts had started up again, screaming like defective smoke detectors. "My ex-husband and I are in a bit of a financial dispute, shall we say, so I'd like to keep this off the books."

If he wasn't irritated enough, Ben also managed to hit rush hour traffic on the way home. He was not happy about Rebecca hitting him up for a four thousand dollar deposit and the worst thing about it was the fears it triggered that Sweeney might have said something to her, spilled the beans about two men's secret arrangement. He was going to have to speak to Sweeney about it.

By the time Ben got to Oltdorf, things had slowed to a crawl. After a couple of blocks Ben saw why.

Several police cars and an EMS truck surrounded the feed store. A crowd of fifty people had gathered outside the barricade of sawhorses and twisted yellow tape. A lone policeman stood in the middle of the street, diverting traffic.

Ben slowed, rolling down his window, but the patrolman was in no mood to answer questions, waving him on. Ben followed the flow of traffic onto the side street and pulled into the first alley he saw. He hurried back, walking and running.

He jostled his way through the crowd. There, leaning against the front door of the feedstore, was a wire shopping cart with one warped wheel. Ben could only stare.

"Long time, no see."

Ben turned. It was Marvin Booth, the hulking musician who'd lived two doors down from them for the past four years. He wore his trademark red suspenders and sucked on a popsicle.

"How you doin'?" Marvin said.

"Fine. What's going on?"

Through the windows of the feed store Ben could see the police shuffling around inside. One of the local TV reporters stood on the far curb, pert as a robin, while her cameraman prowled, looking for the perfect angle.

"It's pretty bad," Marvin said. His lips were still purple from his popsicle. "Some old woman was sleeping in there and they shot her."

"Who shot her?"

"Nobody knows. Fuckin' world we live in, huh?"

"So is she still in there?"

"No, they took her out. They had a blanket over her. But apparently, whoever did this, not only did they blow her face off, they also busted both her hands with a hammer." Ben turned away. Sirens wailed in the distance. Marvin took a long noisy slurp on his grape popsicle to keep it from dripping. "So I hear you're movin'. Sounds like a good time to do it."

When Ben came into the house, everyone was already sitting down for supper. The three of them all looked up at him, waiting for him to say something. His mouth was dry and chalky, incapable of language. The overhead fan spun slowly overhead; a bouquet of fresh flowers adorned the table. What a frail vessel a family was, he thought. He swung his briefcase onto the chair next to the book-case.

"So I guess you heard," Katy said.

"I just did," Ben said. "You guys O.K.?"

Matt nodded and Abby rolled her eyes. "We're fine," Katy said. "You sit down and I'll get you a plate."

She got up and went into the kitchen. Ben took his place at the head of the table and shook out his napkin, scrutinizing his children: his son cutting his meat, his daughter fiddling with her ring. For a second it struck him that it was a scene out of *Father Knows Best*.

"Sort of scary, isn't it?" he said. "Listen, I know it's a terrible thing, but the police are going to find out who did this."

"She was just a poor old woman, Dad," Abby said. "Why would anyone do something like that?"

"I don't know," he said, not looking at her, because of course he did know. He felt his son's clear-eyed gaze on him, his son who believed everything he said. It was his daughter who needed to question everything. "These things do happen."

"But this was so close," Abby said.

"I know," he said. "But it's not as if somebody's going to be coming down the street murdering people."

"How do you know that?"

"Oh, come on, Abby!"

Katy came back with his plate and set it in front of him: steak, twice baked potatos and asparagus, the children's favorite meal. They didn't have red meat often, but Katy felt it was important to have it once in awhile, to keep everyone's strength up.

His hands were shaking. He kept them in his lap, out of sight, trying to regain control. He tried to tell himself that everything was the same, that nothing had changed, it was still just the four of them sitting down at a beautifully set table, the slanting late afternoon light coming in through the windows, but it wasn't the same because he could still hear the old woman screaming at him, thief, thief, and when he shut his eyes for a second he could see her red, blistered face contorted by fear.

Ben took a bite of his potato and then he took two. Abby, still sulking over his reprimand, wasn't looking at him. He sliced into his steak, trimming off the gristle. Lying to the children had turned his stomach to bile. What if he blurted out the truth? That none of them were safe now, that their entire lives dould be torn apart with a single knock on the door, five minutes from now, or ten. He stared down at his meat. A thin pool of blood had gathered in the bottom of his plate. He rose from the table.

"Excuse me," he said.

He left the room and trotted quickly up the stairs. He pulled the bathroom door shut behind him and knelt over the toilet, just in time. He vomited in three long, choking heaves, a yellow cloud mushrooming in the clear water of the basin. He nose stung and tears blurred his eyes. He sat on the floor, depleted, resting his head against the cool white porcelain bowl. A woman had died, a woman Ben had once given a dollar to; she'd died because of what he had done and what he had not done. His passivity had just taken him over the line. He was now an accomplice to murder.

After a moment he took a piece of tissue to blow his nose, cleaning it of the tiny chunks of food, and then flushed the toilet. He washed his face and hands, then opened the bathroom door and stood for a moment on the landing, gathering himself before facing his family. He could still taste the sourness in his mouth.

A little after nine that evening he went out on the front porch. Long arms of colored light still flashed from squad cars three blocks away, pulsing blue and red off the tress. Small groups of neighbors huddled together on their lawns, talking quietly together. A seven year old boy, plastic helmet strapped dutifully under his chin, rode his bike in circles in the street as if was a national holiday, as if there would be no school in the morning.

The police had been down there for a least four hours. What were they looking for? Ben had no idea what police did in a real investigation; all he knew was what he'd seen on television. He imagined them going over the feedstore with a fine-toothed comb. What if they found his fingerprints? But that was laughable. He hadn't been in the feedstore for five months, surely any prints would have been erased by dust and grime by now. But maybe they'd find some fiber from his coat. He might have torn a sleeve on a nail or something might have fallen from his wallet when he'd taken it out to put the four fifties in.

He didn't hear Katy come out on the porch and he started when he felt her hand on his shoulder.

"You O.K.?" she asked.

"Yeah, I'm fine."

"Are you sure?"

"It's upsetting."

"I know." The evening was pleasantly cool for early June and there was a light breeze. They stood silently together, husband and wife, concealed in the deep shadows of the porch. Packing boxes leaned against the wall. The scene surrounding the feedstore was far enough away that it looked as tiny and unreal as a boy's train set, but it was brilliantly lit, as if they were shooting a commercial or a movie.

"I keep thinking about what it must have been like," Katy said.

"What what must have been like?" Ben asked.

"For that poor woman." She slipped her hand in his. "We are so lucky."

The murder was plastered all over the front page the next morning. The homeless woman's name was Audrey Davis and she'd been living on the streets of Austin for seven years. She'd grown up in a series of foster homes in Oklahoma, worked for a time for the phone company and had been institutionalized on and off for years. The photo showed her sitting cross-legged on the steps of a church, flanked by a couple of her street cronies. It was a strange picture. Her face was all screwed up as if she was either drunk or squinting into the sun, but her left arm was raised over her head, the hand curved, the fingers pressed together like a ballerina, like a dim remembrance of grace.

Terry Rossi, the director of the Homeless Center, remembered her as a troubled, fragile woman who loved animals and kept to herself. "She'd had a hard life, but if you were her friend she would give you the shirt off her back." A memorial service would be held on Friday and contributions could be sent care of Ms. Rossi at the Center.

Ben sat at the breakfast table, staring at the article. Whoever had done this had gotten the wrong person and by now they must know that. The house was silent; Katy had already gone for her walk. Ben had the use of the car for the morning so he could move several boxes of books into his office. Now he had another more private task as well. He pushed his chair away from the table and patted his pockets to be sure he had the keys.

The red brake lights of the white pick-up ahead of Ben flickered as they came down First Street. The reaction of the thirty young men, mostly Mexican, lined up along the curb was instantaneous. Hands flew in the air. Some of the men whistled; others began to run towards the truck as it pulled over. Ben waited, watching as a dozen men crowded around the window of the pick-up, negotiating. After a few seconds two of the younger ones leapt up in the back, grinning, pulling their bandannas over their mouths and then hunkering down as the truck sped away.

Ben took the next left and came all the way around the block. An old man pushed a shopping cart filled with bags of crushed cans. It was a dicey neighborhood for parking. The Homeless Center was lodged in one of a dozen old warehouses and on the front steps a group of drunks dug into a bin of old clothes, quarrelling over a pair of boots.

Inside a half dozen men sat waiting on benches. One was asleep and another sang softly in Spanish. A large woman in a wheelchair pinned a picture of a pink cat to the wall. Art was everywhere on the walls, as if they were getting ready for an art show.

"Can I help you?" the woman in the wheelchair asked.

"I'm looking for Terry Rossi," Ben said.

"Her office is back there. Last door on the right."

Ben walked down a narrow hallway, past a water cooler, past a series of cramped offices. His first job in New York had been with the Welfare Department; this had the same underfunded smell.

He peered into the last office on his right. A small woman with curly black hair crouched over her computer. When Ben knocked she straightened up quickly.

"Yes?"

"Hi. My name's Ben Lindberg." She waited for more. "My family and I live in the neighborhood where the woman was shot yesterday. I'd like to make a contribution if I could."

"Please, sit down."

Ben took a seat carefully; an ominous-looking metal stud protruded from the frayed vinyl covering. Every inch of wall space was in use. There were bumper stickers, newspaper articles, government notices. On Ms. Rossi's desk was a tiny framed photo of a group of women in front of a raft with their paddles, a raging river in the background.

"You didn't know her?"

"I used to see her in the neighborhood. And I spoke to her once."

"She wasn't an easy person. But she had a sweetness too, once she learned to trust you. Sometimes she would write poems and give them to me." She closed her eyes for a second, pinching the bridge of her nose. "I'm sorry. I'm just so tired of this. I've worked in this job for seven years. And last night I counted it up, how many people

I've known here who've died. Nearly a hundred. A woman drowned while she was sleeping in a culvert, three men burned to death in an abandoned house because one of them owed somebody three dollars . . ."

"The police must have spoken to you."

"Yes."

"Do they have any idea what happened?"

"No." The intercom blatted, but she ignored it. "Do you know what they did before they killed her? They broke both of her hands. With a hammer. And then they shot her eight times."

Both of them were silent. "The one time I spoke to her she accused me of stealing something," Ben said. She looked up at him with steady brown eyes. "Did she ever say anything to you about that?"

"You mean about *you*? No. She was always accusing people of taking things from her . . . her sleeping bag, her money, her shoes. She would come in here, she would be just furious. It was usually when she hadn't been taking her medicine. Not that she was always wrong. One way to look at it, people took things from her, her whole life. Apparently she had a child once. She was working for the phone company then, but she started drinking and lost her job and then the county came and took the baby away. She never saw it again. So don't think it was just you." She frowned, her eyes misting up again.

Ben took out his wallet, counting out four fifties and a one hundred, and set them on the desk. "I'd appreciate it if you didn't mention this to anyone," he said.

As he left he walked down the steps and stared out across the lot for the day laborers. There were still a handful of men lined up along the curb, but it was nine-thirty now and most of the jobs were gone. A majority of the men had retreated, some to sit on the benches under the tin-roofed shelters, while others shared a bottle in the back of an ancient van.

"Hey, mister! You got any spare change?"

Ben turned. A broad-shouldered drunk shambled towards him, his dirty blonde hair matted as a Rastafarian's.

"Sorry," Ben said. "I'm broke."

"Broke? How can you be broke? America is the richest country in the world!"

The men gathered around the van were staring at them now. A young Mexican boy sitting under a tree rose to his feet.

"My name's Bobby. What's yours?" the drunk said. Ben shook his head. Traffic still droned down First Street. From the far side of the lot a half dozen men began walking towards them. In another minute Ben would be surrounded. "I said, what's your name?"

Ben backed away. "You take care."

"Take care? What the fuck is that supposed to mean?"

A second group of men was coming from across the street. One of them had a towel over his head and he tripped and nearly fell in his haste. Ben waved his hands, like a referee waving off a basket.

"No jobs," he said. "No jobs."

Chapter Ten

It took Ben five minutes to drive home. He jogged up the porch steps, opened the front door and called Katy's name. His voice echoed in the empty house and then there was only the thunking of the dryer; she wasn't back from her walk yet.

He got in the van and drove slowly through Stacey Park. A young mother pushed her toddler on the swings and a couple of fiftyish-looking men in voluminous shorts swatted a tennis ball back and forth across a sagging net. Ben headed up the steep hill and turned right on Travis Heights Boulevard, following Katy's usual route.

As much as he dreaded what he was about to do, it was better to get it over with now, while the children were in school. It would give them a few hours to talk it all through, alone. He tried to imagine what she would think. She wouldn't believe him at first, but when she did believe him, what then? He had always feared her anger. Forgiveness was not necessarily her first reflex and this was not going to be an easy thing to forgive. He had always felt that their marriage could survive anything; he was not convinced it could survive this.

Gregorian monks chanted softly on Public Radio. Ben drove up and down the streets of the neighborhood, but somehow Katy had eluded him. He turned towards home. As he pulled up alongside the curb, the cat, sitting on the front porch cleaning itself, lifted its head and, after a second, flowed down the steps and loped over to the car. Ben opened his door and ran his hand over the cat's arching back.

It was nearly nine-thirty; Katy should have been back by now. She must have stopped off at someone's house. He could feel his resolve slipping away. He had screwed his courage to the sticking point in order to confess, not just sit out here wasting the morning. The cat purred, fidgeting under his touch. Maybe what he should do was go into school, unpack the boxes of books and come back. He shoved the cat gently away from the van, shut the door, and turned on the ignition.

He got a temporary pass at the guard station and was lucky enough to find a parking place directly across from Parlin Hall. He lifted one of the boxes from the back of the van, then turned without looking to cross the street and nearly got himself run over. There was a long screech of brakes and the blast of a horn. Ben stared stupidly, clutching his carton of books. Sweeney sat behind the wheel of his red Bronco, shaking his head. After a couple of seconds he lowered his window.

"Nice move," Sweeney said.

"Hey."

Sweeney scrutinized him. The clanking of metal, the banging of hammers, filled the air. In front of the Main Building a dozen workmen dissembled the graduation bleachers.

"You all right?"

"I'm fine."

"You sure? I hate to say it, Ben, but you look like shit." Out of nowhere, Ben's eyes filled with tears and he had to look away. Not in front of Sweeney.

"Get in for a second," Sweeney said softly. "You can put the box in my car."

"No, that's all right."

"Come on."

Sweeney leaned across the front seat and shoved open the door on the passenger side. Ben stood without moving for another second, utterly lost. Sweeney waited. A truck from Buildings and Grounds pulled up behind them, the driver tapping lightly on his horn.

"Maybe for a minute," Ben said. Sweeney said nothing. Ben walked around to the passenger side, slid the carton of books in the back and then got up front.

They drove slowly past the Architecture Building, past a U. T. cop on his scooter, making out a ticket, then took a right on Guadalupe.

"So is Katy O.K.?" Sweeney said.

"She's fine."

"And the kids?"

"They're great."

It was a hazy June day, moist and warm as a bath, and Sweeney had the air conditioning going full-blast. An old man in a battered cowboy hat leaned against the wall of the Coop, strumming and singing, his empty guitar case on the sidewalk in front of him.

Sweeney turned right on Twenty-Sixth Street. Ben rubbed at his eyes with his thumb and forefinger. Neither man spoke. The story hung in the chilled air, waiting to be told. Ben knew that Sweeney wasn't going to let him out of the truck without some kind of explanation and Ben was too drained to invent one.

"So did you see the papers this morning?" Ben said.

"You mean about the woman they found in the feedstore?"

"Yeah." He leaned forward and turned the air conditioner down a notch. "That's where I found it."

"What are you talking about? Where you found what?"

"Where I found the money."

"In the feedstore?"

Ben was quiet for a long time, knowing that he had done something irrevocable, that there could be no going back. "Yes."

Sweeney glanced over quickly, incredulous, to see if Ben could be kidding, then saw that he wasn't. "Well, mother-fuck."

Sweeney was the last person Ben should have told. A day later, or even an hour later, Ben might have said nothing, but now, still reeling from the death of the old woman, it all came out, haltingly at first and then in a fierce rush of self-loathing.

It was the first time Ben had ever seen Sweeney speechless. His face colored and he rubbed his arms and occasionally he would utter a soft curse— "God damn . . ." and "Good Christ . . ."

The telling took twenty minutes and they were nearly to San Marcos by the time Ben finished. Sweeney drove one-handed, listening, his eyes grave and intent. He offered Ben a stick of cinnamon gum. Ben shook his head no. Sweeney took a stick for himself, folding it before putting it in his mouth. He chewed slowly and looked over at Ben.

"So how much money are you talking about?"

"A lot."

"More than, say, a hundred thousand?"

"Yeah."

"And where is it now?"

Ben shook his head; he told Sweeney enough; he wasn't playing

Twenty Questions. Sweeney balled up the tin foil from his gum, opened his window a crack and tossed it out, the faintest hint of irritation on his pursed lips. Billboards flashed by, advertising snake farms and outlet malls. Ben covered his face with his hands.

Sweeney slid off on the next exit and down under the bridge and then back onto the highway on the other side, heading north towards Austin. Neither man spoke, both lost in their own thoughts. Clouds had started to roll in from the west and across the vast pastures Ben could see cattle and a lone white horse, grazing in shadow as well as in light; it was like a scene painted by one of the Dutch Masters.

"So what do you think of your old teacher now?" Ben said.

Sweeney rolled his eyes. "What are you going to do?"

"I was thinking of telling my wife."

"Jesus, Ben. No offense, but you really can't do that."

"Why not?"

"What good is it going to do? Why would you drag her into this? It's not her problem, Ben. You'll just end up losing everything."

"Then what am I supposed to do?"

"Absolutely nothing. Just go about your business. Go finish your book. You didn't kill that woman. And nobody knows you've got the money."

"Don't they? What if she told them? After they broke her hands?"

"She was nuts. No one would have believed her!" There was a lot of construction south of town and the road narrowed to a single lane, men in orange vests and hard hats moving slowly among the barricades. "Lay low. I'm going to help you."

"How?"

Sweeney leaned forward, both elbows on the steering wheel, stretching out his back muscles like a big cat. "I don't know yet."

That night on the ten o'clock news the police chief bridled at a reporter's suggestion that the fact that the murder victim was a homeless person might make some difference in the way they handled the investigation. There was also a brief, appalling clip of someone who described herself as Audrey's best friend, a stout, middle-aged woman with bad teeth and heavily-tatooed arms. Half-way through the interview she burst into tears. "If they could do something like this to Audrey, none of us are safe. I'm scared, O.K.? You don't know how rough it is out here."

He dreamed that night that he heard something bumping up the stairs, a dull squeaking. In his dream it woke him and he sat upright in bed, listening until the sound stopped. He rose and went into the dark hallway and saw the wire shopping cart with the one bad wheel stationed in front of Abby's bedroom. He went to the door and looked in. The homeless woman sat on the bed, stroking the hair of his sleeping daughter; her hand was bloody and broken.

Ben woke, whimpering, his heart racing. Katy lay asleep next to him, the air conditioning sending a hush through the dark house.

Sweeney insisted that the four of them go out dancing at the Broken Spoke for Rebecca's farewell party. It was not clear that this was her first choice, but Sweeney was determined to send her off with a real Texas evening.

The Broken Spoke was old-time Austin, a throw-back, a dump; the long barn-like building with the wagon wheel out front looked as if it hadn't been painted in forty years. The music was in full swing when they came in—a true country western band with fiddles and accordion and a square-jawed lead singer with his black cowboy hat pulled down almost to his eyebrows.

A dozen dancers swirled across the sawdust floor. There was one old couple who was fantastic; he must have been at least seventy, stooped, and he was missing a hand; his wife looked like Dale Evans in her yoked denim skirt with red bandanna appliques of coyotes and cactus. They never looked at one another, they never smiled, and he backed her around the floor as if they were both on ball-bearings. The other dancers were pretty much from the blue jeans, cowboy boots and white shirts with the sleeves rolled up crowd.

Ben found them a table and they all sat down and had a beer, watching for a few minutes to get their courage up. As the old couple swept by Ben caught a whiff of Old Spice. Sweeney finally rose from his seat and reached across for Katy's hand.

"Shall we?"

Rebecca and Ben followed Katy and Sweeney onto the floor. Ben was generally an acceptable dancer, but this was two step and he didn't do steps. He and Rebecca did their best, but this was serious dancing, and after a couple of songs they made their way by unspoken agreement back to the table.

"I hope you don't mind," Ben said.

"No," Rebecca said. "These really aren't the right shoes anyway."

The band launched into "Your Cheating Heart." Ben stared out onto the floor. What Sweeney lacked in technique he made up for in energy and Katy was a great dancer; it didn't take her long to pick up what people were doing. She never looked more beautiful than when she was dancing.

"So how early in the morning are you leaving?" Ben asked.

"I hope to get away by seven."

"And you're driving by yourself?"

"I'll be fine. I love to drive. And I'll have my dogs to keep me company."

They fell silent for a moment, gazing out at the dancers like two old chaperones. Sweeney jigged across the floor, moon face beaming. Maybe it was just Ben's imagination, but from the first moment of the evening he noticed a change in Sweeney, a new gallantry and confidence, a sly, bright-eyed solicitude. Ben could almost see him savoring the secret that he and Ben now shared, rolling it across his palate like an after-dinner mint. Ben pressed his knuckles to his lips and then turned, aware that Rebecca was watching him.

"You lucked out, didn't you?" she said.

"What do you mean?"

"Your wife. She's a wonderful person."

"She is."

Rebecca brushed a strand of hair from her face and took a swig of beer. She wore a flowered sun dress, her bare shoulders glistening in reflected light. "You know you mean a great deal to Sweeney. He talks about you all the time."

"Really?"

"The right teacher at the right moment, it can change everything." Out on the dance floor Katy and Sweeney linked arms with a group of line dancers. Rebecca seemed sad. There was a fineness to her features, Ben could imagine there must have been a time, not long past, when everyone fell in love with her.

"So it's O.K. between you two?" he said. "You're leaving and all?"

"It's fine." She heistated for a moment. "He's a sweetheart, really, but he's one of those people you don't ever want to say no to."

They both had their elbows up on the narrow table. As she adjusted the gold bracelets on her tanned arm, the back of her hand brushed against his. For a flickering paranoid second it crossed his mind that Sweeney might have told her, but her smile was so rueful, her gaze so unflinchingly candid, it didn't seem possible that anybody could have been that good an actress. The song ended. A black-hatted fiddle-player dipped towards the microphone, taking his bow. Katy and Sweeney made their way back to the table.

. . .

Ben was leaning forward on a ladder, trying to work a screwdriver
into one of the intractable knots of rope that held up the porch
swing, when he saw the man making his way down the block. The
man stopped at every house, ringing the bell, waiting a moment or
two, then moving on. It was curious; at ten-thirty in the morning it
was the wrong time of day for the encyclopedia salesmen and the
Clean Air canvassers. The man was middle-aged, slightly dumpy in
his tan suit and, judging from the hitch in his walk, not that many
months from his first hip replacement.

The man raised a hand in greeting as he came across the lawn.
"Morning."

"Morning," Ben said.

The man squinted, surveying the packing boxes lined up on the
porch, the rolled-up rugs draped across them like exhausted ser-
pents. "Looks like you're moving."

"That's right."

The man leaned over and retrieved a chewed-up rubber football
from the shrubbery below the porch. He came slowly up the stairs
and set the ball gently in the blue crate filled with Matt's tennis rack-
ets, plastic swords and old frisbees.

"My name's Malcolm Hyde," the man said. "I'm with the police
department."

Ben looked over his shoulder and wiped the sweat from his eye
with his forearm. "Uh-huh."

"I've just been going around the neighborhood, talking to people.
See if anybody remembers anything about the night that old woman
was killed. Anything out of ordinary you might have heard or seen."

"No, I can't say that I do."

"No strange cars driving around the neighborhood . . ."

"No."

Ben turned back to his work, twisting the screwdriver in the rock-
hard knot, then taking it out and trying to pry the swollen rope loose
with his fingers. His heart was pounding. The key was to stay calm,
not to give himself away. There was no reason to believe that the policeman knew anything. It was just routine, he was talking to everyone. Maybe Ben should offer him something cool to drink. But, no,
he didn't want to appear too anxious to please.

"You at the University?" Hyde said.

"I beg your pardon?"

"I said, you at the University?"

Ben glanced over his shoulder. Hyde stood at an open boxful of scholarly journals, running his finger across some back issues of *The New England Quarterly*.

"Yes," Ben said.

Hyde smoothed a hand over his halo of wispy hair. "You ever recall seeing this old woman?"

"You mean the woman who was killed?"

"Yeah."

"I think maybe so. Once in a while. You'd see her up and down Congress."

"And did you ever talk to her?"

Ben hesitated for a fraction of a second. "No, not that I can remember."

Hyde looked mournfully out at the street. "So where are you moving?"

"Westlake."

"That'll be nice. I hear the prices are pretty steep out there."

"I think they're pretty steep everywhere."

Hyde fished a blue spiral notebook out of his jacket pocket. "And what did you say your name was?"

"Lindberg. Ben Lindberg."

"That with a g or a gh?"

"Just a g." Ben clutched at the ladder with his left hand, suddenly dizzy.

Hyde scrawled something on his pad and then stared at it, frowning. "Uh-huh. You the one that went by the Homeless Center and made the contribution?"

"Yes," Ben said.

"That was nice," Hyde said. He put the notebook back in his pocket. "Well, good luck with your move."

Chapter Eleven

The plan had been to move early, before it got hot, but, as always, there was more to be dealt with than they realized: a refrigerator to be cleaned out, counters to be washed, an ancient chest of drawers to be carried over to the neighbors, last minute boxes to be packed and taped. It was nearly twelve by the time they finished loading the U-Haul, a quarter to one by the time they pulled up Rebecca's driveway.

The kids were amazed. Abby hopped out of the truck, running around the side of the house to stare at the bright blue pool. "Matt, come here!"

Ben got out, unlatched the back of the truck and pulled down the ramp, giving Matt time to look too. Abby turned back to them.

"Mom, there's a Jacuzzi!"

"O.K., you guys," Ben said. "We need some strong backs here."

They had brought more than they needed. Rebecca's house came fully equipped; all they really would have had to bring was their clothes. With everyone pitching in it took them a little over an hour to unload. The children's excitement was contagious, irresistible. They were both delighted with their rooms and the secret garden with the fountain and the colored fish.

By the time Ben returned the U-Haul, picked up the van and came back again, the kids were already splashing in the pool. Roberto stood on the lawn, watching enviously. It was one of the house rules—Rebecca's or Zoila's, Ben wasn't sure—that Roberto, at three, wasn't allowed near the water.

Ben climbed the stairs and found Katy in the bedroom, hanging clothes in the closet. "So what do you think?" he asked.

"I think it's wonderful," Katy said. "Abby said she feels like she's living in a fairy tale."

Ben walked out on the balcony. The kids played Marco Polo at the far end of the pool, the way they had when they were eight or nine.

For nearly twenty-four hours Ben had been berating himself. He should never have had lied to the policeman about have spoken to the old woman. There had been no reason to lie; he'd just panicked. What if someone had just happened to have been driving by when she'd been ranting at him in front of the cleaners? It was possible. Or even more possible, remembered her verbally assaulting him that afternoon on the Drag, that time with Sweeney? What was wrong with him? It was as if he was losing his grip, making one mistake after the other: going to the Homeless Center, confessing to Sweeney, and now fumbling the ball with the policeman. He leaned forward on the balcony rail, staring down at his children, healthy as young seals, plunging in and out of the water, Abby accusing her brother of peeking.

Ben had tried to convince himself that he was blowing things out of all proportion. What were the odds, after all, of somebody seeing Audrey Davis's face on TV, making the connection to a fleeting glance of a woman panhandling on Congress Avenue three months before and then being concerned enough by it to call the police? It was preposterous. All the same, Hyde had been too alert. The one thing Ben couldn't erase from his mind was the Hyde had recognized his name, that he knew that Ben had gone to Terry Rossi to make a donation for Audrey Davis's memorial.

That night Zoila made them lasagna for supper. They ate in the dining room under a huge dark painting of one of Rebecca's ancestors. Matt was convinced that it was a king and it looked like a king, in his white wig, carrying a golden mace. It felt quite thrilling and a little awkward, having someone serve them, and afterwards Ben carried a stack of dirty plates into the kitchen to find Roberto sitting on a stool in front of the refrigerator eating alone.

The kids went in for another swim while Ben went upstairs to finish unpacking his suitcase. He paused at the bookshelves. Rebecca had an amazing array of titles: contemporary fiction, art books, photography. There was even an entire shelf devoted to theology and it wasn't New Age stuff either, but some of the classics of Tillich, Neibuhr, Buber. How in the world had a woman like Rebecca ended up with Sweeney?

Later, passing Matt's room, Ben looked in to see him laying on the bed, absorbed in Nintendo, with Roberto, full diaper and all, laying on the bed next to him.

It was nearly eleven thirty by the time they got everyone in bed. Ben took a shower while Katy went downstairs to be sure the doors were locked. He let the water get very hot, let it pelt over him. When he was done he found a thick soft towel of Rebecca's under the sink to dry himself. He pulled on a pair of shorts and gathered up his dirty clothes.

As he opened the bathroom door he heard Katy call to him from the balcony. "Ben?"

"Yeah."

"Come here. I want you to see something."

He tossed his clothes in the laundry basket and went to join her. A doe and her fawn grazed out by the pool. In the silence Ben could actually hear the tearing of grass. A single light shone up from deep below the blue green water. The doe looked up for just a second, ears alert, twitching, and then went back to grazing.

Katy took Ben's hand. "So are you still mad about being out-voted?"

"No," he said. "I'm fine."

The following Monday Ben showed up at Sweeney's condo a little before noon. Sweeney had just gotten up and was only half-dressed, padding around barefoot, wearing only a faded pair of jeans. The place was a mess—clothes tossed over the back of the furniture, a half-eaten carton of Chinese food sitting on one of the mammoth speakers, an eternal wave machine rocking back and forth on the bookcase, the softly roiling liquid a snow-cone blue.

Ben stood in the middle of the living room, his briefcase at his side, while Sweeney rummaged through his closet.

"So how's the house?" Sweeney asked.

"Everybody loves it."

"Great. I've got this house-warming gift I want to give you." Sweeney scratched at his bare chest, flicking away some loose hairs. "You all right?"

"I'm fine."

Sweeney pulled a garish Hawaiian shirt from the closet and slipped into it. "You got something for me?"

"So we're going to go on like this? Business as usual."

"Usual is always the best way." Sweeney stared at him blankly. "Why wouldn't we?"

"I don't know."

Sweeney extended an open palm. Ben sat down on the couch and unzipped his briefcase. He took out the tan mailing envelope, heavy with fifty dollar bills, and handed it to Sweeney. Sweeney set the envelope on the mantel, patted the pockets of his jeans, then went to his desk. It took him a minute or two to locate his checkbook.

Sweeney pulled up a chair to write the check, his back turned to Ben. The place smelled of day-old lo-mein. If they had been dealing in dirty money before, it was really dirty now. Ben got to his feet. He stared at the little roll of baby fat above Sweeney's collar; it was like a bear's hump. The idea came out of the blue; he found himself wondering what it would take to go over and snap Sweeney's neck, whether he would have the strength, whether he would have the will.

"So have you been having any second thoughts?" Sweeney said, without looking up. The question caught Ben off-guard.

"About what?"

"About talking to me. Telling me what you did."

"No."

"You don't have to lie to me. It would make sense if you did. Something like this got out, it would be pretty terrrible."

"Yes."

"I'm a jerk, but I'm not that big a jerk. If there's one thing I've learned in my life, it's how to keep my mouth shut." Sweeney pivoted in his chair, smiling, waving the blue paper in his right hand. "Here you go, man."

Ben took the check and stared at it for a minute. "You said you were going to help me," he said. "What did you mean?"

"Oh, the other day?" Sweeney shut the drawer to his desk. "Right now the way I'm going to help you is to take you to this great fish taco place for lunch."

He was, of course, supposed to be working on his book. With the decision about his tenure just a year away, it was crucial that he have a submittable manuscript by the fall, but he'd found it nearly impossible to focus. After dealing with Sweeney day in and day out, the world of high-minded Transcendentalists rambling through the Concord woods seemed as distant as Mars.

He'd struggled with the book for five years. Its genesis was the most remarkable stroke of beginner's luck; working in the Berg Collection at the New York Public Library, he'd found a letter from Thoreau to an unnamed woman, written on the back of one of his botanical studies.

> Dear Sister I want to beg your forgiveness. I have betrayed your faith in me. For all these months your gentle spirit has been my morning star. My misanthropic soul has opened and grown tender under the soft rains of your friendship. At times I could no longer tell where you ended and I began. I know I have destroyed that with one rash act. Be assured that I will never speak of this to anyone. I was your brother and now I am nothing. God have mercy on me.

Though the woman wasn't named, it scarcely seemed necessary. There was only one real possibility: Lidian Emerson. the wife of Thoreau's great mentor. The affection between the two was scarcely news, but the standard interpretation was that it was entirely Platonic. The only dissenter, a critic from the Thirties, was roundly scoffed at when he declared that "Thoreau was what the common man would call in love with Emerson's wife."

But he'd had no ammunition. Ben had the ammunition. The afternoon that he found the letter, sitting at a grime-slicked table with great Bierstadt-like shafts of light pouring in through the high library windows, he stared at it for a half-hour without moving. He'd stumbled onto the Comstock Lode. The letter cast the Emerson-Thoreau friendship and eventual estrangement in an utterly new light. The book that was going to come out of this looked like a slam-dunk.

The argument, which he was able to virtually outline in his head that first afternoon, was a simple one. In the early years of Thoreau's writing life, everything good that had come to him had come through the older man's generosity. It was Emerson who took him under his roof when he was penniless, who pressed editors to publish his work, who bought the tract of land adjoining Walden Pond and allowed Thoreau to build his famous cabin there. Thoreau, in return, was a fervent and dutiful disciple ("Emerson's shadow," James Russell Lowell called him), adopting his mentor's ideas, his manner of speaking, even his walk.

Over time inevitable tensions began to surface—Emerson's disappointment in Thoreau's early writing, his exasperation over the young man's prickliness ("As for taking T.'s arm, I should as soon take the arm of an elm tree—")—but the real breach didn't occur until 1847–48 when Emerson went abroad, leaving Thoreau in charge, acting as surrogate husband and father to his wife and three small children.

Thoreau thrived in the role, rough-housing with the children in the evening (like Sweeney, he seemed to have a full repertoire of party tricks, making a book disappear only to pull it out of young Eddy's nose seconds later), tending Lidian when she was ill, helping plant the spring garden.

When Emerson returned after eight months to take up his old place as head of the household, things were not the same between the two men. It would have been natural for Thoreau to feel some twinges of jealousy. The Big Dog had come back to claim his kennel, with stories of the high life in London and Paris (Emerson had picked up his share of English manners, including the ritual of the after-dinner cigar) and what was Thoreau supposed to do? Slink off into the woods again? He had come to love Emerson's children; he had great fondness for Lidian; America's most famous solitary had found more pleasures in domestic life than he'd ever imagined possible.

The two men were never able to recapture their old intimacy. Each complained about the other in their journals. Emerson on Thoreau: "He wants a little ambition in his mixture. Fault of this, instead of being the head of American Engineers, he's the captain of a huckleberry party." Thoreau on Emerson: "While my friend was my friend he flattered me, and I never heard the truth from him, but when he became my enemy he shot it to me on a poisoned arrow."

Who could have guessed that what lay at the bottom of it all was as simple as sexual betrayal? It was classic, straight out of Sophocles or Freud or Harold Bloom: the need to destroy the father. The article Ben published in The New England Quarterly a year after his discovery created a furor. The traditionalists were incensed, the Young Turks filled with glee. A half dozen editors called, putting their bids in to see the finished manuscript.

Ben's problem, five years later, was that he had lost faith in his evidence. Did he actually believe that Thoreau and Lidian Emerson had slept together? There was, after all, other rash acts than the sexual one; there were other ways to betray people's trust besides seducing them. Lidian Emerson was forty-five, fifteen years older than Thoreau, had borne four children and buried one of them, a sad, strange woman in black who fed the rats in her house for fear they might go hungry and burst into tears over her husband's supposedly spiritual friendship with Margaret Fuller.

Ben had played the scene backwards and forwards so many times, trying to convince himself that it could really have happened: Thoreau swinging the children on his arms and then putting them to bed, coming downstairs to find Lidian in the drawing room, reading her husband's latest letter (he hadn't written nearly as often as she'd hoped) about his dinner with Thomas De Quincey and Sir Walter Scott. The house would have been still, the only sounds the ticking of the clock, the pop and rustle of the fire in the fireplace.

He tried to imagine the author of *Walden* coming up behind her chair, putting a hand on her shoulder (now if it had been Sweeney, Ben could imagine it all too easily!) He tried to conjure up the surprise on her face as Thoreau touched her grey hair, coiled up in a twist, held by a single ornate comb.

Ben found it preposterous. One could make the case, just the way you could make the case that Jefferson had children by his slave mistress, that Melville beat his wife, or that Hemingway was impotent, but what was the point? To make a stir? To publish a book he didn't believe in? He'd struggled to make the manuscript less reductive, but that only led him into the murk; the reality was that the more reduced the argument the more pithy and striking it was. The enterprise had come to disgust him. He'd lost his appetite for scandal, for exposing another man's shame.

For the first time in his life Ben was a true hero to his wife and kids. It wasn't just the pool or the incredible views or the fact that life was so much easier with no beds to make, no laundry or dishes to be done; it was something more, some sense that they were all being taken care of, some sense that life contained possibilities that they had never before imagined.

Their first weekend in the house they invited the Stricklands out for a barbecue. Ben had to run to the store for some last minute items and when he returned everyone was already gathered around the pool with their drinks. Tom Strickland rose to greet him, spreading his arms wide: "Il Padrone!"

It felt as if they'd just won the lottery. The kids had their friends over to swim in the afternoon and it seemed as if they were having people over for dinner almost every other night. With Zoila to help, it was a lot easier to entertain.

The only one who had any trouble adjusting was Dusty, their cat, who was intimidated by Rebecca's parrot. It was a formidable bird; not only could it squawk and hiss, it could also bark like a dog, imitate a doorbell and call for tea. Dusty ran away twice. The first time they found her trotting along the road nearly a mile from the house, as if she was determined to walk all the way back to South Austin, and the second time they found her cowering in a storm drain.

Katy was happier than Ben had seen her in years. Something had been liberated in her. He could hear it in her voice, when she talked to her mother and her sister on the phone, insisting that they had to come and visit their new home. Suddenly it was as if there was breathing space in their lives. Several times she and Ben went walking along the road at night. There was no traffic and the only lights were the lights on the radio towers a couple of miles off. The only sounds were the crunch of gravel under their feet, the occasional rustling of birds in the cedar, the distant barking of a dog.

Yet at the same time Katy knew something was not right with him. She was so attune to his moods it was nearly impossible to hide. He had more and more trouble sleeping and had been uncharacteristically short with the children. At first she thought the problem was the house, that he was uncomfortable living in such luxury. "Maybe I'm just more materialistic than you," she said. "I'm a more superficial person."

No, he said, it wasn't that. It was just that there had been so much disruption in their lives; he needed to get back to his work.

Every day he scrutinized the papers, but the story of Audrey Davis' murder had been replaced by more recent atrocities, a policeman who'd stopped to help a stranded motorist and been run down by a drunk driver, a gunman taking a child hostage at a day care center.

Ben bought a car. For Katy to drive him in every morning and then pick him up again every afternoon was madness, so for five hundred dollars he purchased a ten year old Cutlass that he found in the ads in the paper. When he brought it home Abby was mortified. She swore that she was never riding in it, ever; she would die first. Ben didn't argue. The car was not a beauty. The upholstery on the ceiling sagged, the windshield was cracked and the roof and hood looked as if they'd spent too many nights under flocks of roosting grackles, but all Ben needed was something to get around in. It solved any number of problems.

Having the eight coolers hidden in Dick's office worked out better than he could have imagined. It was reassuring to be able to walk past three or four times a day, just to calm his fears. He had mentioned to several of his colleagues that he would be using the office as a hideaway, a place to get his writing done.

Every other day at eight in the morning, when the building was virtually deserted, he would come in and pack one hundred thousand dollars in a Kinko's box and slip the box in his ragged, ink-stained briefcase.

It took only four or five minutes. The key was not to rush, not to get clumsy and make a lot of noise. The walls were thin. When the phone rang in the Africanist's office next door, Ben could hear the message on the answering machine, clear as a bell. Sometimes as he counted out the stacks of fifties and one hundreds he would hear students laughing as they passed beneath his window. Leaving the office, he would walk quickly across campus to his car, the strap of his over-laden briefcase cutting into his shoulder, stopping for no one, waving to the departmental secretaries as they plodded up the hill, nursing their morning coffee.

He never went to the same bank twice. He used Bank One, Texas Commerce, Cattleman's, Franklin and Frost, driving his sputtering Cutlass as far out as Dripping Springs, Georgetown and Taylor. The first couple of times it was terrifying, walking up to a strange bank (they all seemed to have planters full of red geraniums out front and a Texas flag snapping on a flagpole), but he soon came to realize that he had nothing to fear. What reason did they have to suspect him? He was a middle-aged white man with pleasant manners. All they wanted for identification was a driver's license. Often there were duck hunting prints on the wall. He would fill out the forms, chatting with the bank officer about the weather, and then she would take him back to the vault.

In the larger banks the safety deposit boxes were located in their own sealed-off rooms, but in others all that separated the vault from the lobby was a simple metal gate. The safety deposit boxes all had two keys, one for him, one for the bank. The bank officer would unlock her lock and then leave him to conduct his business in private.

During the first three weeks of June Ben secreted one million dollars in safety deposit boxes in ten banks, scattered across three counties. He was as busy as a squirrel, getting ready for winter, the Johnny Appleseed of cash. Yet he had emptied, in its entirety, only one of the eight coolers and part of a second. He kept the ten keys for the ten safety deposit boxes in a small brown envelope in his desk at his office.

. . .

They kept getting calls for Rebecca. There was the woman with the heavy German accent who phoned to say that Peter DeVries had died and that there would be a memorial service in Connecticut; she was sure that Rebecca would want to know. There was the famous playboy English publisher who happened to be in town for the night and was hoping that Rebecca was free for the evening and there was a very pissed-off house-painter who Rebecca still owed eight hundred dollars.

There were also the hang-up calls. Not a lot, maybe one every two or three days, but enough to make Ben wonder.

Katy kept asking when they were going to have Sweeney over for dinner, for Ben please to remember to ask him, and when Sweeney finally came over on a Saturday night, three weeks after they'd moved in, Katy really put on the dog. She'd baked her grandmother's cream cake and driven in to Central Market for a whole Alaskan salmon that had been flown in fresh that day.

They ate out by the pool and Sweeney was at his most charming. He had seconds of everything and entertained them all with tales of his escapades in the music business. When he casually mentioned that he'd once met Elton John, Abby was dumbstruck.

"You did?" Her eyes were wide as saucers.

"Yeah, but it was no big deal. This friend of mine was one of their sound men, and he had me come backstage and we talked for maybe two minutes. And you know what he wanted to talk about? Fishin'! Can you believe it? He wanted to know about fishin' in Texas."

"And what was he like?" Reflections from the candles shimmered on the pool. Ben sipped slowly on his wine, the taste faintly bitter as he watched his wife and daughter lean forward in their chairs, utterly transfixed. He saw something tonight he hadn't really seen before: behind all of Sweeney's joking around, the country-boy shtick, a true malevolence. . . .

"Sort of a weird little guy, to tell you the truth. I hate to bother you, Katy, but could I have a sliver more of that cake?"

"Of course."

"It's got to be about the best thing I ever put in my mouth." Ben watched as Katy cut the cake; the piece she laid on Sweeney's plate was big enough to strangle a horse. "And what do you think of him?"

"I think he's a genius," Abby said.

"A genius!" Sweeney said. Sweeney gave Ben a wink, reaching

across to give him a playful punch on the arm. "Your father's the one who's the genius!"

Carlights bouncing up the driveway made them all turn. A horn sounded and Abby got up from her chair. "I guess that's Kim."

"You've got your keys?" Katy said.

"Mom, I'm fine." Abby turned to Sweeney, her face shining. "It was nice talking to you."

Sweeney bounded to his feet, a real gentleman. "It was nice talking to you. So don't have too wild a time out there tonight." Abby could only continue beaming, not knowing what to say. Sweeney remained standing, watching her as she skipped down the walk to the house. "So how old is she?"

"Fifteen," Katy said.

"Fifteen." He shook his head. "My God, is she going to break some hearts!"

They waited while Sweeney polished off his cake, then gathered up the dishes, snuffed out the candles and went inside. Katy put on the water for coffee while Sweeney went to use the bathroom. Ben scraped the plates, stacking them in the sink, his fingers smelled of salmon.

"Is something wrong?" Katy asked.

"No. Why?"

"You seem out of sorts."

"I'm just a little tired." The parrot eyed them warily from his cage. "You're not mad at me?"

"I'm not mad."

"Ben, it's something . . ."

They heard the toilet flush in the hall bathroom. Ben opened the door to the dishwasher, pulling out the top rack.

"Just leave all that," she said. "We can get it later."

When Sweeney returned they went into the living room. Sweeney rummaged through the liquor cabinet, found a bottle of Drambuie and then got down three of Rebecca's brandy glasses. He poured a glass for himself and one for Katy. Ben passed. Sweeney sprawled on the big yellow couch, making himself at home.

Katy asked about the photographs scattered around the room, who the people were, and before they knew it Sweeney was launched on Rebecca's entire life story: her brilliant, roue father and her futile attempts to win his approval, her various marriages and liaisons. At one time or the other, Sweeney claimed, her romantic entanglements included a high-ranking member of Parliament, the star of the national cricket team, and an American television commentator.

"But what about your family?" Katy asked.

"My family?" Sweeney waved the question away, as if it were beneath consideration.

"No, I want to know."

"I've already told Ben."

"But you haven't told me. Tell me about your father."

Sweeney leaned forward and refilled his brandy glass with Drambuie. "You want to know about my father? I'll tell you *the* story about my father. I've never even told Ben this one. Houston. Summer-time. I was thirteen years old. My mother had been sick, so she and my little sister were in Arkansas where my aunt could take care of them. For the first time in my life it was just me and my Dad and I was lapping it up. He'd been in and out of the family for years, on the road a lot, and I just followed him around like a little dog, going out on the job, carrying his toolbox.

"One day we went by this rich lady's place, this mansion across the street from Rice. She was married to some doctor and they'd just moved down from the north. It was their first summer in Houston and she was hysterical. Big barn of a house and all they had in it was window units. I mean, they were dying.

"As soon as we walk into the place I could see the dollar signs going off in my father's head. This place had everything—Tiffany chandeliers, marble statues, stained glass windows with the family seal—everything except central air. We took the tour, checking out the vents. My father started joking around with her. She was not that old. Sort of pretty in this shiny wax-doll way. Every time he made a suggestion about what needed to be done she would go, 'Uh-huh, uh-huh,' as if it was no problem at all. He got her laughing—he was a totally charming guy when he wanted to be—and whenever she looked the other way he would give me a wink like, do we have ourselves a pigeon here or not? Pigeons were what he used to call them, when he found somebody who could pay our rent for a couple of months.

"Then he told me, 'Danny, we're going to have to do something to keep this poor lady from asphyxiating. I'm going to have to go check up in the attic, why don't you take the car and go get some lunch?'

"I was like, God! I was thirteen. He'd never let me drive before, unless it was in somebody's pasture. 'Give me a couple of hours,' he said. 'Get yourself a magazine, get a nice booth and sit up in the cool for awhile until I figure this one out. You can bring me back a malt and a burger.'

"He gave me the keys and twenty dollars. I walked out of there so proud. We had a red Fifty-seven Cadillac . . . whether we were in the chips or not, my father believed in driving a good-looking car. When I got behind the wheel I could barely see over the dash; I hadn't gotten my growth yet. I must have driven down that road about seven miles an hour. When I saw somebody coming up behind me I'd just pull over to the curb and let them pass. People must have thought I was crazy."

Sweeney stopped for a second to take a sip of his brandy. He was telling the story almost as if he thought it was funny, but nobody thought it was funny, not at all. Ben looked over at Katy, who was hunched forward in her chair, listening intently.

"I drove up the Avenue to this place where my father and I used to go. They had the thickest malts in town. The problem was there was this huge line, twelve million Chinese guys with slide rules in their pockets; there must have been a physics convention or something. The lady said there would be a forty-five minute wait. I didn't know what to do. My father had said for me to take my time, but I didn't think he meant that much time, so I went to the take-out window and ordered two malts, two burgers and some fries. It was the best day of my life. I had wheels, I had two big creamy malts in my hands, my father was going to score this major job and pay off all our bills. God bless air conditioning, I was thinking. Houston, air conditioning capitol of the world!

"I drove back to the house. When I went inside there didn't seem to be anybody around. I called out, but there wasn't any answer. I looked in the kitchen. Nobody there. Living room. Nothing. I started up the stair with the carton of food in my hands, trying not to spill anything. It was sweltering hot in that house and a little scary; big smooth bannisters and pictures of men in black suits on the walls. I thought maybe my Dad might still be up in the attic, but I could figure out where the woman might have gone.

"Then, on the second floor, I saw the door partially open to this little maid's room and I saw my father's work boots sitting on the rug. When I took a step closer I could see the cot and I could see my father's feet. He still had his socks on and there was a hole in one of them. Funny, what you remember, isn't it? I'll always remember that little hole. Pink little dime of flesh. I could see his toes digging into the mattress and I could see her white knees waving back and forth.

There I was thirteen years old, holding the best malts in Houston. I could hear the rattling of one of those old window units and once in a while I could hear her moaning. Sweat was stinging my eye, but my hands were full, I couldn't touch it. I tried to wipe my face on my shoulder, but I must have banged against something. All of a sudden he was on his feet, scrambling to pull up his pants and coming at me. Screaming. 'What are you doing, sneaking up on me, boy? What the hell do you think you're doing?' With one hand he was holding his trousers and with the other he whacked me across the face and then it all went, malts, hamburgers, fries all over the lady's rug. . . ."

"And what did you do?" Katy said.

"I should have killed him."

"But what did you do?"

"Nothing. He paid me to keep quiet. Five dollars a week." He waggled his hand, as if trying to wave it all away. "You asked me, right?"

"Yes," she said. "I asked you."

Sweeney locked his fingers behind his head. "So are you loving it here?"

"We are," Katy said. She was flushed now and upset. "I don't know if Ben's enjoyed it as much as I have . . . "

"Oh? And why is that?"

"I guess I'm just a more superficial person. It's so beautiful here. He's not so interested in physical things."

Sweeney took a sip of his Drambuie and set down his glass. "Don't worry, we're going to loosen him up."

Chapter Twelve

Sweeney started to show up a lot—not every day, not even every other day, but a lot. He had a knack for appearing just at dinner time and two or three times he came out to swim. Once he came by with a litter of basset hound puppies he wanted to show the kids and once he arrived with a huge tray of Mexican food from the restaurant, all wrapped in silver foil.

As far as the kids were concerned, Sweeney was just part of the family. He played Prince of Persia on the computer with Matt and argued with Abby over who was the most beautiful of all the Super Models. He would stand in the kitchen with Zoila and Katy, grating cheese and making them laugh with his endless stories. Katy was like a mother to him. One afternoon Ben came home to find him stretched out on the bed chatting while Katy folded the laundry.

He had fastened onto the family like a blood-sucker. Sweeney seemed, at times, almost pathetically eager for something resembling normal life. He was full of plans for them all; he had a friend named Al Jackett who had a beautiful ranch an hour west of town and Sweeney was determined to get them out to see it. He was constantly trying to sit down with Ben for earnest discussions and every time Ben suggested a book—Trilling's *The Liberal Imagination* or D. H. Lawrence's *Studies in Classic American Literature*—Sweeney would be back in three days ready to talk about it.

What were his motives? Ben had spent hours thinking about this. Ben's taking him into his confidence was without doubt the most flattering thing that had ever happened to Sweeney. He had become the family's protector, all that stood between them and ruin. He clearly loved the idea of himself as the stalwart friend, but he was human too, he had his own appetites.

Ben knew the time would come when Sweeney would start asking what was in it for him. Ben hadn't told him how much money was involved and it was no doubt good that he hadn't, but that just made it that much more tantalizing; he knew how Sweeney's imagination could run. It was an inherently untenable situation. What Ben needed was for Sweeney to remain silent forever and how likely was that? One word to anyone—to Katy, to one of the bartenders at the club, a drunken brag to a girl after a couple of margaritas—and everything became disaster.

Sweeney had said he would help and yet he had never told Ben how he would help. In his darkest moments it occurred to Ben that Sweeeney might be deliberately delaying the moment to make Ben suffer, to make him beg.

They were the rankest of amateurs when it came to dealing with servants. Ben had to admit there was a certain awkward pleasure in coming down every morning and having Zoila serve him tea and toast while he read *The New York Times*, but it also offended every democratic bone in his body.

Zoila did a good job. It was a matter of some pride to her. Unfailingly polite and good-natured, she got along with everyone in the family and, in spite of the lack of a common language, they all found their own way to communicate. Abby would carry Roberto around on her hip and Matt would play a version of ping-pong with him in the yard, tossing the ball softly to him and letting him swing wildly at it, missing most of the time, but every so often swatting it into the flowers.

Yet there was always a gulf. When guests came over Roberto would be confined to the kitchen while the rest of them swam and splashed in the pool. At night Zoila and Roberto would go to their bedroom and close the door while the rest of them had the run of the house, watching television, reading, playing hearts around the kitchen table. Sometimes Ben, passing down the hall, would hear the radio in Zoila's room, turned down low, playing Mexican music. Once a week Ben would put five twenties in an envelope for her, always finding a way to give it to her when no other members of the family were around, as if there was something implicitly shameful about the transaction.

She had Sundays off and her uncle would come pick her up. He

lived in a housing project in East Austin and the ancient Ford Fair-
laine he drove was in worse shape than Ben's Cutlass. He never came
to the house. His routine was to park out on the road and sometimes
in the evening when be brought her back they would stand out by
her car and talk for a hour.

This arrangement bothered Ben. Several times he nearly said
something. There was no reason the uncle couldn't come up to the
house, unless this was something they'd worked out with Rebecca.
Ben, after all, was new to this, he didn't want to upset the apple cart.
But he didn't like it, complicit now in a drama he didn't remember
auditioning for, waking up on Sunday mornings, looking out the
window of the second-story bedroom to see the uncle waiting pa-
tiently on the road as the early morning light crept down through the
cedars.

One night he dreamed of Walden. In his dream he stood in the snow
outside Thoreau's cabin, just before dawn, and there were foxes
barking deep in the woods. He knocked several times and when
there was no answer he finally cracked open the door and peered in.
Several books lay open on the simple writing desk, embers still smol-
dered in the fireplace, the bed was still unmade, but there was no one.

He turned finally and spied the tracks in the snow, leading down
to the pond. He followed the tracks down through the white pines.
An owl hooted softly from the boughs overhead. It was bitterly cold.

A lantern glowed far out on the frozen pond. As Ben drew closer,
he saw a figure squatting over a hole in the ice. Ben began to walk
faster, his rubber boots squeaking on the snow. When Ben got within
ten feet, the man finally glanced up. It was Thoreau—he looked just
the way he looked in all the old daguerreotypes, with strong features,
a piercing gaze and a slightly misshapen beard. A heavy woolen cap
covered his ears and came down so low it nearly reached his eyebrows. He smiled, almost as if he'd been expecting Ben.

Thoreau held one end of a slender cord that disappeared into the
black water of the raggedly-cut hole. Ben knew perfectly well what
it was: a sounding line. Thoreau was mapping his pond.

Ben crouched on his haunches, balling his hands tight inside his
mittens. His toes ached from the cold, but he was so excited. There
were so many things he wanted to ask, but he didn't want to disturb
him. Scholarship didn't matter now—books, articles, citations—
nothing mattered as long as he was allowed to sit here. It was the
happiest moment in Ben's life.

Thoreau kept pulling the sounding line up, hand over hand, letting it coil at his feet. It seemed as if it had been going on forever. Maybe Thoreau had been wrong; maybe Walden was one of those bottomless ponds after all.

Thoreau turned and gestured to him. When Ben hesitated, Thoreau gestured again, somewhat crossly, motioning him to come look. Ben rose and went to his side. Thoreau pointed down into the hole.

Ben couldn't see anything at first; the water was too dark. He got down on his knees, both hands on the ice. From up close, the water was remarkably clear, tinted a faint green. Thoreau kept pulling, the cord sawing across the sharp edges of ice.

Finally Ben saw what Thoreau intended him to see. Clinging to the stone at the end of the sounding line was the old woman. She was not alive. If anything, she looked frozen, her eyes open but lusterless and vacant as a pike's, but somehow that hadn't loosened her grip as she trolled upwards in the sacred water, her Mardi Gras beads drifting around her neck like eels.

The next morning Ben left the house before eight and drove in to the University. Crossing campus, the only people he saw were a couple of maintenance men fooling with some sprinklers and the owners of the Korean egg roll stand setting up in front of the fountain.

The empty halls of Parlin smelled of fresh wax. He let himself into Dick's office and switched on the light. He'd done this so many times by now he was nearly as quick and efficient as a meter-reader; it took him less than ten minutes to move the cartons of books, count out the forty packs of fifty (fifty to a pack, one hundred thousand total) and tape them securely inside two Kinko's boxes. He put the two Kinko's boxes in his briefcase and zipped it shut.

A new Cattlemen's Bank had just opened in Lockhart. If the traffic wasn't back, he could get down there, have the money in a safety deposit box and be back at work by ten-thirty. He shoved the cartons of books into their original positions and draped the rolled-up rug artfully across them.

Leaving the office, he instinctively looked both ways; the only think moving in the hallway was a Study Abroad notice on a distant bulletin board, blowing softly in the air conditioning. Ben pushed out the double doors into the muggy summer morning, hustled down the stairs and, as he turned the corner, nearly knocked Sweeney down.

Sweeney staggered back a step, putting a hand out to catch himself. "Jesus Christ!" he said. In his sunglasses, cut-offs and flip-flops, his hair wild, Sweeney looked as if he'd just emerged from an all-night luau. "What are you doing here?"

Ben hefted his briefcase back onto his shoulder. "I was just heading over to the library, see if I could get some work done. What about you?"

"Me?" Sweeney rubbed at his nose. A dead grackle lay under one of the bike racks, swarming with ants. "I was supposed to meet somebody for breakfast, but it looks as if they stood me up."

Ben stared at Sweeney. What a glib bastard, he thought. "So who was that?"

"Who was what?"

"Who was it you were supposed to meet for breakfast?"

Sweeney put his fist to his mouth and belched softly. "Just some lady. It's not a big deal. She said she needed somebody to talk to . . . you know. Listen, you got time for a cup of coffee?"

"I should probably get to work."

Sweeney reached out and gave Ben's briefcase a thump with his fist. "So this is it, huh?"

Ben felt all the blood drain instantly from his face. "What?"

"The opus. The magnum fucking opus."

"Yeah," Ben said, trying to recover.

Sweeney sucked at his teeth, regarding him quizzically. "Tell you what," he said. "I've not nowhere to go. Let me walk you down to the library."

There was no real way to say no. They headed down the hill together, Sweeney's flip-flops slapping on the sidewalk as he rattled on about how baseball had gone to hell. It was all those expansion teams, he said, every two-bit second baseman was on track to break Ruth's record.

Ben was still having trouble breathing. He didn't believe the story about Sweeney meeting someone for breakfast for a second. What was the truth then? Had he been following Ben? Or worse yet, maybe he *hadn't* been following him, maybe he'd been on his way to Dick's office, about to empty the place out. As they crossed the street, a bicyclist whooshed down on them and Sweeney grabbed Ben by the elbow to keep him from being run over.

They stopped in front of the library. Sweeney seemed in no hurry to leave. For a moment Ben thought Sweeney intended to follow him into the library. A student in a knee brace sat on a low wall, watching them, having his first morning cigarette. Pigeons strutted in wide circles before the newspaper racks.

"So you working all day?" Sweeney said.

"We'll see."

Sweeney bent down and scooped an Arby's Two for One coupon off the concrete. "Whatever. Good writing, all right?"

Ben went in through the revolving doors and then stood for a few seconds, watching through the tinted glass as Sweeney slouched off. The guard at the turnstile dozed, a paperback mystery propped on his lap. When Sweeney reached the curb he stopped and looked back over his shoulder as if to see if he was being observed. That was the moment that Ben knew, with utter certainty, that Sweeney knew.

Ben waited until Sweeney had disappeared from view and then pushed on through the doors, cutting ahead of a young Chinese couple holding hands. He walked fast at first, head down, and then began to run, the briefcase banging at his side. What he had under his shoulder was nothing compared with what he was about to lose. He looked up and down Twenty-First Street; Sweeney had vanished.

He began to run again. Someone waved to him from a car. It was the graduate coordinator from the department, being dropped off by her son. Ben didn't even acknowledge her, running up the steps, past the rearing metal horses, across the lawn.

By the time he reached Parlin Hall his shirt was drenched in sweat. If he found Sweeney, what was he going to do? There was no light under the door to Dick's office. Ben flipped through his keys, found the right one, inserted it into the lock. He shoved the door open, faced the same mountain of boxes, the rolled-up rug, the same neatly-organized shelves of books that he'd faced just a half hour before. Nothing had been touched. He stepped inside and the door closed after him. He let his briefcase drop.

Something slithered behind him. He whirled, thinking it was Sweeney crouching in the corner, waiting for him, but it was only a yellowing notice for an old creative writing contest that had slipped to the floor. He picked it up and crumpled it in his hand. He rested his forehead against the wall and pounded the rough stucco just once, with both fists, and then pulled back, trying to gather himself. From the framed portrait above the desk, James Joyce eyed him through lenses think and round as onion slices, eyed him with utter suspicion.

. . .

Ben never did get to the bank in Lockhart. He went in to the library the next day, but was too distraught to work and took the afternoon off, driving west into the Hill Country, through Dripping Springs and Johnson City. He had no plan, no sackful of money; he was just driving to calm himself down.

Maybe Sweeney hadn't discovered Dick's office yet, but he suspected, Ben was sure of it. The man had the nose of a bloodhound. Ben was going to have to move the coolers and move them quickly. But where?

Ordinarily being in the country soothed him. When they'd first come to Austin he hadn't understood why everyone made such a big deal about the Hill Country, it seemed like yet another case of Texas boosterism, but he'd come to love the vistas, the way you could hit the top of an incline and suddenly be able to see for miles; he'd come to love the trickling creek bottoms, the sight of wild turkeys waddling across the road, the stone farm houses set back in the trees.

Heading home he took the back roads out of Johnson City and managed to get himself thoroughly lost. There was no place to ask directions—the one gas station he passed looked as if it had been closed since the Eisenhower Administration—and he seemed to have gone miles without seeing a marker. He roller-coasted over the hills, great parachutes of dust swirling in his wake.

Finally coming across a pick-up parked in the middle of the road, he slowed, pulling over to the shoulder. A heavy-set man in overalls looked up from hammering a FOR RENT/ FOR SALE sign in the rocky soil along the fence line.

Ben leaned across and rolled down the window. "How you doin'?"

"All right." The old man held his five pound hammer loosely at his side. He was not just old, he was big. He must have gone at least two-fifty, but his eyes were watery and there was a frailty in his voice, as if a locust had lodged in his throat.

"Listen, I seem to have gotten myself turned around here. I'm trying to get back to Austin."

The old man walked slowly to Ben's car. He pointed back up the road. "You'll need to go back here to the fork and take a left. That'll take you back out to the highway." Insects sang in the grass.

"So you're getting rid of your place?"

"It's my sister's place. She's gone in the hospital."

"I'm sorry to hear that."

"She'll be all right," the old man said. Behind him the sign had blown down softly in the weeds without his noticing. "She's just gotten too old to live out here by herself anyway."

"So how big a place are you selling?"

The old man nudged a rotting armadillo shell with the toe of his boot. "About a hundred acres. You interested?"

"I don't know if I am or not."

"It's pretty back there. If you've got the time I could show you around."

"All right."

They got in the old man's truck. His name was Harold Smeltzer. It was a long way back in and they had to stop twice to unlock gates. The property was mostly woods with a couple of prickly pear-ridden meadows. They passed a collapsed shed, rolled down to a stream and bumped across a treacherous-looking cattle gap.

The house sat at the top of the next rise. It was the simplest of buildings, four small rooms with a long porch, some beautiful live oaks in the front yard and a badly neglected garden in the back. Mr. Smeltzer's sister hadn't raised vegetables for a couple of years, but it was a good plot, the old man said, you just had to be sure to put up a stout fence to keep out the deer and the feral pigs.

The old man moved at a snail's pace as they surveyed the front yard. A massive long-horn skull sat on a weathered bench. The best thing about the place was the view; the stream, a hundred yards away, widened into a swimming hole under high limestone cliffs. People still did catch fish in there, Mr. Smeltzer said, you just had to watch for snakes.

"Pretty remote out here," Ben said.

"It's quiet all right," Mr. Smeltzer said. "If you like quiet."

"So how much are you asking?"

"Two hundred and fifty thousand. That would include everything."

Ben whistled softly. "Pretty steep."

"Not for around here. Not any more."

Ben put his hand on a worn cedar post. "I don't know if I could do that," he said. "All at once. But maybe we could work something out."

"I should let you know I don't like dealing with those fancy real estate people."

"Me either," Ben said. "What if I rented it from you for awhile? Say for a couple thousand a month?"

The old man bent over and picked up a fallen branch, tossing it over the barbed wire. "That's something to think about."

He moved the seven coolers late on Tuesday night. This time he was very careful to be sure no one was in their office before he lugged the forty-pound containers down the Parlin hallways. The risks moving the money out were just as great as they had been moving it in, but he wasn't nearly as nervous; maybe he'd finally accepted that it was all in the hands of the Fates, or maybe he was just developing the instincts of a second-story man. Because Katy had the van in Mississippi he had to use the Cutlass and it took him two trips out to the ranch and back, almost three hours of driving. He stacked the seven coolers in the old machine shed behind the house and then covered them with some half-rotted bales of hay.

It was nearly two in the morning by the time he got back to Rebecca's house. He crept up the stairs as quietly as he could. Zoila had left the hall light on for him; God knew what she thought he was up to with his wife out of town.

In the morning Zoila was noticeably cool towards Ben as she served him his breakfast of tea and toast. Roberto at least was talking to him, tugging at his leg and calling him El Senor. Ben found Rebecca's yardstick hanging in the cupboard, then drove into the hardware store to buy a roto-tiller, a shovel and a pick-axe. He stopped by Church's on the way out of town and got a basket of chicken and a jug of Coke.

It was nearly eleven by the time he got out to the ranch. The thermometer read ninety-six. It took him two hours to roto-till the garden plot behind the house. When he finally stopped to eat, his t-shirt was soaked and his arms ached, but he knew he'd only gotten through the easy part.

He measured out each hole with a yardstick. The coolers were twenty-six by fifteen by thirteen and he figured he needed to make the holes at least a foot deeper than that to protect them against burrowing animals and sudden rainstorms.

He set to work with the pick-axe. It went well at first, each ripping stroke releasing the rich aroma of top-soil, popping roots, but after he got down ten or eleven inches there was a new clicking sound as he began to hit limestone. Some of it he could shatter or work around, but at other spots he found himself slamming away at an impenetrable ledge. The first hole he tried he had to abandon, the second was fine, the third no good again.

After two hours he had one cooler buried. Despair was taking him over. He had underestimated the size of the task, underestimated badly. His shoulders throbbed with the effort and the sun was killing. He took a break again about four, went to the stream and just lay motionless in the water for a half hour.

When he came back his luck improved. He dug two good holes in a row, lowering the coolers into their resting places, stomping them down with a foot until they were snug, then shoveling the dirt back on top.

He was too tired to think; the world had narrowed to this plot of plowed ground, the field of prickly pear and thistles that surrounded it. He had forgotten to bring gloves and his hands were blistering. He was losing all judgement. At one point in the late afternoon, as he sat panting on one of the coolers, taking a break, he thought he heard a car coming up the road. He panicked, convinced that it was Smeltzer, convinced that he was about to be discovered. He grabbed the cooler and stumbled towards the machine shed, the thirty pound container banging against his thighs, but by the time he reached the shed the sound had disappeared.

By seven-thirty he had four of the coolers buried. He went into the house, ate the rest of the cold chicken and drank some water. He went into the empty bedroom and lay on a dusty mattress; when he awoke it was nearly nine.

As he stepped out of the house a huge croaking bird flapped up from the live oaks next to the stream. The sun glowed a dull red, sinking behind the limestone cliffs. The plot was a mess; it didn't look so much like a garden as if did like a battlefield or a mass grave.

He bent down stiffly to retrieve his pick-axe. Birds twittered in the brush and the crickets had started their twilight chants. It was going to be a matter of will now.

Setting to work again, his t-shirt was utterly drenched within fifteen minutes. Whippoorwills were calling, somewhere across the front lawn. It was easier now that darkness had come. He lost track of time, but he buried the fifth cooler and then the sixth. His muscles trembled in protest.

The moon came up over the trees just as he finished digging his last hole. He carried the last cooler from the machine shed, nearly tripping over some snarled barbed wire.

He knelt to lower the cooler into the hole, gentle as a father lowering a baby into a cradle, but it wouldn't go. He tried to force it with a foot, but all he got for his effort was the grinding sound of rock and plastic. He tugged the cooler free and stared down into the dark mouth of the hole, trying to see what the problem was, but he couldn't see anything.

He grabbed the pick-axe and went to work widening the hole. He shoveled out the loose rubble, but when he tried the cooler again he still couldn't get it to go down more than half-way. He sat on the edge of the hole, pushing with both feet, but it got him nowhere. It was as if the jaws of the earth had swallowed enough for one day.

He was near tears with frustration. He yanked the cooler free a second time, then got on his belly and reached down into the hole as far as he could, like a kid trying to retrieve a lost baseball from a sewer. He patted his way along the rough walls, pulling at roots, digging out limestone shards, tossing them over his shoulder. Was there no one else in the whole world on his side? He was a sweating, rooting, exhausted animal. He felt something wet on his hands and then he realized that his knuckles had begun to bleed. He stopped for a second to suck them. He heard a rustling in the woods.

He lay still. The sound stopped and then started again, moving closer. It was too noisy for deer. He reached out for the pick-axe at his side. There was a snuffling and a grunting and then something jangled the barbed wire.

Two armadillos waddled along the freshly turned-up soil. They came directly at Ben, dim-witted and blind. When Ben finally rose to one knee they stopped five feet away, sniffing the air with their prehistoric snouts. When Ben stood up one of them gave a hop and began to scurry away; the other wasn't quick enough. Ben drove the pick-axe squarely through the shell. The animal shuttered, its tongue flickering in the throes of death.

Chapter Thirteen

Katy and the children got back from Mississippi about six-thirty. She'd done all the driving herself, but she seemed in great spirits and delighted to see Ben. They'd stopped in Shreveport for lunch and brought him a strawberry cream pie from Strawn's. Everyone at home had asked about him, she said, and hoped his writing was going well. They'd had no rain and the soybeans were drying up, but otherwise things were good.

That night Katy and Ben lay side by side in bed, holding hands. "So are you happy to be back?"

She gave his hand a squeeze. "Very happy," she said. "This is a wonderful house."

"Do you think you'd like to own a house like this? If we could afford it?"

She hesitated as if it were some sort of a trick question. "Yes."

He turned onto his side, putting his hand on her hip. "Say we didn't have to worry about money. Ever. What would you want most of all?"

"I don't know. It's hard to imagine." She had brought magnolias back with her from Mississippi and one of the huge white blossoms sat in a bowl next to the bed, filling the dark room with the scent of yearning.

"I don't know. It's hard to imagine."

"But try."

"I suppose I'd like to take my mother and my sisters on a trip to England."

"And what else?"

"I can't think of anything else. What about you?"

"I don't know."

"Would you quit your job? Would you want to go back to New York and write plays?"

He thought for a long time; the question had caught him off-guard. A siren sounded far, far away. "No."

"Why not?"

"I just don't think you can ever go back."

Ben and Sweeney leaned forward on the iron bench staring at the ice skaters, waiting for Matt and his friends to get out of the movie. Sweeney dug about in a carton of buttered popcorn. Behind them the Saturday night crowd drifted past, sucking on smoothies, checking out the t-shirt stands. Outside it was ninety-seven degrees at nine in the evening. It was August in Texas and all over the state, the malls were full.

"So what are we going to do, Ben?" Sweeney said.

"What do you mean?"

"We've got to do something."

Ben glanced at him swiftly, taken by surprise. Sweeney tossed back a handful of popcorn, like a man tossing back tequila. Out in the middle of the ice a man with a shaved head, dressed all in black and lean as a wolfhound, skated backwards, weaving his way among the stumbling novices.

"Your wife keeps asking me what's wrong with you. What at I supposed to say?" Sweeney asked.

"I hope you don't say anything." Ben watched an awkward teenager flail his arms and them slide slowly into the far wall of the rink to stop himself. Almost mournfully, Ben remembered the pond behind their house, growing up in Wisconsin, the make-shift games of hockey they would play on gray February afternoons, two or three on a side, scrambling back and forth of the rough ice for hours.

"These guys," Sweeney said, "whoever they are, they haven't forgotten about the money, don't kid yourself. I've been thinking a lot about this, Ben. There are people I can put you in touch with, people who could help you."

"What kind of people? Crooked bookkeepers?"

As soon as it was out of his mouth, Ben knew he shouldn't have said it. Sweeney's face underwent an instantaneous change; suddenly he was glum and offended.

"No. Some pretty classy people, as a matter of fact."

Neither of them spoke for a minute. A man walked out of Furr's cafeteria, picking his teeth with a toothpick, one arm around his wife. His t-shirt read Reel Men Play With Their Flies. Ben looked down at his hands, still nicked and cut from the night he'd buried the coolers.

"I think I'll pass on that right now," Ben said.

"What do you mean, you'll pass on it?"

"I'm not ready to do this yet, Sweeney." They were close enough to the ice that they could feel the coolness coming up at them in waves. Sweeney flipped a bum kernel of popcorn away with his thumb.

"And when do you think you'll be ready?"

"I don't know."

Sweeney pulled a cowboy boot over his knee. "Whoa," he said. The corners of his mouth glistened with butter. For the first time Ben could see the flaring of undisguised anger. "Whoa. So what's the deal here? You think I'm after your money?"

"No."

"The only reason I'm offering you this is because I love your family and I don't want anything bad to happen to them. It's nice to be nice, but let's deal with reality here. This is really big-time crap you've fallen into. It's going to take more than a damn Ph. D. to get you out of it." Ben nearly came back at him, but decided against it. "I've been protecting you in ways you can't even know."

"What do you mean by that?"

Sweeney shook his head, stony-faced. "I don't know. Sometimes I feel a little like I'm being used."

"Being used? How have I used you?"

"I've done a lot for you."

"I know that," Ben said.

Ben had had enough. He stood up. The crowds were just letting out of the seven-thirty movie; he thought he saw Matt and his friends goofing around at the video games. Sweeney stood up too, right at Ben's elbow.

"That gun you bought, you still got it?" Sweeney said.

"Why?"

"Because one day you're probably going to have to use it."

It was the first time they'd had a dinner party for people from the department and it was a roaring success. They had the Steinbachs, the Stricklands, Mike Howarth, back from a month at Bellagio, and his girlfriend, a striking third year graduate student who could more than hold her own. If Ben had been concerned about the grandiosity of his new house, his fears were quickly laid to rest; everyone thought it was splendid. Sam Steinbach told the story about a student of his who, for several years, had house-sat for a wealthy art-collector in Westlake and used to throw the wildest all-night bacchanals, but this house was so much more tasteful than that one had been.

Zoila was an immense help, rushing back and forth and keeping track of everything in the kitchen. The wine flowed freely. They had grilled chicken and salad by the pool (Mrs. Steinbach said she felt as if she was on the Amalfi Coast) and came in afterwards for coffee and dessert.

Everyone got along famously. It was as if the house itself had put them all in an expansive mood; didn't this stroke of good fortune for the Lindbergs really mean good fortune for them all? Mrs. Steinbach, who had the reputation for being the person no one wanted to get stuck in the corner with, had everyone in stitches with her stories of growing up in small-town Vermont. Mike Howarth, who Ben had secretly considered rather grim and full of himself (his Ring Lardner article in *The New York Review of Books*, the paper he'd given at a cultural studies conference in Dublin), ended up trading reminiscences with Tom Strickland about the old Mr. Magoo cartoons.

As the evening wore on the group inevitably segregated itself, the academics settling in the living room to discuss the department's prospects under the new dean, Katy taking the two other wives on a tour of the house.

The doorbell rang a little after eleven. Ben rose to his feet, baffled. He had no idea who it could be; both children were spending the night with friends. Katy, already on the stair, came down to open the door.

It was Sweeney. He stood there grinning, holding a small wooden crate. In his Caesar's Palace t-shirt, cowboy boots and dark glasses he could have passed for one of Wayne Newton's bodyguards.

"Hey!"

"Hey," Katy said.

Eyeballing the roomful of people, Sweeney leaned over and kissed her on the cheek. "Listen, I'm sorry if I'm interrupting."

"You're never interrupting. Please, come in," Katy said. Ben stood with one hand on the back of his chair, feeling the acid rising in his stomach.

"I just came from the club," Sweeney said. "They had this extra crate of Fredricksburg peaches they didn't know what to do with and there was no point in letting them spoil."

"That's really nice," Katy said. "Please, come in and have some dessert."

"No, you've got real company here."

"You're real company. I insist." She took him by the arm and led him into the living room. "Everyone, this is Daniel Sweeney. He's a good friend of ours. As a matter of fact, he's the one who found us the house."

Sam Steinbach raised his coffee cup. "Hear! Hear! The hero of the evening!" Everyone else applauded lightly, their faces raised and genial. Sweeney almost seemed abashed.

"Hey, everybody," he said. He had yet to look in Ben's direction; he knew what he was doing. Katy took the crate of peaches from him, making a ballet spin towards the kitchen. "Do you want your pie with or without ice cream?"

Sweeney snapped off his sunglasses and put them in his back pocket. "With would be great," he said.

There was an awkward moment when no one said anything. "Let me introduce you," Ben said. "Sam Steinberg, Mike Howard, Tom Strickland, Emily Chassen . . ."

"Like your necklace," Sweeney said.

Mike Howard's new girlfriend, caught off-guard, seemed flustered for a second. "Thank you."

"Please, everybody sit down," Sweeney said. As Sweeney wove across the room to get a chair from the hallway Ben realized he was drunk. Everyone there had had a lot to drink, but Sweeney'd had more.

Sweeney bumped the chair across the rug, pivoting it around so he could sit on it facing them, his elbows resting on the back.

"So what were you all talking about?" he said.

"Oh, not much," Mike Howard said. "The future of the English department."

"Is that right? From what I hear, there isn't one." Everyone looked a little stunned.

"What do you mean?" Mike Howard said,

"Didn't somebody write a book about it? I don't mean your department, I mean all English departments. With all this lesbo stuff, Chicano lit, my body is a text kind of thing . . ." He reached out and touched Emily Chassen's arm. "I hope I'm not offending anybody."

She didn't answer yes or no, her face a mask, but that wasn't going to stop Sweeney. In the dining room, Zoila moved silently around the table, removing dessert dishes.

"From what I read, it's like nobody knows what an English department is supposed to be any more. I'm not blaming you guys. It's not like you can go back to the days of raising well-rounded young gentlemen . . ."

"I think it's a little more complicated than that," Mike Howard said, gearing up for a fight. The sadness had returned to Sam Steinberg's great beagle eyes; he'd been having such a nice evening; did they really need to get into this discussion again? Did they really need to have some stranger dressed like a croupier telling them that their lives had no meaning?

Tom Strickland shot Ben a quick glance, waiting for him to do something. Ben should have thrown Sweeney out on his ear, but he couldn't do it and Sweeney knew that. This was payback for the other night, payback for telling Sweeney no.

"Hey, but what am I doing, shooting my big mouth off when I could be learning something?" Sweeney rose from his chair as Katy entered the room with a plate of apple pie, adorned with two glistening scoops of vanilla ice cream, a dessert fit for a king.

Ben had a total of twenty-one thousand dollars in his retirement account. He sat at his desk with Stan Gancher, the dapper consultant from his pension fund, going over the numbers. It was mind-boggling. Ben was forty-four years old, more than halfway through his life, and he had twenty-one thousand dollars set aside for what Gancher insisted on referring to as his and Katy's golden years.

"So what would this turn into?" Ben said. "By the time I'm seventy?"

Gancher loved to use his pocket calculator. He punched the buttons, nimble-fingered as any rag-time virtuoso, then held the calculator up for Ben to see. Ben squinted at the figures pulsing behind the smoky plastic. It wasn't much. It was a lot less than half a cooler.

"Of course that doesn't factor in your raises," Gancher said.

"I got seven hundred dollars this year."

"Yes." Gancher was a tall, gentle man from East Texas, a golfer and a church-goer, a fancier of expensive silk ties and tassled loafers. How he could make a penny coming to see Ben once a year, Ben had no idea. "So let's see. That will make it thirty thousand, seven hundred."

Ben leaned back in his chair. It was just two days after the dinner party debacle, it was late in the afternoon, and he wasn't in the mood for pity. "Tell you what," Ben said. "I want you to max me out."

Gancher looked stunned. "Are you sure?"

"Yeah. I want you to take the maximum out of my salary next year and put it all in retirement."

"But what will you live on?"

Ben rocked forward and slapped Gancher on the knee. "We'll figure something out."

It was nearly six by the time Ben got back to Rebecca's. As he pulled into the driveway he saw Sweeney's Bronco parked under the magnolia tree next to the garage. The van was gone. He opened the front door and called out, but the only one in the house was Zoila in the kitchen, snapping kernels off a cob of corn one by one with her thumb; she had nearly an entire bowl full. Ben gave her a smile and then looked up; he could hear shouts and splashing coming from the pool.

He stepped into the yard. Matt, Abby and Cameron, all in their dripping swimming suits, teetered on the concrete edge of the pool while Sweeney bobbed up and down in the water, eyes closed, his back to them, counting. They were playing Sharks and Minnows and Sweeney was the Shark.

Roberto stood in the middle of the lawn with his plastic gun, watching enviously. Matt was the first one with the nerve to ease into the water. He made it maybe a third of the way across before Sweeney heard him. With a roar Sweeney turned and threw himself at Matt like a blitzing linebacker. Abby and Cameron, seeing their chance, dove in at the other end, but Sweeney was wise to them, reversing his field. Cameron was out of range, but not Abby.

Sweeney lurched through the water, hairy-backed, arms held wide, love handles showing above his trunks. He wasn't interested in the others, just in her; Matt and Cameron coasted to safety. Abby backed off, laughing at Sweeney, trying to splash him, and he splashed back, carving out great bucket-sized scoops. Ben stood, invisible on the grass. Abby tried to dive to escape, but Sweeney made one last ursine-like belly-flop and caught her by the ankle. He rose up, swinging her through the water. She tried to keep her balance on one foot, but he wouldn't let her and she fell back.

"Hey, Dad!" Matt said.

"Hey," Ben said.

They all turned. Sweeney let go of Abby's leg. "Hey, Ben, how you doin'?" he said. Water was everywhere; the deck was soaked, *The New York Times* sitting on the glass-topped table was sopping.

"I'm fine," Ben said. He was so angry he could barely see. Roberto ran back to the house. "So where's Mom?"

"She had to go to the store," Matt said. He clung to the side of the pool, regarding his father with wonder, knowing something was wrong, but not knowing what it was. Abby wrung out her wet hair while Sweeney bounced from foot to foot, chest high in the water, grinning, man in his larval state.

"You guys need to get out and get dried off," Ben said. "We're going out to supper."

"But Dad," Matt said. "Mom said she was making hamburgers."

"Plans have changed. We're going to meet the Stricklands downtown."

The kids groaned. It was a clumsy lie, but Ben didn't care. It was more than he could take, the idea of Sweeney touching his daughter.

"Aww, come on, Dad . . ." Abby said.

Ben clapped his hands. "I said it once, that's enough. Cameron can go with us. Let's go, guys."

He bent down to retrieve a pair of wet goggles. The two boys struggled out of the pool while Sweeney glided over to the ladder. Ben could not bring himself to look at him. Sweeney padded across the deck and grabbed a towel.

"Feel free to stay and swim," Ben said.

"No, that's all right." Sweeney scrubbed his head hard, drying his hair, looking as sullen and injured as a child. He knew perfectly well what was going on. "I should be pushing along anyway."

Ben didn't hear from Sweeney for a week. On Monday, the day they were supposed to meet to exchange cash and check, there was a message from Sweeney on the answering machine saying that something had come up and he'd call later. Ben didn't like the feel of it. If there was one thing worse that having Sweeney around all the time it was not having him around at all and not knowing what he was up to.

All evening he brooded about it and finally, just as he and Katy were getting ready for bed, he said, "Katy, I think I'm going to see if I can find Sweeney. I think I may have really hurt his feelings."

Katy stood at the bathroom sink. Her face was covered with white cream, all but two circles for her eyes. "You could just call him."

"No," he said. "I want to do this face to face."

He got to the club a little after eleven, but Sweeney wasn't there. Toby the bartender was busy throwing out a group of Austin High girls with fake I.D.s, but through the melee managed to say that Sweeney'd left a half hour before. Toby thought he'd been headed home, but he wasn't sure.

Ben drove MOPAC to Bee Caves, the jagged crack in the windshield of the Cutlass gleaming in the headlights of the passing cars. His stomach was raw; this was not a scene he was looking forward to, but he needed to somehow clear the air. He waited for a break in the Monday night traffic and finally took a left up through thick cedars into the condo complex. The parking lot was jammed and he had to park near the front and walk all the way back, passing a raucous pool party.

Sweeney's apartment was on the first floor, with a big picture window overlooking the woods. Ben was glad to see that the lights were on, but as he came up the sloping walkway it struck him that there was something odd about the far wall of Sweeney's living room. It took him a second to figure out what it was: the bookcase wasn't there. Then he saw the shattered mirror above the mantel.

He stopped dead in his tracks. Splashing and shrieking from the pool party echoed through the humid night air. Ben reached out for the railing and took two steps up onto the landing. He stared in through the picture window. A three hundred pound man sat on the couch in Sweeney's living room, resting his chin on the knob of a baseball bat.

The apartment looked as if a bomb had gone off. There was almost too much to take in at once: the slashed furniture, the contents of Sweeney's desk spewed across the floor, the shattered remains of the beloved wave machine, the electric blue stain on the rug.

Off to the left side of the room and partially concealed by an overturned bookcase, a sixteen year old boy, Mexican-American, in t-shirt and crinkly black running pants, was down on the floor, pitching forward and back as if he was riding a mechanical bull. But it wasn't a bull he was riding. As the boy reared back, nearly standing for a second, Ben saw that the boy had Sweeney by the hair, even though it scarcely resembled Sweeney any more, one eye shut already, his face swollen and bloody and looking vaguely Chinese.

Ben couldn't stay where he was. A bug-spattered bulb above the entryway cast a flickering half-light and though they hadn't seen Ben yet, they would have if they'd looked. He moved back off the steps and slipped under a low chair into a landscaped area of woodchips and lariope. He was in darkness again, under the twining shadows of an ancient live-oak.

As he moved closer to the window he stumbled on a pile of broken flagstones. When he stood on top of it he was within a foot or two of the glass and could see the upper half of the enormous man, the gold chain and the neatly trimmed goatee. One of the louvered side panels of the window was open four or five inches, but it was enough to funnel the sounds of their voices.

"So where's our money, Mr. Sweeney?" There was a muffled answer, but Ben couldn't make out what it was. "What did you say?"

"I don't know what you're talking about." Sweeney sounded half-strangled, like a man in a dentist's chair.

"No?"

"No."

Off to Ben's right, around the corner of the building, he could see the crowd gathered around the pool. It was a young Westlake crowd and they had started to do the limbo, men in golf caps and bermuda shorts bending low, staggering like crabs, then collapsing on the grass. Everyone was laughing and having a beery good time.

The giant man rose from the couch. He moved awkwardly, as if he'd been through his share of knee operations. He crossed to the picture window. Ben stared at the back of the man's stout calves, only inches away.

"Come on, shitface, where are you hiding it?"

"I don't have it!"

"Why have you been talking then?" The big man swayed like a genie, filling the window. "You've been talking like you got it. You told our friend Calvin. . . ."

"I was just asking . . ."

Ben felt something sting his left ankle. He bent down to swat at his sock and nearly lost his balance, teetering on the flagstones.

"You were talking like you wanted some finder's fee."

"I was talking hypothetically. . . ."

"You know what your finder's fee is going to be? Just staying alive!"

The hulking man moved away from the window and disappeared

from view. There was a thud, followed by a shuddering groan. Around the pool they were singing, here we go loop the loop . . .

"So are you saying we made a mistake?"

Sweeney's answer was inaudible. There was another thud and this time Sweeney cried out. Here we do loop de lie . . . It was utterly clear to Ben what had happened. Whether out of stupidity or greed or hurt feelings, Sweeney had betrayed him. He had tried to sell Ben out and ended up outsmarting himself.

An air conditioning unit cut on somewhere above Ben. He was soaked with sweat. If he did nothing, Sweeney was going to die and what was terrible was that Ben had to acknowledge that there was some part of him that would have been almost willing to let him die and yet another part of him, no less low and calculating than the first, knew that Sweeney would offer up names before he died and Ben couldn't let that happen.

He bent down, groping among the broken flagstones until he could a dagger-shaped shard, with slightly more heft that a softball. He moved back from the window, back through a shoulder-high yaupon hedge. He was a good thirty feet away. He hurled the stone with all his might, felt the rough edges spin off his fingertips. The window came down in an avalanche of glass.

For an instant, everything was still—inside and out—and then three guys came running around the corner from the pool party to see what had happened. The sixteen year old boy stared out from where the window had been, looking rather slight and forlorn. Ben crouched low behind the hedge.

"What the fuck are you doing?" one of the men standing on the grassy slope bellowed. He sounded belligerent enough, but neither he nor any of his pals were willing to come any closer.

The boy disappeared from the window and a moment later he and the three hundred pound man, his bat under his arm, came out of the building, moved briskly across the parking lot and roared off in a big Land Cruiser.

Ben rose to his feet. About a dozen other party-goers had come from a look. One of the men, tall and red-headed, finally came up the walk and disappeared into the entryway.

Ben stepped backwards off the curb. No one seemed to have noticed him, everyone pointing at the shattered window, talking among themselves.

"Oh, shit!" The voice came from inside the apartment; it wasn't Sweeney's. "Oh, shit! Somebody call an ambulance!"

Ben felt for his keys, walking quickly across the parking lot to his car.

It was Toby who called the next morning with the news that Sweeney was in the hospital. He'd been banged around pretty good, Toby said, but he was going to be fine. If there was one thing Sweeney had going for him, it was a hard head.

"So what hospital?" Ben asked.

"Seton."

"And do they have any idea who did this?"

"I'm not really sure," Toby said. Katy stared up from the breakfast table, her eyes dark with alarm. She did know who or what was being discussed, but she knew from Ben's questions it was bad.

"So will they let him have visitors?"

"I don't see why not. But you might call," Toby said. In the walled garden outside the kitchen window Zoila sprinkled fish food in the fountain, sunlight gleaming off the lilypads like something out of a Monet painting. Ever since the night that Ben was out until two a.m. burying the coolers Zoila had been sullen around him. It was as if she was somehow onto him. It used to be she would have his tea ready for him as soon as he came down in the morning, greeting him with her radiant smile; now, he had to shift for himself.

When he hung up, Katy was waiting for the story. Ben repeated everything that Toby'd told him and she sat stunned for a second. "But how could this happen?" she said.

Ben turned away from her, scanning the room for his car keys. Deceit lay at the back of his throat like some imperfectly dissolved capsule. "Things like this happen all the time," he said.

Driving in to the hospital, Ben was in a fury. He kept going over it again and again in his head. How many ways, really, were there to interpret what he'd seen the night before? Sweeney had betrayed him. Whether Sweeney intended to do it all along or whether it was because he'd gotten his feelings hurt, got impatient and greedy, or couldn't resist talking big, it didn't matter. There was absolutely no one Ben could trust now. The thugs would be at his door if he didn't act and act immediately. Sweeney had gotten Ben into this and now Ben was going to have to use Sweeney to get him out.

He rode up on the hospital elevator with a one-legged woman in a wheelchair and her husband, a crewcut ex-Marine whose face was a map of defeat. Ben held the door for them and then followed them out.

He wandered down the hallway, a box of chocolate brownies under his arm, looking for Sweeney's room number. He passed the nurse's station and a scrub-suited doctor making a golf date over the phone. Hospitals always gave Ben the heebie-jeebies.

Sweeney's room was at the far end of the corridor and the door was open. Looking in, he saw a willowy woman with Joni Mitchell hair ladling soup out of a plastic bowl. When he gave a soft knock, she turned.

"Hey," she said. "Come in."

Ben entered almost sheepishly, poking his head around the corner. Sweeney lay under a white sheet, one hairy foot protruding, and his neck was in a brace. His nose looked like a bratwurst about to pop and his right eye had narrowed to a slit. He tried to smile, but it didn't quite work.

"Hey," he said.

"Hey," Ben said.

"Marina, this is Ben," Sweeney said.

"How are you?" Ben said. The TV set blared overhead and Sweeney's attention was divided.

"I've had better days," Marina said. She was an attractive woman, though not exactly what Ben would have called Sweeney's type. She was thirty at most, in cut-offs and hiking boots and sported a butterfly tatoo on her inner thigh.

Ben raised the box of brownies. "Got something for you."

"What's that?" Sweeney asked.

"Brownies."

"Great. Why don't you just set them over there?"

Ben put the carton down on the window sill, amid the artfully ribboned bouquets. When he looked over his shoulder, Marina was leaning across the bed with the spoonful of soup and Sweeney was puckering up to receive it, eager as a baby bird.

"So how'd you hear?" Sweeney said.

"Toby called me."

Marina wiped Sweeney's lower lip with a napkin. "Pretty pathetic, huh?"

"I never think of you as pathetic," Ben said.

They all stared at the television for a second. All the guests on the talk show were people who'd made love to their pets and the studio audience was in an uproar of glee and disgust.

"I think I'd better be going," Marina said. Sweeney hit a button on his tray and the screen winked off. She got up and kissed Sweeney tenderly on the forehead. "I'll be back later." She turned to Ben. "It was nice to meet you."

"Nice to meet you too," Ben said.

After she was gone, Ben took her chair. Sweeney's eyes followed him, even though he couldn't move his head. "So what's the prognosis?" Ben asked.

"Got myself a nasty little concussion. And my ribs don't feel so great, though the doctors are telling me they're not cracked. They want to keep me around for another twenty-four hours to observe me."

"So what happened exactly?"

"What does it look like? I got the shit kicked out of me."

"Over what?"

"The usual stuff."

"And what's the usual stuff?"

"Over a girl. You'd think I'd know better by now." Sweeney rested his head against his pillows. Ben marvelled at the off-handed ease with which Sweeney lied.

"And you told the police?"

"I told 'em what I could." Sweeney stared mournfully at the brilliantly yellow cubes of jello shimmering on his lunch tray. "I'm not holding my breath about it."

Ben leaned forward in the chair, pressing his fingers together. "Listen, I want to apologize," he said.

"About what?"

"About the way I've been lately. And I wanted to say . . . I've been thinking about your proposal."

"What proposal was that?"

"The other night. At the skating rink." Ben raised his head, meeting Sweeney's gaze directly. "I was thinking maybe we should go ahead with that."

Sweeney didn't say anything for a long time. "You're sure?"

"I'm absolutely sure."

Sweeney fingered the edge of his tray. Ben rose, thinking he needed help, but Sweeney waved him off. Sweeney's eyes glistened with tears. "You won't regret this," he said. "I promise you. Scout's honor."

Ben and Katy lay on a quilt on a patch of grass under the Congress Avenue Bridge, waiting for the bats. They were supposed to have their friends the Stricklands, but for some reason the Stricklands hadn't arrived (Anna's sisters were visiting from Ohio and taking them to see the Mexican free-tailed bats was one of the obligatory tourist things to do).

Dusk was falling fast but it was still nearly one hundred degrees. Eighty or ninety people were hunkered down on the scraggly lawn around them: parents feeding popsicles to fussing infants in strollers, some German college students, adorned with tatoos and a variety of piercings, their heads propped against their backpacks, a romantic young couple in white ducks who'd had the foresight to bring their own cooler and wine glasses.

Lined up along the railing of the bridge were several hundred others. It was Austin's nightly show. A paddle-wheeler, lit up like a Vegas casino, drifted back and forth under the bridge while out in the middle of the darkening water a canoeist sat with his paddle across his lap just an Indian scout in some nineteenth century painting.

Katy was out of sorts. She'd been quiet in the car. When he asked her if anything was wrong, she said it was just that it was so ungodly hot but on their walk from the parking lot he could see that she had a definite look. When he tried to put his arm around her, she pulled away.

"Maybe I should call them and see what happened," Ben said. He could hear the bats twittering and chirping under the girders. There were a million and a half of them, incredible as it seemed, living in the one inch expansion joints of the bridge.

"No, I'm sure they're on their way," she said. "I went down to Sweeney's club today."

"Oh. And why did you do that?"

"Because you've never taken me. I wanted to see it." One of the German students had gotten to his feet and was pointing; several of the bats were starting to swirl, flying in tight circles beneath the great concrete pillars.

"And?"

"I met one of the owners."

"Which one was that?"

"I forget his name. A big muscly ex-football star. I introduced myself. He didn't know who I was."

"Well. . . ."

"And he didn't know who you were either. I told him that we'd invested in his club. He said he hadn't heard anything about it." More and more of the bats were venturing out now, the whirlpools of tiny bodies beginning to thicken, but still spinning under the bridge. The smell of marijuana sweetened the air.

"Come on, it was five thousand dollars. Why should he even remember? That's peanuts to these guys."

"I mentioned Sweeney's name and he got this look on his face."

"So what are you trying to say?"

"I'm saying that I don't know what's going on here! I'm not stupid, Ben! I never saw any residual check, all I see is that our bank balance goes up five hundred dollars a week. . . ."

"Katy, listen. About the money. I did it all through Sweeney. It was more like a loan. He needed the money to even be a partner."

"But you didn't tell me that."

"Maybe I didn't."

"No, you didn't." A great shout went up. Further on down the bridge a great stream of free-tailed bats was heading out over the lake. "You know I went back and checked our bank statements. You lent him five thousand dollars, right? And we started getting five hundred dollars a week in the middle of May. This week will make it fourteen weeks. That's a two thousand dollar profit in four months. Forty percent interest. Hard to beat that."

"What are you accusing me of? That was the deal, that I was going to be paid off first! Jesus Christ, I don't believe this!"

She pushed up from the quilt and walked towards the lake, her arms folded tightly around her chest. He watched her go, hesitating for a moment. She was so close to the truth; one more step and they were lost. He got to his feet and went after her. This time when he put his hand on her shoulder she didn't pull away.

"I took a job," she said.

"What are you talking about?" An old man with perfect posture stared through his binoculars, standing just a few feet away from them.

"They called me from my old school today. They need someone to teach reading half-time. I told them I'd do it."

"But Katy, you don't have to do that."

"Don't I? Maybe not. But I think it would be better for all of us."

She stared out over the lake. Clouds of bats stained the sky, drifting south and east like smoke from a great conflagration, like a genie let out of his bottle.

Chapter Fourteen

A week later they all drove out to visit the ranch of Sweeney's friend Al Jackett. They took the van, Sweeney playing Botticelli with the kids in the back. Other than a scab over his right eye and an engorged nose, he seemed to have returned to robust good health.

It was a cloudless morning and it was hard to believe that summer was almost over; Abby and Matt would be back in school in a matter of days. They drove for nearly an hour, deep into the Hill Country. Sweeney had promised to show them the real Texas and he was doing it.

Turning off the highway, they followed a dirt road for a couple of miles, passing a creaking windmill and herds of longhorn cattle. As they rumbled over a bridge, a red fox dashed across ahead of them.

Jackett's place was perched on a high ridge and the rutted road up to it nearly tore the bottom out of the van, but the view on top was magnificent. The house sat behind stone walls and the Texas state flag snapped from a twenty-foot high flagpole; it looked like the kind of place John Wayne and four good men could have defended for weeks.

They parked in the shade of some mesquite trees and no sooner had they gotten out of the van than two cowboys came thundering over the rise on their lathered-up horses. Matt's eyes went wide with wonder; this was better than the movies.

The older of the two cowboys swung off his horse and tossed the reins up to the younger. He took off his hat, wiped the sweat out of his eyes with his elbow, grinned a winning grin and extended a hand to Ben.

"Al Jackett," he said. Ben stared for a second. He had seen this man before and he couldn't remember when. Sweeney was nearly squirming with pleasure.

"It's nice to meet you," Ben said. "Ben Lindberg."

"Sweeney here has told me a lot about you," Jackett said. He was in his late sixties, Ben would have guessed, but looked as tough as nails. The horses stomped their hooves, still blowing hard, anxious to get to the barn. Matt reached out to touch the wet flank of one of them.

"Johnny, why don't you take the horses down and get them some water?" Jackett said. "I'm sorry to be looking like this, but some cattle busted down a fence and our neighbor was mad as blue blazes. Hey, you kids must be starving after driving all that way. Let's see if we can find you something to eat."

Unpretentious from the outside, from the inside the house was sneakily grand. Picture windows overlooked miles of rolling hill country and glassy-eyed heads of deer and bighorn sheep, lion and water buffalo stared down from the walls. A huge stone fireplace that wouldn't have been out of place in one of the old railroad hotels loomed in the living room.

"Shelby? We've got visitors here!" Jackett shouted. Ben kept looking at him, racking his brain, trying to figure out where he could have possibly met him.

Mrs. Jackett came out of the kitchen, wiping her hands on a towel. A trim and attractive woman in a black and white print dress, she was horrified by the grimy state of her husband and sent him off to wash. She was as gracious and welcoming as Mr. Jackett, kissing Sweeney lightly on the cheek and taking everyone back to meet the cook, an elderly man with a gold tooth whom they'd just brought up from Monterrey.

When Jackett returned, fresh-faced in a seer-sucker shirt and clean blue jeans, they all sat down for dinner. The food was remarkable: the best enchiladas Ben had ever tasted, an avocado salad and peach cobbler with home-made ice cream for dessert. There was still a part of Ben that was wary, trying to puzzle out what part the Jacketts could possibly play in Sweeney's schemes. He squeezed Katy's hand under the table.

Mrs. Jackett entertained Matt and Abby with stories of her grandmother, a hardy woman who'd homesteaded in West Texas and had once killed a Comanche who'd come to her door while she was alone with her three young children, then given him a dipperful of cold water as he lay dying. Mrs. Jackett had been an English major at the University and Frank Dobie had been her favorite professor.

"And we like that chairman you've got over there now," Mr. Jackett said.

"My chairman?" Ben said.

"A few of us have been talking about maybe coming up with a new building for you all."

It suddenly all came back to Ben: outside the chairman's office, later January, the gathering of men in nice suits. Christ, leave it to Sweeney to introduce him to a donor.

"That's terrific," Ben said.

"See if you can get this guy an office with a window while you're at it," Sweeney said.

"We'll do our best." Jackett pushed away from the table. "What do you say we go for a little ride around the place?"

In Texas, Jackett said, people always take you to see their water and that was what Jackett did, though in late August there wasn't much of it. The creeks were down to a trickle and the tanks nothing more than circles of trampled mud.

They bounced from ridge-line to bottom, trailing clouds of dust, Jackett pointing things out. Jackett was the kind of man any man would like to be his father, charming to the point of seeming a little simple-minded, but sharp-eyed as well—quick to spot turkey buzzards soaring on the thermals a mile away or a strange pick-up parked next to a distant deer stand. He was originally from the Panhandle and had started in the oil business, but for the past ten years had been in trucking in Mexico. The ranching was just a diversion, but it was good to get some dirt between your toes from time to time.

Jackett wanted to check on his bee-hives. A man from North Dakota came every year and in exchange for a place to raise and winter his bees he gave the Jacketts free honey.

"He's from your part of the country," Jackett said. Sweeney and Ben both braced themselves as Jackett gunned the pick-up over an embankment. "Nice fella. Hard-working. Those people can be a little quiet, though, I'll tell you. Here we go." A half dozen square white boxes sat under a grove of pecan trees. "Want to take a look?"

"Sure," Ben said.

The three men got out of the trunk. A huge longhorn swung its head around to stare at them from a fenceline fifty yards away. Sweeney let Ben and Jackett walk on ahead.

"This fellow from North Dakota is amazing. He'll walk in among them, never get stung. I guess the key is staying calm."

As they moved closer Ben could see some of the bees looping in and out of the boxes. The longhorn ambled toward the truck as if he thought he was about to be fed.

"So I hear you've got some money to move," Jackett said.

Ben stepped over a dried cowpie, taking a quick, involuntary breath. So this is it, he thought, the moment he knew was coming. The moment he wanted. "So where did you hear that?"

"Sweeney told me a little about your situation."

"This is the guy, Ben," Sweeney said. "You're not going to do better than this."

Jackett bent down and picked a couple of pecans out of the tall grass. He rolled them together in his fist, pressing hard until they cracked. He offered Ben the handful of shattered shells. "Want some?"

"No, thanks." Ben could hear the bees droning, the low, throbbing warning.

"So you just *found* this money, is that right?"

"That's right."

"When Sweeney told me the story I had a hard time believing it. I thought the guy's got to be either a cop or a crook. But you're not either, are you?"

"No. Just a lucky guy."

Jackett put one of the fractured bits between his teeth and crunched down on it, then wiped the bitter fragments off his tongue with his thumb.

"Let me put my cards on the table. I work closely with a number of Mexican banks. If you wanted to deposit your money in one of those banks, it could be arranged. We could set up the accounts for you and we have people there who know how to stay discrete. It may sound complicated, but it's a lot less complicated that driving a herd of cattle to Montana. You just want to be damn sure you don't make any amateurish mistakes."

Ben glanced over at Sweeney. For a second it crossed his mind that this was all part of one vast conspiracy—the Colombians in the liquor store, Jackett, the pair who'd beaten Sweeney up—but he didn't really believe that. No, Sweeney was looking for a way out of the jam he'd gotten himself into, just the way Ben was.

"And how much would it cost me, your assistance?" Ben said.

"Forty percent."

"Forty percent."

"I believe that's the going rate."

Ben whistled softly, kicking at a clump of weeds. Grasshoppers sprayed up in front of him. "And so what would I do? Just turn all the money over to you?"

"These things are based on trust. That's what it always comes down to. You just have to decide." Jackett reached out and flicked a bee from Ben's collar. "Remind me when we get back to the house. I want to give you some of that honey."

The children had had a great afternoon. They'd both gotten to ride on a one-eyed stallion named Spook and the horse had nearly run Abby into the low-hanging branch of a tree, a cause of much excited conversation on their trip back to Austin. Katy'd had a good day too; Mrs. Jackett had invited her to lunch with some of her museum friends. It was only the men who were quiet: Sweeney, staring out the window, lost in his own thoughts, Ben at the wheel, battling the late afternoon traffic.

As they came up the driveway a raccoon scurried away from an overturned garbage can. Everyone got out of the van, Katy leaning back to retrieve the red plastic bucket of honey and the rusted horseshoe Mrs. Jackett had given Matt for good luck. She called the children back from the front door to thank Sweeney for the lovely day. Sweeney put a hand on her shoulder and gave her a feathery kiss.

"I'll walk you to your car," Ben said.

The two men trudged silently down the driveway. Neither spoke until they heard the door to the house slam.

"So what did you think of Jackett?" Sweeney said.

"I liked him."

"You ready to do this?"

"Probably so. If you could just give me a couple of days. It's a lot to think over." Sweeney shot him a quick glance. The setting sun stabbed through the tops of the cedars like a glowing cinder.

"Sure," Sweeney said. "Just don't think about it too long."

The plan had been for the whole family to go to Wimberly for their last weekend before school started and they'd rented a pair of simple cabins on the Blanco River with the Stricklands. Katy was dismayed when Ben announced that he had too much work to do and they should go on without him. It wouldn't be nearly as much fun without him, she said. Couldn't he bring his work with him? Or they could come back early on Sunday. Ben held fast; there was no room for negotiation on this one.

Katy and the children left a little after ten on Saturday morning. Ben went into his office and futzed with his syllabus for an hour and then drove up to Julio's for lunch. As much as he loved his family, this was a time when he wanted them out of the way. He was about to take the biggest chance of his life and what he needed was time to think and move.

In the afternoon he returned books to the library, stopped by Kinko's to pick up his course instruction packet and went to the gym. He got back to the house about six-thirty and was surprised to find a brand-new Honda Accord parked in the driveway. He sat with his hands in his lap, just staring at it for a minute. Zoila and Roberto were spending the weekend with her uncle in East Austin; he had no idea who this could be.

The front door was unlocked. Ben pushed it open and stepped into the cool blast of the air conditioning.

"Hello?" he called. The house was utterly still. Through the living room windows he could see the tiny head of a turtle moving across the surface of the fountain, a green nub. Something thumped softly on the second floor.

Ben set down his gym bag and moved silently up the stairs. The door to the spare bedroom stood open and suitcases were strewn across the landing. Rebecca had her back to him as she sorted through a stack of summer dresses on the bed. When she finally turned and saw him she gave a start.

"Hey," he said.

"Hey." She wore white pants, a tightly rolled blue bandanna to hold back her tawny hair and the kind of Gucci sandals that showed lots of tanned foot.

"What are you doing?"

"Just looking for some of my clothes," she said. All the closets in the bedroom hung open and a David Hockney print, bowing slightly in an inadequate frame, leaned against the wall.

"And when did you get in?"

"This morning," she said. "I tried to call three or four times, but I didn't get anyone, so I just came by. I hope it's all right. I was going to leave you a note."

"Of course it's all right." There was something about her that seemed off, something desperate and harried. Ben didn't believe her story for a second.

"So where is everybody?" Rebecca asked.

"Katy and the kids went down to Wimberly for the weekend. Zoila's at her uncle's."

"So it's just the two of us."

"Apparently so," Ben said. He scratched his nose. His heart still raced wildly. "You have plans for dinner?"

"No."

"Well, let's see what I can whip up."

Still more than a little pissed—who likes people breaking into their home, even if it is their landlord?—Ben went downstairs and found a couple of chicken breasts coiled inside a container of lemon marinade. He got the grill going and then rustled around for salad makings. Rebecca—acting as if she'd done nothing wrong—opened a bottle of wine and sat at the kitchen table while Ben sliced tomatoes.

Her summer in Santa Fe had been a mixed bag. The air was wonderful and she'd gotten a lot of work done, but the crowds in August had turned the place into a zoo and sometimes she yearned to have a conversation with someone other than a massage therapist.

"So have you seen Sweeney?" Ben asked.

"No," she said. "And I don't imagine that I will."

"And why is that?"

She rolled her wine around in her mouth for a second before swallowing. "Sweeney, I believe, is occupied."

"How do you mean?" In the corner the beady-eyed parrot chewed on sunflower seeds, the hulls dropping to the floor of his cage.

"Oh, come on, Ben. You must know."

"Know what?"

"Sweeney's got a girl friend."

Ben slid the tomatoes into the salad bowl, feeling his face beginning to color. "Well, yes."

"Well, yes, indeed. You must see him."

"We saw him yesterday as a matter of fact. We went to see a friend of his. A man named Al Jackett."

Rebecca got up from her chair and stared out the window. In profile she seemed noble and ruined. "You've done a wonderful job with the flowers," she said. "Everything looks so nice. You and Katy are doing well?"

"Oh, yeah. She loves it here."

. . .

It was nearly dark by the time the chicken was ready and they ate by the pool. A breeze had come up from the north, for the first time in months it seemed, and the temperature dropped ten degrees. Ben was still wary; it was too strange, her appearing tonight of all nights; it felt too much like a set-up.

Most of her women friends were becoming Episcopalian priests, she said, maybe she would give it a try herself. Not that she believed in God exactly, or at least not in the God with the long white beard peering down from Heaven, but there were things about religion that had always drawn her, the part where you ask God to forgive you your trespasses as you forgive those who trespass against you. Perhaps it was simple-minded, but just saying those words always made her feel cleaner. If she could only make it a practice, forgiving her enemies, clearing the slate, and allowing God to forgive her, getting rid of all those terrible poisons.

Ben said nothing, staring out at the breeze rippling the surface of the pool. It was cool enough now, but tomorrow it would be a hundred again, without doubt. Between the two of them, Ben and Rebecca had finished the bottle of wine.

They did the dishes and went for a walk on the road. The cat followed them, meandering off in the bamboo from time to time to search for baby birds. Rebecca made Ben tell her the story about his and Katy's courtship, their years in New York. For all of his wariness, he found himself talking to her almost eagerly, talking more openly than he'd talked to anyone in months. Some time during their stroll, he decided he'd been wrong to be so suspicious of her. She was just lonely and wounded. Sweeney had really hurt her—not a difficult thing to imagine.

When they got back to the house it was nearly eleven. They went upstairs and she finished her packing, filling two travel bags and a leather suitcase the color of caramel.

"So do you have a place to stay?" he asked.

"No, but it won't be hard to find one."

"You're welcome to stay here. It is your house."

Her smile was wry. "It wouldn't be awkward?"

"Not at all. You can sleep in Abby's room."

He got her fresh towels from the hall closet, kissed her on the cheek and they went to their separate bedrooms.

He got into bed and tried to read for awhile, thumbing through an old *Best American Poetry* anthology. He heard Rebecca go out to her car and come then come in again; a few seconds later he heard the shower.

He snapped off the bedside lamp and lay in the dark for a long time, just thinking. In the morning he would have to call Sweeney; he'd let him sweat enough. He rolled over on his side, scrunching up his pillow. He didn't remember falling asleep, but he must have, because the soft knock on the bedroom door took him out of it with a rush.

"Yes?" he said. He was aware of his voice sounding oddly strangled. He propped himself on an elbow as the door swung open. Rebecca stood in the half-light from the hallway, wearing a simple cotton nightgown.

"Hello," she said.

"Hello." She stood there for a long time without saying anything. "Is anything wrong?" he asked.

"No," she said. She came in. The bed creaked as she sat down. "It's just that it's so strange, being here again."

"Why is that?"

"I don't know. It's as if I don't quite know where I belong in the world." He reached out for her hand; her grip was surprisingly fierce.

"Why did you come back?" he asked. She shook her head and then turned away from him, surveying the dark room.

"You moved the bureau," she said.

"I hope it's O.K."

"Of course it's O.K. Everything's O.K."

She leaned forward and kissed him gravely. He didn't move away from her at first but then he did, touching her lips with two fingers.

"I don't think we should do this," he said.

"But you want to, don't you?"

"Part of me does. But I can't . . . I can't lie to my wife."

"But you already are."

"What do you mean?"

"You already are, lying to her." There was just enough moonlight coming through the window for him to see the long line of her bowed neck.

"About what?"

"You know what."

"Sweeney told you."

She let go of his hand and got up from the bed. "Of course he told me. You think Sweeney can keep his mouth shut about anything?" She moved across the room to the window. "Why do you think he talked me into giving you this house? He's going to rob you blind. He and his friend Jackett."

"You know Jackett?"

"Of course I know Jackett. He and I were once quite . . . close." He heard her stumble against something in the dark. "I better go."

"Yes," he said. "You better go."

"Give my best to your wife."

She closed the door when she left. He heard her bump down the stairs, heard her start the car. Lights slid across the ceiling of his bedroom as she backed down the driveway. He got up and opened the window. The cool breeze was gone; even at midnight he could feel it heating up again. He stood for a long time, staring at the blinking lights of the radio towers and listening to the chant of the cicadas.

He called Sweeney as soon as he got up the next morning. It was a little before nine and it was clear that Ben had woken him.

"Any chance we could get together today?" Ben asked.

"Sure. Whatever you say."

"How about two this afternoon?" Ben leaned over on one foot to retrieve the two wine glasses from the dishwasher and then set them back in the cupboard.

"Great," Sweeney said. "You want me to come over there?"

"No, I want you to meet me. You know where Camp Chatauqua is?"

"You mean that place out by Spicewood?"

"Yeah."

"It takes forty-five minutes to get out there!"

"It's Sunday, Sweeney, what else do you have to do? I'll see you there."

Ben took the towels from Abby's bedroom and put them in the washing machine. He toasted a bagel and ate it standing at the kitchen counter. When he was done he went out to the garage and found the shovel. As he was putting it in the trunk of the Cutlass he heard the phone ringing. He raced back inside, thinking it was Sweeney, that there was some problem, but it was just Katy, calling to see how he was.

"The kids have had a great time," she said. "Really, it's so beautiful. We're right down by the water and there are all these big cypress trees. Everybody misses you. We were thinking if you could come down and have a swim with everybody. . . ."

"I probably shouldn't," Ben said.

"Is anything wrong? You sound rushed."

"No," he said. "I'm just trying to get a couple things out of the way."

He filled up at Chevron and headed out. The evening with Rebecca was still with him, but what remained wasn't so much alarm as a deep sadness. He was weary of imagining conspiracies. She had come to warn him, nothing more, but he was already warned. What had she told him that he didn't already know? Sweeney had been setting him up from the start: big surprise. Nothing she'd said was going to change anything. What he needed to do now was act.

There were readings for the blind on Public Radio, articles from the week's newspapers; a woman had been married at the Central Park Zoo. Ben listened for awhile and then snapped it off. Driving through Oak Hill he caught a glimpse of a red Bronco eight or nine cars back in traffic and his heart leapt. His first instinct was that it was Sweeney, following him, but after a mile or so, the Bronco vanished. It was nothing but his jumpiness; it had gotten to the point where he was seeing Sweeney behind every tree.

Once he got into the high, rolling country he started to relax. The turns were almost second-nature to him now. He passed the crossroads store and the rusted windmill and labored up the big hill. Getting out to unlock the gate, he picked a half dozen flattened beer cans from the weeds and tossed them in the back seat of the car. Dust billowed behind him as he drove in; it had been almost a month since they'd had any rain.

A relief welled up in him, just seeing that the house was still standing. He parked under the live oak tree, got the shovel from the trunk of the car, and walked to the plot; it was untouched. He stood for several minutes, staring at it.

He knew exactly where every cooler was. He'd buried them in a simple crossing pattern, five in a row north/south and two east/west, with two long paces between each, using the line between a rotting fence post and the corner of the house to get his bearings.

He scooped out two shallow shovelfuls and then turned the shovel upside down, plunging the handle down into the earth, jabbing it again and again until he heard a reassuring thunk—the hard bottom that Thoreau had always been looking for, below freshet and frost and fire, a place where you might found a wall or a state.

It took twenty minutes to dig up the cooler and wrest it from its rocky hole. The heat was withering and by the time he finished he felt as if he might pass out. He lugged the cooler into the shade of the porch before he opened it.

It was all there, fifty dollar bills packed in tight and orderly. Ben tore open one of the cellophane wrappers and counted out twelve thousand dollars (six hundred a week times twenty weeks, the equivalent of everything he'd already given Sweeney). He put the twelve thousand in a rusted coffee can and stuck it under the front porch, his only witness the longhorn skull, staring blankly with its cavernous eyes. Ben closed the cooler, went back out in the heat and shovelled the dirt back into the hole. He stamped it down with his feet.

He glanced at his watch. It was just eleven-thirty and he wasn't meeting Sweeney until two. He walked down to the creek and took off all his clothes. He waded up the shallow stream, watching the minnows dart ahead of him. The high grasses rustled on the shore and a red-tailed hawk circled high above the limestone cliffs.

The water was warm at first, but as he moved downstream it got deeper and cooler and when he came to one of the gouged-out pools he bent low and launched himself, breast-stroking his way to the middle. At the deepest the water was neck high. He rolled over and spread his arms, letting the pool hold him, only his face exposed to the intensity of the one hundred degree heat. He remembered being baptized at a small Wisconsin church, the minister's hand covering his face with a cloth; he remembered how he had struggled, afraid of going over backwards, afraid of surrender. Insects sang on the bank and tiny fish nibbled at his ankles.

He must have floated on his back for a couple of minutes, letting the combination of sun and cool water lull him nearly to sleep. It was only when he shook his head, waving a hovering dragonfly away from his nose, that he saw the flash of light in the trees above the limestone cliffs. He scrambled quickly to regain his feet and stood chest-deep in the creek, staring upwards. It had been just a sudden splash of light, like the reflection off a mirror or a windshield, but he hadn't made it up. He stood for a long time, shielding his eyes, but he didn't see it again. A jay called from the nearby cedars. Ben looked back towards the house where the cooler still sat on the porch, undisturbed. He sloshed back to the shore; it was time to get going.

On his way out he stopped at the crossroads store and picked up a six-pack of beer and a chopped beef sandwich. He ate the sandwich in the car, wiping his greasy fingers on a Dairy Queen napkin and then pitching the crumpled paper out the window, watching in the rear view mirror as it tumbled down the pavement and into the tawny weeds.

It took him a little over thirty minutes to get to Camp Chatauqua. There was no attendant at the guard state so Ben put two dollars in one of the camp envelopes, carefully writing down his license number and time of arrival on the flap, and slipped it in the drop box.

He found a picnic table a hundred yards from the water, sheltered from the sun by a rough wooden roof. A clown reunion seemed to be going on across the road, four or five of the men in full costume, the others wearing their Shriner jackets, and they were having a great time. They had a fire going, mothers slathered their children with sunblock and a group of swim-suited teenagers picked their way carefully through a field of cockle-burrs, heading for the water.

Ben sipped at a Corona, staring at the lake, the sixpack sitting on the table in front of him. The afternoon had turned hazy. He had never quite accepted the fact that Central Texas lakes were lakes; they were just dammed-up rivers. There were stories he had heard, he didn't know if they were apocryphal or not, of entire Western towns still down there, buried beneath a hundred feet of water.

Sweeney pulled in a little after two. He looked rather confused when he got out of his Bronco.

"This your idea?" he asked. He gestured to the clowns across the road. A man in a Shriner jacket was twisting balloons into giraffes for his grandchildren.

"No," Ben said. "You want a beer?"

"Why not?"

Sweeney lifted a Corona from the six pack and sat down on the opposite side of the table. He twisted off the cap and tossed it in the general direction of the trash basket. It came up a couple of feet short. Far out on the lake two cigarette boats bounced across the choppy water. Ben took a swig of his beer and Sweeney did the same.

"I hate circuses," Sweeney said.

"Is that right?"

"I never thought they were that funny. A bunch of clowns beating the crap out of each other with clubs.I remember buying a ticket once to see the world's fattest man. It was just this guy in a trailer, he couldn't even get up. It was like he was just swimming in this pool of flesh. Eight hundred and fifty pounds. I didn't really enjoy it." Sweeney took another swig of his beer. "So what's the deal here?"

"I've got something for you," Ben said.

"What's that?"

"It's in my trunk." He fished his car keys out of his pocket and lay them on the table. Sweeney gaped at him. "Go on."

Sweeney took the keys, got up and went to the Cutlass. The closest possible witness was a father in wingtip shoes and no socks changing his daughter's diaper in the backseat of a van thirty yards away. Ben pulled at his nose; in the heat, one beer was enough to make him dizzy. Sweeney popped open the trunk and stared at the cooler.

Ben rose from the table. "Open it," he said.

Sweeney hesitated, as if it had to be some sort of trick, then undid the plastic latch and lifted the lid. Ben stood five feet away, just watching Sweeney's face. For a second there was no reaction at all—as if Sweeney didn't know what he was looking at—and then he let go with a big puttering noise of amazement.

"So how much is this?" Sweeney asked.

"A little under a million," Ben said. Sweeney ran his hand lightly over the stacks of money. He seemed oddly baffled, a shadow of disbelief lurking behind his clear blue eyes. "You can take it to your friend Jackett."

"You don't want to take it yourself?"

"I thought it would be better if you did." Across the road one of the clowns danced around the table with a can a beer that cascaded with foam and everyone was laughing uproariously.

"Either way," Sweeney said.

"You want to count it?"

"No, I'll take your word for it," Sweeney said. He was still staring down at the money, fingering the torn cellophane, mulling over the one shortened stack. Somewhere in the distance speedboats droned like angry hornets.

"I guess this means no more of our weekly meetings," Ben said.

"No, I think we just graduated," Sweeney said. He handed Ben his keys back. "So how do you want to do this?"

"I'll help you load it in your car."

Sweeney gave a short laugh. "So I'm the guy who gets to drive back into Austin with this in my back seat, right?"

"Just make sure you don't get stopped," Ben said.

Together they lugged the cooler to Sweeney's Bronco and set it on the floor in the back.

"So this is all of it?" Sweeney asked.

"Yeah, this is all of it," Ben said. Sweeney rubbed gravely at his ear for a second and then patted Ben on the shoulder. "I'll get it to Jackett tomorrow. I'll call you."

"Whenever."

A white Camry was coming slowly down the road towards them. As it passed, Ben saw that all three passengers were in full clown costumes—curly orange wigs, cheery-red noses, the corners of their painted mouths curving downward in horse-shoes of irrevocable sadness. One of them raised a hand in greeting; Sweeney refused to acknowledge him, glowering back.

Driving back to Austin, Ben was filled with elation. Let them rob him, let Sweeney disappear with the money if that was what he was going to do; it was a small price to pay. The solution was so simple; the only astonishing thing about it was that he hadn't thought of it before. The one advantage Ben had was that Sweeney didn't know how much money there was. As long as Sweeney thought he'd gotten his, he wasn't going to be turning Ben over to a bunch of drug dealers for some lousy ten per cent. Ben still had millions, more than anyone would ever need. Next time around he wasn't going to be so stupid. He would talk to no one, trust no one, let the money bake in its sun-hardened plot for ten years or twenty if he had to, until everyone had long forgotten. The million he'd lost he could just chalk off to the rising cost of education.

Katy and the children pulled into the driveway ten minutes after he did. The tops of Matt's feet glowed with sunburn and everyone was tired. Ben hugged them and kissed them all as if he hadn't seen them for a month.

Abby wriggled out of his grasp with a sardonic smile. "Dad, is something wrong with you?"

"No, honey, I'm just in a good mood."

It was school the next day and everyone needed to go to bed early. They ordered pizza and spent a quiet night watching television and searching for ring notebooks and protractors. It was a nice evening; the only jarring note was when Abby stomped down from her room just as the weather came on.

"Mom, somebody's been in my closet."

"Oh, yeah," Ben said. "Rebecca was here last night."

"Rebecca?" Katy said. Her face furrowed with confusion. "Did she *stay* here?"

"No," Ben said. "No. She was only in town for the day. She came to pick up some of her stuff."

Chapter Fifteen

At nine-thirty the next morning he stood in front of one hundred and fifty strange faces, talking about the origins of American writing, of the desire to create a literature to match the energies released by the Revolution, the desire to burn away the past.

"If you want to understand this country and its literature," he said, "a good place to start would be with the accounts of the early hunters, the descriptions of skies blackened by flocks of passenger pigeons and wild turkeys, of buffalo herds stretching to the horizon. This has always been, in the world's imagination, the land of plenty, the country of limitless possibility, a place where the streets are paved with gold. But everything comes at a price. If you listened to the political speeches during the last election, you might come away with the impression that the essential American is just a good-hearted Joe temporarily misled, perhaps, by a few unscrupulous leaders of the opposing party. But as you will see as we move through the semester, our greatest writers have a more complex story to tell. Putting it most charitably, Emerson said that heroes do not fix but flow, bend forward and invent a resourse for every moment. Less charitably, Simon Suggs tells us that it's good to be shifty in a new country."

Two burly football players at the back of the room exchanged swift glances; this was a course to drop. A young blonde woman in bobby-socks scribbled furiously. After class a dozen students crowded around the podium—the scruffier ones, by and large, the ones with the nose rings and the burning eyes and the Berkeley t-shirts. They thought they had found their man, their closet radical.

His second class wasn't until three-thirty. On his way over to the Coop to check on textbooks the sound of pan-pipes pierced the air, sweet and melancholy. Ben jostled his way through the crowd that had gathered on the West Mall to listen to the music of two tiny Peruvians and an old hippie. A gentle pear of a man in a Robert Hall suit was passing out pocket-sized copies of the New Testament and newspaper salesmen were offering free copies of *The Statesman.*

He'd started the morning free and easy, almost gleeful, but as the day wore on he felt himself growing increasingly edgy. Sweeney had said he'd call; Ben guessed there was less than a fifty-fifty chance of that happening, but he couldn't help wondering about it. The big question was, if Sweeney did go to Jackett, was Jackett going to buy the story that the million dollars was the all of it. Maybe they knew more than Ben thought they knew.

After he straightened things out with the textbook people he stopped at Texas French Bread for lunch and then walked all the way across campus to Parking to see about a new sticker for his car.

The bell had already rung when he walked into his three-thirty class. He strode quickly to the podium, unzipped his briefcase and arranged his notes. He glanced up. Every eye in the room was on him. It was usual, on the first day, for a class to be wary, but this was more than that. He nodded at an Indian student in a sari who quickly averted her gaze.

"Hot enough for everybody?" he said. "I've always thought that if they're going to ask us to start our lit classes in August in Texas it would make a lot more sense to begin with Dante's *Inferno* than Ralph Waldo Emerson . . ."

He surveyed the room. Not a glimmer of a smile anywhere. What had he done? For a second he thought he must have walked into the wrong room. A couple of late-comers peered in through the door.

"Come on in," Ben said. "We've got plenty of room down front."

Ben waited until they made their way to their seats and got settled. The rest of the class was still staring like a herd of transfixed cattle. Then he realized that the students weren't looking at him, they were looking past him. He turned. Scrawled on the blackboard, in huge juvenile print, was the message: WE WANT OUR MONEY BACK.

Ben turned back to face the class. He ran his fingers through his hair, taking a second to gather himself. "I'm sorry, everyone, but there's been an unexpected emergency. I'll leave copies of the syllabus here in front, you should all pick one up before you leave, and I'll see you on Friday."

The students seemed dumbfounded. Ben jammed his lecture notes back in his briefcase, stumbled down from the podium and set the stack of syllabuses on an empty seat in the front row.

"Professor Lindberg?"

Ben glanced up and saw the hand waving in the back, but there was no time. He shook his head no, reaching for his briefcase, and left the room. As soon as he was outside the door he began to run. He raced down the hallway, through the clutch of students gathered in from of the course listings board, nearly knocking over Ernestine Bryce as she came out of the Undergraduate Office. He took the two flights of stairs to the basement three steps at a time. He fumbled with his keys, picked them up, and opened the door to his office. His fingers danced, punching the numbers in on the phone.

"Hello?"

"Hey," Ben said. Out of breath, he leaned against his desk. "Are the children home yet?"

"No, but they should be any minute."

"I want you to go to school and get them."

"What are you talking about?"

"Please, Katy. Just do it. I'll explain when I get there."

She heard the fear in his voice and it frightened her. "I'm sure Ann's already picked them up. What is this? What's wrong?"

"Go anyway," Ben said. "Please. I'll be home in twenty minutes."

He hung up and stood for a minute, staring for a moment, then swept his hand across his desk, sending books and papers flying.

His car was parked all the way down by the stadium. Walking and running, it still took him five minutes to get there. It was four o'clock and the traffic on Mopac wasn't bad. He was on autopilot, terror coiled in his stomach like a spiny sea-creature. It was all he could do to remember the way home. His tires squealed as he took the long curves on Bee Caves. Maybe he'd over-reacted. Maybe he'd scared the wits out of Katy for no reason, made a fool of himself, but that didn't matter. All that mattered was that his children were safe.

He'd said he'd be home in twenty minutes; he made it in fifteen. Pulling into the driveway he saw their neighbor Tracy Howarth's Suburban parked next to the house. The back door of the van was open and Matt was getting out, crouched low to keep from hitting his head. Katy stood on the far side of the satiny black and gray vehicle, talking to Tracy.

Ben snapped off the air conditioner, listening to the long hushed sigh, and then turned off the ignition. He sat with his hands in his lap, like the last man to leave the stadium after a hair-raising game. Matt looked back, crooking his neck and gave him a shy wave. Ben opened the door and pulled himself out of the Maxima.

Katy came around the front of the van. Her face was so hard that Ben didn't know what to think—could Sweeney have somehow called her and spilled the beans? The image flashed in his mind of the two of them sitting in Rebecca's living room, under the photograph of Clint Eastwood and Ronald Reagan, Sweeney gesturing as he talked as if he was juggling unseen balls in the air, presenting it all as if he was doing her a favor, as it was something she really needed to know, reaching across to touch her hand, offering consolation, a glass of untouched iced tea on the table between them. Ben really wouldn't put it past the guy—but then he realized that he didn't see Abby.

All eyes were on him as he moved up the driveway of crushed limestone, Tracy leaning forward on the steering wheel, the three kids solemn as owls in the back, still strapped in seat belts.

"Where's Abby?" Ben asked.

"We're not sure," Katy said. She could not bring herself to look at him, her voice low and throttled.

"We waited fifteen minutes," Tracy said, "and then I sent Vivian to look. One of her friends said she thought Abby had said something about going home with Claire."

"Did you call Claire?" Ben asked. He squinted from one woman to the other, the sun glaring mercilessly off the huge white house.

"I just tried," Katy said. "There was no answer." Matt stood at the front door, his green backpack sagging at his side. Tracy took her sunglasses out of her hair.

"I should get the rest of these kids back," Tracy said. She was wise enough not to want any part of this. "If there's anything I can do, please call me."

"Of course," Katy said. As they watched Tracy back down the drive Ben put his hand on Katy's elbow. She slid away from him. "What is this? Ben, what is happening?"

He looked at their son, shadowed in the door. "We'll be in in a minute, O.K.?" Matt hesitated and then went inside. A jet had left its stuttery Morris Code trailing across the cobalt sky.

"So where is she?" Katy said. She'd been working in the yard and a pair of heavy cloth gloves protruded from her back pocket.

"I don't know."

"Then why did you call me like that?" The phone rang inside the house.

"I need to get this," Ben said.

"Answer me, Ben!"

As he turned away she tried to catch his arm. The phone rang a second time and he tore free, running for the house. She stood stunned for a second and then she began to run too.

He slammed open the front door. Matt, already on his way to get him, froze in the hallway, startled by the violent entrance. He pointed to the receiver laying on the table in the breakfast room.

"It's for you," he said.

"Thank you, Matt, thank you." He patted his son quickly on the shoulder as he passed. When he picked up the phone all he could hear at first was a grainy hum, as if the call was coming over the transatlantic cable.

"Hello?" Ben said. Zoila stood at the kitchen counter, chopping red peppers. "Hello!"

"Mr. Lindberg?" The voice was gravelly, male, with the hint of an accent.

"Yes?" Ben turned, the phone cord spiralling around him. Katy stood behind Matt, her face flushed, her hands on his shoulders.

"You got our money, right?"

"Who is this?"

"What does it matter, who it is? You got a whole lot of money that doesn't fucking belong to you, right?" The hum grew stronger and for a second Ben thought they'd been disconnected. "What did you say?"

"I didn't say anything," Ben said. The parrot clattered in his cage, ruffling his green and yellow feathers.

"So you've got something that's mine and I've got something that's yours."

"What do you mean?"

"Your daughter."

"Where are you?"

"Don't you worry about where I am. What you need to worry about is getting all that fucking money back to me."

"That's fine."

"By five-thirty." Zoila kept at her task, slicing vegetables, rock-solid reliable at one hundred dollars a week.

"I can't do it that fast."

"Don't you fucking tell me how fast you can do it! You're not the one making the rules around here!"

"But the money isn't here!"

"Then where is it?"

"It's out in the country. I buried it. On this piece of land. I can take you there. Or I can tell you where it is, either way. Just let her go."

There was only silence on the other end of the line for several seconds and then, in the background, a heated conversation in Spanish. Ben glanced at Katy and Matt, saw the wonder in their faces. Katy had taken Matt's hand. The blender sat on the counter, full of strawberry smoothie that she had made for the children's after-school snack.

"So how far out in the country is it?"

"Seventeen, eighteen miles," Ben said.

"We're going to have to call you back."

"What do you mean, you'll call me back? I can take you there right now, whatever you want."

"I just told you, man. We'll call you back. So stay off the phone, all right? And don't even think about calling the cops."

"No, wait . . ." There was a series of short, castanet-like clicks and then the steady hum of the dial tone. Ben set the phone down.

"Bye-bye," the parrot called. "Bye-bye."

Ben turned. The only sound was the steady snap of Zoila's knife against the chopping board. Matt pulled free of his mother's hand. Katy, a million miles away, stared out the window at the rose bushes, dappled in the late afternoon sun, the water splashing in the fountain.

There was a sudden patter of feet. Roberto raced in, beaming, holding aloft two ping-pong paddles. "El Senor!"

"No, Roberto, not now," Ben said.

The boy stopped short, his diaper sagging. His smile turned tragic. Zoila put her knife down and gathered him in, prying the paddles out of his hands.

"If you could take him upstairs for a few minutes," Ben said.

Katy said something in Spanish and Zoila nodded, moving Roberto toward the hallway. Matt stepped out of the way to let them pass.

"Matt? You too, pal," Ben said. "Mom and I need to talk."

Without a word Matt was gone. Ben could hear Roberto complaining loudly to his mother on the stairway.

"Someone has her," Katy said. Her voice had fallen to a whisper.

"Yes."

"Who?"

"I don't know."

Katy rose from her chair. "You said something about burying money. What money?"

"There is this money. That I found."

"How much money?"

"A great deal of money."

"Zoila!" the parrot screeched.

Katy fingered the basket of apples and browning bananas on the side table. "You mean the residual check. . . ."

"There was no residual check."

"And the money from Sweeney's club. . . ."

"That was all part of it."

She slapped him, catching his flush on the cheek, the sound loud as a shot in the still room. The parrot cocked his head, first left and then right, regarding them with a curious, unblinking eye. Ben reached up to touch his face.

"How long have you been lying to me?"

"Katy, listen, let me explain."

"How long, Ben?"

"Since, I don't know, January."

"I'm calling the police."

"No, you can't."

"What do you mean, I can't? It's my daughter's life we're talking about here."

"I know that. But the police aren't going to be able to get her back. I'm the only one who can get her back."

"My God, Ben. . . ."

"They're going to call me."

"When?"

"I don't know."

"And if they don't?"

She waited and then saw he had no answer. She pivoted away from him, trying not to cry. It was not in her nature to be pitiable. When he tried to touch her shoulder, she spun around, knocking his hand away.

He walked to the far end of the room and leaned against the back of a chair. The parrot began to bark, going through his whole repertoire. Katy picked the ping-pong paddles off the floor and put them in the drawer of the china cabinet.

Without looking at him she said, "So tell me. Tell me what you did."

He told her the story from the beginning, about the night he found the coolers under the feedstore, about moving it to the storage unit, about the arrangement he made with Sweeney. He did not tell it well. He kept having to go back over things and she didn't make it any easier for him, staring at him without expression as if he was explaining how he'd just spent the last nine months walking on the moon.

"So when we all went out for dinner on my birthday it was with this money?"

"Yes," he said.

She pulled a napkin from one of the blue ceramic napkin rings, folding and refolding it on the table in front of her. "And you never asked yourself whose money it was?"

"Of course I did. All the time."

"But you thought you could get away with it?" She spoke as if she was talking to a simpleton. Ben could see it sinking in, just how deeply tainted everything was. "So you were both in on it, you and Sweeney?"

"Katy . . ."

"And Rebecca? I suppose she knew too? This is where the house came from?" He made a futile wave of his hand. He didn't even begin to know how to answer that one. "How could you do this, Ben? How could you go on lying to me like that?"

Suddenly he was hollering. "I lied to you because I thought you would have made me turn it all in! I lied to you because I want you to have a home you could be proud of! I lied to you because I was tired of us being at each other's throats every time we had to send the car to the shop! I lied to you because I wanted there to be some possibility of hope in our lives, because, let's face it, it was getting pretty god-damned clear what our lives were going to be like on thirty grand a year or even forty and it wasn't the life you were counting on."

Her face filled with disbelief. "So it's all my fault, is that what you're saying?"

The dull ring of the phone made them both jump. Ben picked it up, heard the fizz of the cellular phone.

"Hello?"

"Mr. Lindberg?"

"Yes?"

"Do you know where the Seven-Eleven is on Cedar Breaks Trail?"

"Yes." Ben stared out at the empty pool, the brilliantly blue water riffled by a slight breeze; he remembered how excited Katy had been, the first time she'd seen it, how she'd cried out for them to come look.

"There's a pay phone outside the store. I want you to be at that phone in fifteen minutes."

"And what about my daughter?"

"Your daughter is the least of your worries. You just be there, all right? And I don't want you bringing anybody with you."

"I understand."

There was a sudden click and then nothing. He looked back at Katy.

"So what did they say?"

"I'm supposed to go down to the Seven-Eleven on Cedar Breaks."

"And are they bringing Abby?"

"I don't know."

"I'm going with you," she said.

"You can't. He said not to bring anyone."

"He said! And this is what we're doing? What he says? Whoever he is?"

He stared at her with a look that could have been mistaken for contempt. "You need to stay here. If there are two of us, they'll never show their faces."

"And what am I supposed to do then?"

"Wait. If you don't hear from me in an hour, call the cops."

When he walked past her she never moved. He made it all the way out to the car before he heard the door to the house open behind him. He turned and saw Katy running toward him. In the distance an electric lawn mower droned and sputtered. Ben stepped in front of the Maxima to intercept her. As she lunged for the door handle he caught her by both wrists.

"I'm going. I have to see her. I have to know . . ." She tried to pull free and they pirouetted in the white gravel.

"You can't, Katy! You can't! Listen to me! I'm the only one who can give them what they want! I got us into this and I'm going to get us out!"

He still had both of her wrists. They were locked tight against one another, like the bride and groom atop a wedding cake. Her face dissolved. She lunged, hitting him on the chest with her forehead, once, twice, three times and then she was sobbing deep, inconsolable sobs. Ben let go of one of her wrists so he could put his arm around her.

"I'm sorry," he murmured. "I'm so sorry."

He put his other arm around her then, trying to comfort her. She let him. Leaning against the car, he felt the hot metal sear his back like a brand. He looked up. Matt stared down at them from his bedroom window, one hand holding back the white lace curtain.

He sped down the twisting mountain roads, narrowly avoiding a slow-moving gravel truck on one of the blind curves. The Seven Eleven was at a four way stop a half mile up from the lake. The road had been built before the housing boom and what had been a quiet country road was now a major thoroughfare for rush hour traffic.

When Ben pulled up there were cars at all six gas pumps and a couple of kids lounged in front of the store with their Big Gulps. A sign for the Texas Lottery was taped up in the cashier's window.

Ben pulled himself out of his car. The pay phone stood unoccupied next to the dumpster. Checking his watch, he saw he had five minutes to spare.

He leaned against the side of the store, staring at the traffic. The four-way stop was a miracle of cooperation, the bulky grey and black Suburbans taking turns like trained elephants. Every so often a Jaguar zoomed down from the hills. A blonde woman in a lime-green aerobics outfit went into the store and came out a couple of minutes later with a Diet Coke and a bag of chips. She smiled uncertainly at Ben; anybody who was going to just stand out in the ninety-eight degree heat had to be crazy.

Five minutes passed. A large man in a sweat-stained white shirt and loosened tie came out of the bathroom. He dug down in his pants pocket for change and headed for the pay phone. Ben pushed away from the wall.

"Excuse me, sir," Ben said. "I'm sorry, I'm waiting for someone to call me back. I think they've got another phone inside. I appreciate it."

The man looked at Ben for a couple of seconds, and then decided it was too hot to make anything of it. The man shook his head as he lowered himself into his car.

The air smelled of gasoline and burning brakes. The heat was making Ben dizzy. What if they'd changed their minds? What if something had gone wrong, if they'd been scared off? Part of him still refused to believe any of this was real. Maybe it was just another of Sweeney's pranks. Maybe Abby was perfectly safe at a friend's house, drinking lemonade.

He looked at his watch again. Nearly fifteen minutes had passed.

He scrutinized the passing traffic. It could have been just his imagination, but he was almost certain that the beige Land Cruiser with the tinted windows had been by more than once. Two girls about Abby's age came out of the store, giggly and gangly-legged, aware of the boys' stares.

The ring of the phone was anemic. Ben grabbed the receiver, the plastic hot to the touch. "Hello?"

"Mr. Lindberg?"

"Yes?"

"Here's what we want you to do. There are some batting cages out on Riverside, all the way out, past Montopolis. They'll be on your right. You think you can find them?"

"Yeah, I'll find them."

"We'll meet you there." Ben put his fingers to his left ear, trying to drown out the passing cars.

"And what about my daughter?"

"She'll be there too."

"And how are we going to handle this?"

"You're going to take us to the money."

"But she doesn't have to be part of this."

"Not once we have you."

Riverside was all the way across town and it was rush hour; there was no good way to get there. Ben drove in on Bee Caves and cut across the park. Traffic slowed to a crawl and then stopped altogether. He snapped the radio on and then off again, trying to get hold of himself. For a second he considered being a real asshole, pulling onto the shoulder and zooming past everyone, but it looked as if it was bumper to bumper all the way to the Barton Creek Bridge and the last thing he needed now was a cop pulling him over. It was unthinkable, what had happened. His mind leapt, like a grasshopper in a jar. Even if he got Abby back, how were they ever going to recover from this? A terrier scrambled in the car next to him.

"Fuck it! Fuck it!" he shouted, hammering on the steering wheel. The traffic began to move again, almost as if someone had heard him. On the soccer fields the players ran relentlessly up and back, through a haze of dust.

Once he got to Riverside, traffic improved. The cars suddenly got cheaper and older. These guys, he thought, do they have any idea how many years they could get for this? He drove past the shopping center, past the half-built apartment complexes and the empty, wooded lots. Just when he was about to turn around, thinking he'd gone too far, he spotted the netting high above the trees.

He turned off onto a narrow dirt path. A low clubhouse was set fifty yards back from the road and behind it were the cages and three or four sand pits for horseshoes. Beyond the cages was a junkyard. The place looked as if it had been closed for awhile. The front door had been kicked in and huge, untrimmed mulberry bushes made it invisible to the passing traffic.

Ben got out of his car. There was a pay phone on the patio of the clubhouse. As he walked towards it a sparrow burst out of the rotting eaves and winged its way into the trees. Ben picked up the phone; he was surprised to find that it had a dial tone. On the wall of the low building someone had scrawled a crude picture of a man with a huge erect penis.

He walked to the cages and pushed open one of the creaking metal doors. A half dozen yellow softballs nestled under the pitching machines. He walked down the sloping concrete and picked up a couple of them.

He remembered the first time he had taken Abby to a batting cage. She had gone reluctantly and when they got there she fussed over not being able to find the right-sized helmet, but she'd ended up being delighted, hitting ball after ball while he sat outside on a wooden bench, watching. They must have spent three dollars worth of quarters.

He whirled and threw one of the balls high into the sagging nets. The ball snagged for a moment, rolling along a seam, and then dropped to the concrete. It rolled back towards him. As he bent to pick it up he heard the low thumping of a boom box. He turned to look.

The beige Land Cruiser with the tinted windows swayed along the dirt path and pulled to a stop behind the Maxima. The music was loud enough to shake the windows. The doors opened on both sides and two kids got out. They were both Mexican-American, baseball hats on backwards, with expensive sneakers. One, wearing a Seventy-Sixer t-shirt, carried a baseball bat. The other had what looked like a water pistol crooked under his arm, but Ben figured it wasn't. Neither of them could have been older than seventeen.

Ben dropped one of the softballs and stepped out of the cage. He thought he heard someone else bumping around inside the van, but he couldn't see through the tinted windows. The kid with the gun looked a little Vietnamese and his shoelaces weren't tied. He shouted something, but the music was so loud Ben couldn't make out what he said. The one with the baseball bat moved off to Ben's left, making his own independant appraisal.

A second Land Cruiser, identical to the first, rolled down the dirt path. The door opened and a giant of a man got out, the same man Ben had seen that night in Sweeney's apartment. Ben took a quick, deep breath. The man wore the largest pink shirt Ben had ever seen and he walked with difficulty. Irritated, he waved his arm at the first Land Cruiser and shouted something. The music went off.

"Mr. Lindberg?" the big man said.

"Yes."

"You ready to go for a ride?"

"Where's my daughter?"

"Hey, Doctor No, put that shit away, would you?" the big man said to the kid with the gun.

"But Whale . . ."

"Just do what I tell you, all right?"

The boy shrugged and stuck the gun in the back of his belt. The big man turned back and made a sweeping circular motion with his arm.

"Hey, Tavo, let her go!"

A door opened and Abby stepped out. Someone inside handed her her backpack. She stood there in her khaki shorts from the Gap and her new sandals, looking like every other Westlake schoolgirl. She didn't seem angry or scared, but profoundly embarrassed.

"Hey, pie," Ben said.

"Dad?"

Ben walked towards her. The nets of the batting cage seemed to have been slung up against the sky. When he ran his hand along her arm she flinched, her eyes darting from the huge man to Doctor No to the van and back again.

"Dad, what did you do?" Abby asked.

A stoop-shouldered boy got out of the second Land Cruiser and then reached back to pull a bat from under the front seat. The boy Ben had seen before too, riding Sweeney's face into the floor, that terrible night.

"I'll tell you all about it," Ben said. He could feel the tears welling to his eyes. "Just not here."

"Does Mom know?"

"Yeah, Mom knows. Listen, I'm going to have to go with these guys for a little while, O.K.? It's nothing to worry about, I promise.

Here." He dug down in his pocket and found a quarter. "You call Mom, she'll come pick you up."

"Hey, hey," Whale said. "Not so fast." He scratched at his neatly trimmed goatee. "I think she should go with us."

Ben stared at Whale for several seconds and then down at his feet. Birds flitted in the mulberry bushes. "But that wasn't the deal."

"I didn't know that we had a deal."

Ben drew himself up, frowning. "I'm not going through with this unless you let her go," he said.

"You're not what?" The big man hitched up his jeans and walked off a few paces. Doctor No, squatting by the vans, took the gun out of the back of his belt. "You think we're going to leave her out here in the middle of nowhere? That doesn't seem smart, does it? Who knows what kind of crazy person might come along?" Abby looked at her father and then at Whale, unable to hide her alarm. "I mean, hell, we're just going for a little ride in the country, right? If it goes the way it's supposed to we'll have you both back by supper-time."

Ben considered the quarter in his hand. Rush-hour traffic droned thirty yards away, behind the high hedges. It had been stupid to think they would just let her walk away, but Ben had a major problem. What were these guys going to do when they discovered that Ben only had six coolers, not eight? Whatever they might do to him, he didn't want Abby around when that happened. On the other hand, these guys were just foot soldiers, maybe they didn't know how many coolers there were. At least there was a chance, a lot better chance than their trying to bolt for it now. The boy in the Seventy-Sixer t-shirt picked at his teeth, the bat hanging loosely at his side.

"O.K.," Ben said.

"Good," Whale said. "I want to ride with Mr. Lindberg here, so Doctor No and Ricky, you come with us and Tavo, why don't you take the young lady in the other van?"

Abby took a step back. "I don't want to do this," she said. Doctor No rose to his feet and Ricky wiped his hand across his Seventy-Sixer t-shirt, amused.

"Abby, please," Ben said.

"I don't know what this is about. No one has explained anything to me." Her face shone in the heat; she had never been a child you could boss. "Are you selling drugs or something. . . ."

"No, honey, no," Ben said.

"You want to tell her what you did?" Whale said. "Go ahead. Tell her. Your Dad ripped us off."

Abby stared at her father, waiting for him to deny it, to say it wasn't so. He couldn't. Her chin began to quiver.

"Honey, we don't have a choice, please. It will all work out . . ."

Tavo came and took her by the elbow, gentle as a prom escort; she did not resist him.

Chapter Sixteen

Ben sat in the back next to Doctor No, with Whale and Ricky up front. As they bumped up onto the paved road an empty Colt Forty-five bottle rolled out from under the seat.

"So where are we going?" Whale said.

"Two Ninety West," Ben said.

"You got it." Glancing back, Ben saw the other van easing into traffic. The tinted windows made it impossible to see Abby.

They skirted the city. It was a quarter to seven and the worst of the traffic was over. The car smelled brand new and was loaded with accessories—when Whale hit a button on the dash a little compartment opened overhead holding his sunglasses.

No one spoke for a long time. Doctor No held the semi automatic between his knees and Ricky resumed his task of trying to dislodge whatever was stuck between his first and second molars. Whale caught Ben checking the rear view mirror.

"Don't worry, we're not going to lose 'em," Whale said. He drove like a man sitting on a throne. "So you teach college?"

"That's right."

"So what do you teach?"

"English."

"Is that right? Maybe you could teach these guys something. I keep telling 'em, they're not going anywhere in this world if they can't speak correct English. Hey, Doctor No, you even know what a pronoun is?" Doctor No was silent. "You see what I'm saying?"

A car in the right lane had its blinker on, trying to cut in, but the two Land Cruisers were bunched up as tight as a church camp caravan. Whale leaned over and turned on the oldies station. Neither of the boys looked happy with the choice.

"So how'd you end up with all that money?"

"I was out looking for my cat," Ben said.

"You were out looking for your cat! That's a good one! Were you scared?"

"I guess I was."

"I guess so." Bobby Darin sang "Dream Lover" on the radio. "There are people out there on the street, they'll shoot you over twenty dollars."

Without warning Whale hit Ricky across the mouth with the back of his hand. It was a blow of astonishing force, the teen-ager's head ricocheting off the headrest, and Whale hadn't even taken his eye off the road. Ricky reached for his mouth, checking for blood.

"It's such a god-damned dirty habit, picking your teeth! You ever heard of floss?"

Everyone was quiet for awhile. They passed two girls riding their horses by the side of the road. Ben was furiously considering his options. It wasn't as if he was just a couple hundred dollars short and he'd already seen what they'd done to Sweeney. If it really got down to it, he was going to have to come up with a great story. It occurred to him that he hadn't told Katy the location of Smelzer's sister's ranch.

"So how much further?" Whale said.

"We'll be turning off in three or four miles," Ben said.

"Hey, Doctor No, pay attention, you might see a real cowboy."

The vistas were magnificent once they turned off Two-Ninety. Long shadows crept across the pastures. Ricky leaned his head against the window, staring at a half dozen white goats scampering under a distant windmill. The roads were gravel now and Tavo dropped back a hundred yards to avoid eating the first van's dust. Ben tried to imagine what Abby could possibly be thinking, what the conversation was, between her and Tavo.

"Up there on the right there's a gate," Ben said. "I'm going to have to unlock it."

Whale eased the Land Cruiser over to the side of the road. "Doctor No, I want you to go with him."

Doctor No got out and Ben got out after him, his legs stiff after the long ride. He fished his keys from his pocket as the other van pulled up in a halo of dust. Ben unlocked the gate and it made a low groan as he swung it open. Whale rolled down the window, leaning across the front seat.

"Hey, Tavo!"

The window of the other Land Cruiser slid down and Tavo poked his head out. The two men exchanged a dozen words in Spanish. Standing at the open gate, Ben caught just a glimpse of his daughter, sitting on the far side of Tavo, rigid and forlorn as a statue in some distant gallery.

"Yo, let's get the fucking show on the road!" Whale said.

Both windows hummed shut and the two Land Cruisers rolled through the gate. Doctor No, his face scrunched up against the billowing dust, waited while Ben rewrapped the chain and snapped the lock.

The two vehicles waited. As Ben and Doctor No passed the second car Ben could just make out Abby's outline through the shadowy glass. He tapped lightly at the window. It was a stupid thing to have done. The gesture startled her. She turned, the look on her face blurred and terrified as a drowning child, sinking into an amber murk.

Doctor No shoved Ben in the shoulder. The back door of the lead car hung open. Ben climbed in first and Doctor No followed him.

The Land Cruisers rumbled down the washboard road. A couple of deer grazing at the edge of the woods raised their heads, but didn't run. Ricky leaned forward, hands pressed together in front of his mouth. As they rolled over the cattle gap a great blue heron flapped up from the creek.

"Nice out here, huh?" Whale said. "We should get out to the country more often. Hey, Doctor No, you ever been to any of those Fresh Air camps?"

"Can I ask you something?" Ben said.

"What's that?" Whale said.

"The old woman who died. Did she tell you about me?"

The van was utterly still. "No," Whale said. "She couldn't tell anybody anything. She was nuts."

Sure, she was nuts, Ben thought. He remembered that they had taken her child away from her; that would be enough to send anyone over the edge. "It's up here, just ahead," he said.

The tin roof slid into view, shining in the sun. The long-horn skull still sat on the front porch and the plastic water glass was still under the chair where Ben had left it. The first thing he saw that struck him as out of place was the pick-axe leaning against the live oak tree— Ben didn't remember ever putting it there—and then he saw the plot.

It looked as if it had been blasted by mortar shells. Great holes were everywhere, the plastic top of one of the coolers tangled in the barbed wire fence.

Whale pulled under the live oak tree, frowning. "This is it?" He saw what Ben saw, but only Ben knew what it meant.

"Yeah," Ben said.

They all got out, Doctor No taking his gun with him. The second Land Cruiser eased in behind the first, parking on the steep incline. When the doors opened, Whale turned.

"Leave her in the damn car!" he shouted.

Tavo, one foot already on the ground, hesitated, then leaned back to say something. The door on Abby's side closed. Tavo yanked the bat from under the seat, slammed his door, and came to join the rest of them.

Doctor No had wandered on ahead, scouting out the back of the house. Ricky, sensing something had gone wrong, looked as if he was about to giggle.

"You sure this is it?" Whale said.

Ben moved slowly towards the plot. "Yes," he said.

He tried to count the holes to see if any of the coolers could have been overlooked, but it was hopeless; the plot looked as if it had been torn apart by amphetamine-crazed bears, dirt and shattered rock thrown everywhere. Sweeney, Ben thought, it has to have been Sweeney.

Whale lurched up behind him on bad knees. A mockingbird scolded them from a fence post, tail jerking like a metronome.

"So what the shit is this?" Whale said.

"It's gone," Ben said.

"What are you talking about?"

"It's gone." Ben turned to face him. "It was all here yesterday, but now it's gone."

Ben didn't see the swing coming. The punch caught him in the face, knocking him down. It was the first time in his life Ben had truly been hit. It felt as if the chemistry in his head had been permanently altered.

"Aww, man, how fucking stupid do you think I am?" Whale said.

Ben put a hand out to steady himself and staggered to his feet. There was the warm taste of blood in his mouth. He prayed for Abby to stay in the car. "It's the truth, I swear to God."

"Fu-u-ck!" Whale's head snapped in frustration. "Fu-u-ck! If it's not here, then who's got it?"

"I don't know."

Whale gaped at him for a moment as if he hadn't understood. Huge half-moons of sweat shone through his nice shirt. The others watched him, tense and excited, waiting to see what he would do.

"Give me that thing," Whale said. Doctor No handed over the gun. Tavo and Ricky grabbed Ben's arms and Whale laid the gun barrel gently along Ben's temple.

"So tell me again, where is it?"

"I don't know." Sunlight glinted off the windshields of the Land Cruisers. What was it like for Abby, he thought, being forced to watch this? It was as if she was trapped at a second-rate drive-in movie, only it was her father up on the screen, about to be done in, and there was absolutely nothing she could do about it.

"It must have felt pretty good, having all that money, huh?" Whale said. Ben kept his mouth shut. If only Tavo had somehow forgotten the keys in the van, maybe Abby could just get the hell out before it all started, but no, Tavo would never be that stupid. The barrel of the gun moved up into his hair.

"It must have made you feel like a real big man. So what did you do? Spend it all?"

"I didn't spend any of it."

"Aww, come on, man! Somebody has all that money and they don't spend it, they're not human. These guys here, whatever you give them, they'll piss it away in twenty-four hours."

"But I'm not them," Ben said.

"Now that sure is right. Still driving that shitty car. So where the fuck is it?"

"I don't know." Ben could see waves of heat rippling in front of the limestone cliffs, a hundred yards away. He remembered the splash of light he'd seen in the trees when he'd been laying on his back in the creek. He understood now. It had been Sweeney who'd followed him. . . .

"You better come up with some ideas real quick, teach, or I'm going to blow your brains all over this fucking garden!"

"I don't know. You think I would have brought you all the way out here if I didn't think it was here?"

It was a point. Whale lowered the gun and stepped back as if he was thinking it over. He looked down at the gun, taking the barrel in both hands and then swung it underhanded like a man shovelling snow, hitting Ben in the groin.

Ben fell to the ground. The pain was excruciating. He clawed at the dirt, the ring of young faces staring down at him.

"Hold him down!"

Fighting back the waves of nausea, Ben could scarcely see. He felt his arms and legs being yanked and he was suddenly spread-eagled, face down in the dust.

"Give me the bat! Where's the god-damned bat?"

Ben tried to raise his head. With one eye he could see Whale walking around him, strutting like a professional wrestler before the big pin. He had gotten rid of the gun; he carried Tavo's baseball bat over his right shoulder. The mockingbird flew from the fence post to the top of the machine shed.

Whale squatted next to Ben. "Nobody's playing here, teach. Somebody's going to tell us, one way or the other. Because if we finish with you and we still don't have what we want we're going to go back and burn your house down, do you understand? I don't care how fucking fancy your zip code is. You ripped us off. Do you know what would happen if word got around that I let you get away with this?"

"There's a guy named Sweeney," Ben said. "Daniel Sweeney. He owns a club in town, *The Railyard*. You know him." Ricky had a knee on Ben's right arm; Tavo straddled his left.

"Yeah, I know him. We've been following that guy around for a month. How the hell do you think we found you?"

"Go ask him where the money is."

"Well, fuck."

Whale straightened up and walked off a few paces. His shirt-tail hung out at the back and there were big dirt stains on the knees of his jeans. He held the bat out in front of him, spinning it so the trademark was on top. So this is how he got his name, Ben thought. It wasn't W-h-a-l-e, it was W-a-i-l.

Whale turned and raised the baseball bat over his head, his cheeks puffed out like a man gathering every ounce of strength to ring the bell at the county fair. Ben tried to jerk his hands away, but the kids on his arms held fast. The sound of his right hand breaking was like the crunching of a mallet on fishbones. Blood flew. Ben bucked twice, but his captors rode it out. Someone screamed; for a second Ben didn't even realize it was him.

He was blacking out. Whale let the bat drop, disgusted. "Somebody go get the bitch in the car," he said.

Tavo rose to his feet, letting go of Ben's left arm. Ricky let go too, rolling back on his knees, his face flushed. Ben grovelled in the dirt, cradling his mangled hand to his chest; bones protruded from the skin, the blood welling up dark and red. Everything was spinning, but only one thing mattered. No one was going to call his daughter that, no one was going to do what they intended to do.

Whale and Doctor No both had their backs turned, watching Tavo stroll toward the van. Ben pushed up on his left elbow. Only when he got to one knee did Ricky realize what was happening and try to collar him, but Ben pulled free.

"Hey!" Ricky shouted.

Doctor No and Whale turned, but not in time. Ben plowed into them with his shoulder, grabbing for the gun, but only succeeded in knocking it loose, sending it cart-wheeling across the loose dirt into one of the freshly-dug holes. All three men went sprawling. Pain flashed up Ben's right arm as if he'd just stuck his finger in an electrical socket, but he couldn't stop. He rolled over once and staggered to his feet.

The gun was out of reach, Doctor No already scrambling after it. The bat lay in the grass. Ben and Ricky both went for it, Ricky getting there first, but Ben shoved him past it and scooped up the Louisville Slugger with his one good hand.

Ricky spun back to face him. Ben swung, the bat missing the boy's head by inches. Ricky's eyes went wide with disbelief. Ben flailed again, missing again, but this time Ricky stumbled backwards, sprawling onto the porch.

Somewhere Whale was bellowing like an Old Testament prophet. Ben turned, waiting for the shot, but Doctor No was banging the gun in the palm of his hand, trying to get the dirt out. Whale lay on his side, holding his left leg, beached.

Ben ran for the vans. The only one in his way was Tavo, who stood his ground, arms spread. Ben swung the bat one-handed. Tavo ducked, making a futile swipe at the bat as it blurred past his face.

Ben panted, trying to get his wind back. His right hand felt as if it was about to come off, bones stabbing into places where they never should have been. He rocked back for a moment. Red spots swirled like gnats in front of his eyes and it almost seemed as if the second Land Cruiser was silently sliding away from him. Ricky and Doctor No were both sprinting towards them, Doctor No tossing the jammed gun into the weeds.

Tavo gave a little juke, as if he was going for Ben's legs. It was a mistake. Ben chopped down with the bat, hitting Tavo on the shoulder, the sound sharp as a solidly hit golf shot. Tavo crumpled at his feet.

Ben bolted for the vehicles. To his astonishment he saw that the second Land Cruiser really was moving away from him, rolling down the steep incline, gathering speed as it went—somehow Abby had managed to get it out of gear. Ben stumbled on the gravel road and then righted himself, flying down the hill with the teenagers in pursuit like something out of the Keystone Kops.

With only one usable hand he had to toss the bat away in order to jerk open the car door. Abby crouched over the steering wheel, tears streaming down her face. Ben kept pace for three or four more steps and then, grabbing hold of the passenger seat, lunged, banging his knee, wriggling his way in. Abby glanced across at him and sobbed.

"Honey, honey . . . ." he said.

The van hit a rock and pitched to the right, nearly throwing Ben out again. He slammed the swinging door shut and then reached across to help Abby, but with no key and the ignition off the van's power-steering made any kind of control nearly impossible. They careened backwards like a runaway caboose, slamming through thickets, banging over culverts, heading for the creek.

Ben glanced up the hill. Tavo was still curled motionless on the ground and Doctor No seemed to have given up, going back to the other Land Cruiser for something, but Ricky, who'd retrieved the fallen bat was right on their trail, broken-field running through the yucca and the prickly pear.

There was a high-pitched rasping sound, like a badly-tuned violin and then a series of sharp pops as the van broke through a fence. Suddenly they were over the bank. The van reared like a frightened horse and then slid backwards into the shallow water.

For several miraculous seconds they seemed to float, the whole car eddying around like a boat and then water began to bubble through the floor. Ricky stood on the bank, gaping, while Doctor No bounded down the hill carrying the other bat.

Abby shook uncontrollably, covering her face with her hands. When he reached across to comfort her, she gave a small cry, but there was no one else for her to turn to and she buried her head in his chest as if she was six. He kissed her hair—it smelled of vanilla—his left arm around her, his bloody right hand erect in the air as a flag.

He looked down suddenly; his shoes were wet. The water pouring into the car was warm, heated by the August sun. The van rocked softly and finally touched bottom in three feet of water.

The two teen-age boys stood side by side on the bank. Ricky looked uncertain, almost as if he's had enough, but then something made them turn. Whale limped across the lawn, screaming orders. He grabbed the pick-axe that had been leaning against the tree. Ben reached across and locked all the doors.

The two boys sat down in the dry grass and took off their shoes and socks; they weren't about to ruin their two hundred dollar sneakers. Ricky eased into the water and Doctor No waded in after him. Ben pushed Abby's head down, knowing what was coming. Ricky took the first swing, the bat bouncing off the windshield, and lost his balance, splashing backwards into the creek. Doctor No swung second, to no greater effect.

Abby clung to Ben's hand. When she was small, he remembered, she would squeeze his thumb as she was falling asleep to keep him from slipping away. Whale limped heavily down the hill. He swung the pick-axe at his side like an old prospector.

"Get in the back, Abby," Ben said. "Just get in the back and get down!"

Ben helped her squeeze past him. The water was ankle deep now in the car. He reached down under his seat, groping in the silty water, looking for a tire iron, something he could use.

The two boys had figured out that they would have better luck with the side windows. One solid hit transformed the pane on Ben's side into a glistening spiderweb. Blow followed blow, Ricky and Doctor No swinging in tandem, spirited as apprentice carpenters. Abby was curled up in the back, her eyes bright with fear, not making a sound. We are rabbits in a burrow, Ben thought, being dug out by dogs. Ben opened the glove compartment, raking out maps, gas receipts, a jumble of cassettes; there was nothing.

Whale, on the bank now, let himself down into the stream like the shyest of bathers. A direct hit by Doctor No made the window sag inward like wire mesh, but it didn't give. Ben felt along the ceiling, yanking open the overhead compartments.

Whale swayed through the waist-high water. It was one thing to steal seven million dollars, but you don't fuck with somebody's car. He took a round-house swing, but lost his grip on the wet handle. The pick-axe glanced off the roof of the van and splashed a dozen feet downstream. Whale flailed like a circus bear and nearly went down, but when Ricky tried to help him he pushed the boy away and wrestled the bat from him.

Ben turned and glanced at Abby. She knew there was no way out;

he could see it in her eyes. It was then that he saw the shoe box under her seat. He reached back and yanked it free. The cardboard was sopping wet. He yanked off the top. Inside was a damp cloth case of some sort. It was heavy; he fumbled with it and finally managed to unbutton it. The gun was huge. Sweeney would have known what caliber; Ben didn't. He wiped the moist barrel dry under his arm.

Whale sloshed through the water, getting himself into position. One blow sent glass flying all through the Land Cruiser. Suddenly there was no window, nothing between them. Whale extended his bat like a triumphant fencer daring his opponent to make another move.

Ben raised the gun with his left hand. His crippled right hand was clutched over his heart as if he was giving the Pledge of Allegiance.

Whale gave a short, mirthless laugh, running his tongue along his lower lip. It was only the second time Ben had ever held a revolver in his hands; the first had been at the Gun and Knife Show, but that had only been playing. He had no idea if the gun was loaded or if it was too wet to fire and Whale didn't seem to know either.

Ben flinched, startled by the touch of his daughter's hand on his cheek, a reminder of some other world. "Shoot him, Dad, shoot him . . ."

He gave an impatient shake of the head, signalling her to get back. For several seconds there was utter silence, just the sunlight glowing off the limestone cliffs, a dragonfly flitting above a clump of thistles, the only sound the soft rippling of the stream.

Whale lowered the bat, letting it slip into the water. He rubbed at his nose with his thumb and then looked back at Ben, trying to decide what he was capable of. Ben strained to keep the gun steady, but the barrel had started to waver. His right had pulsed at his chest like a fierce, wounded animal. There was no more than two feet between the two men. Whale sucked at his teeth and took another slow step forward, open-handed, as if it had all been in good fun, counting on Ben not to do certain things in front of his daughter.

The shot was deafening, echoing in the enclosed van. Ben felt a quick spatter on his face like rain and Whale pitched backwards into the stream. Doctor No broke for the bank. Ben lowered the gun, resting it against the broken glass of the window. He could feel Abby's head against the back of his seat; he could hear her sobbing.

Ricky didn't move, standing knee-deep in the water, stricken. When Whale floated down to him Ricky bent his knees, trying to grab him under the arms, trying to get Whale's face out of the water, but as the boy wrestled the huge body around Ben saw there was no face there anymore, only a red pulp.

Ben turned away. He slammed the glove compartment shut with the barrel of the gun. His ears rang, but there was some other sound too, rising and falling, coming from far-off. It was a siren. Ben looked up and saw Doctor No crashing into the woods.

Two green sedans and a police car bumped over the cattle gap. Ricky let Whale's body slip back into the water. The front of his Seventy-Sixer t-shirt was rose-colored with blood. A policeman stepped out of the lead car, barking orders. Ricky raised one hand, but still clung to Whale's shirt with the other, refusing to abandon him. Abby touched Ben's arm. He set the revolver down on the driver's seat and reached back to pull his daughter's head to him. The baseball bat floated downstream, gleaming in the late afternoon sun like a golden otter.

Chapter Seventeen

The soft rustling of a newspaper woke him out of a drugged sleep. Ben opened his eyes, blinking at the beige ceiling of his hospital room. It was several seconds before he realized that there was a man looking vaguely familiar sitting in the corner, reading the sports section. The man put the paper down and stared at him intently.

"Mr. Lindberg?"

"Yes?"

The man was avuncular, on the far slope of middle age, with thinning hair and a Save the Children tie. He got up and moved toward the bed. "So how are you feeling?"

"Not so good."

Ben's right arm was immobilized and elevated, propped up on a pillow and encased in a stocking that was tied to an I. V. pole. It made him feel a little absurd, as if he was permanently frozen in the position of a New Yorker hailing a cab. The metal pins prickled in his hand. The man sat down in a chair next to the bed. Ben watched him out of the corner of his eye, not wanting to move his head.

"Sounds like you had yourself one hell of a day yesterday."

"Yeah."

Not that he could remember all of it. He had passed out in the police car and once he got to the hospital they had pumped him full of sedatives and pain-killers. The operation on his hand had taken hours, nearly all of the bones having to be rotated back into place. All through the night and early morning he'd drifted in and out of a drugged fog, waking several times in utter panic, not knowing where he was, having to be restrained by nurses when he swore he heard Abby calling for him in the hallway.

"My name's Hyde. Malcolm Hyde. You may remember me. We spoke out in front of your house, two, three months ago. I'm with the police department."

Ben's mouth went dry; he grimaced and wipe his mouth with his left hand. "So where is my daughter?"

"She's home. I was over there this morning. She's doing fine."

Ben waited, hoping for more, but Hyde seemed satisfied that he'd said enough. Ben had tried to call the house, several times, but the line had been busy for more than an hour. His guess was that she had taken the phone off the hook. As far as he knew, he'd had no visitors—except, of course, for Hyde.

"I just want to tell you, you're quite a hero down at the station," Hyde said.

"Why is that?"

"This guy Whale . . . a really bad guy. There are a lot of people who would have liked to have done what you did." Hyde took a small tin of Altoids out of his shiny jacket and popped a breath mint into his mouth.

"So have you talked to the kids who were with him?"

"Yeah."

"So how did they find me?"

"You went to see Sweeney, right? Apparently they were watching the hospital. They started following you. And when they saw you living in the big house, it wasn't hard to figure out." Hyde sucked hard on his breath mint. "I'm just here to make sure nothing bad happens to you. I thought we could just go over things. . . ."

"It's a long story."

"I've got time. You want a little water?"

"Yes. Please."

Hyde leaned forward and poured some water into a tiny plastic cup. Ben drank it greedily.

Hyde didn't take any notes and didn't seem to have a tape recorder; they just talked. It all went very easily. Even though Hyde was a cop, it all felt strangely inconsequential—maybe it was just the effect of the painkillers. He told Hyde about the feedstore, the weekly exchanges of cash and check, the safety deposit boxes, the visit to Al Jackett.

Hyde didn't seem paticularly surprised by any of it, but as Ben went on there was a slow and noticeable change. Hyde got up and went to the window, staring out at the parking garage. He took another breath mint and hitched up his ample trousers.

At first Ben thought he was just restless. Maybe Ben was boring him, or being too cavalier not showing enough remorse. As Hyde lowered himself back in his chair, Ben thought he detected the shadow of a frown on the older man's face.

A nurse came in with lunch. She had bobbed hair and a Sandy Duncan bounce to her step; she did a lot to improve the mood of the room. She set up Ben's tray, adjusted the bed and fluffed up his pillows. The doctor was making his rounds now, she said, she should be by soon.

Hyde stayed to watch him eat. It was classic hospital food: a slice of cardboard chicken, some watery vegetables and butterscotch pudding. Ben tried a couple of awkward, left-handed bites of the pudding and then put the spoon down.

"So when you shot him. . . ."

The voice of the detective startled him. Ben's hair was damp with sweat. He turned his head. Hyde stood in the doorway, looking as solemn as a basset hound.

"Was he actually coming at you?"

"He'd taken a step forward, yeah."

"And he still had the bat in his hand?"

"Well, no, actually. He'd put it down."

"Uh-huh," Hyde said. He pushed away from the door. The taste of cut-rate butterscotch still clung to Ben's palate. "But what did you think he was about to do?"

"He wanted the gun. He didn't think I had the nerve to do it." A bell sounded in the hallway, soft as the ring in a department store elevator. "What else could I have done?"

"Yeah, well, these things are not exactly like *Gunsmoke*. You're not obliged to shoot the guy in the arm."

"So what's going to happen now?" Ben asked.

"We'll probably need to take a statement from you, but we don't need to do that today. It'll go before a grand jury, but I can't imagine they're going to find anything but justifiable homicide, given the circumstances." He gave the rail at the bottom of the bed a light tap. "Now there may be some other people who are going to want to talk to you."

"Like who?"

"We'll have to see. I'm just a lowly homicide detective, all right? I should let you get some rest." Hyde retrieved his paper from the chair. All of a sudden Ben didn't want him to leave.

"So how did the police find us yesterday?"

"Somebody called."

"Do you know who?"

"No. They didn't leave a name." Hyde folded his paper neatly and stuck it under his arm. "It was nice talking to you."

"Something bothers you about this, doesn't it?"

"Bothers me? No, nothing bothers me."

"It does. I can tell." Ben had to wrench his neck around, still tethered to the pole. "What is it?"

Hyde straightened his belt. "It's none of my business, but I don't know how you could not tell your wife, all that time. My wife would've killed me."

Ben had the cab drop him off at the foot of the drive so he could walk up on his own. He carried the paper bag of pain-killers in his left hand, his right protected by a blue sling and wrapped in a roll of gauze the size of a boxer's mitt.

He was surprised to find the van gone and more surprised still to find the house empty. Even the parrot was missing, the wire door to the cage open and birdseed scattered on the floor. Ben walked into the backyard, calling out for Katy and then Zoila, but there was absolutely nobody there. A slice of watermelon sat in a puddle of red juice on a plate in the middle of the lawn. It had evidently been there for some time because an army of ants had found it.

It was as if everybody had been swept away by extra-terrestials in one of Matt's *X-Files* episodes. Ben threw the watermelon in the garbage, brought the plate inside and checked the answering machine. There was a worried call from Sally Strickland, offering to bring over food, whatever she could do to help, and a wary message from his chairman, asking him to call when he got in. The number of Ben's hospital room was scrawled on a pad next to the phone and breakfast dishes were still piled in the sink.

He trudged up the stairs, looking for some clue to what had happened. The door to Zoila's room was shut, Abby's clothes were, as usual, scattered across her floor and Matt's mud-encrusted Michael Jordan basketball shoes propped against the laundry hamper.

He entered his and Katy's room. The white bedspread looked as if had just come in off the line, stiff and clean and fresh, frilly throw pillows tossed against the oak headboard. He went to the window.

Everything was so still he could hear the splashing of the fountain in the walled garden below. Orange carp drifted in the dark water.

He wiped at the back of his neck; he had started to sweat again. He lay down on the bed, his heavily-swathed hand extended out in front of him like a wounded paw. He was asleep within seconds.

The slam of a car door woke him. He lay without moving, still groggy, uncertain how long he'd been asleep, and after a moment he heard the key in the downstairs lock, a rustling and then his children's voices. He pushed himself out of bed and went to the top of the stairs, They were all below him—Matt holding the door for his mother, Abby a couple of steps behind, wrestling with two sacks of groceries. They did not see him at first. His heart ached the way ghosts' hearts must ache.

"Hey, guys," he said.

Startled, Katy dropped her keys. Abby leaned her bags against the sideboard, staring at the blue sling on her father's arm. She looked well, he thought; this was going to be all right.

"How did you get here?" Katy said.

"I took a cab," Ben said. He could feel them all braced against him. He came down the stairs. "Is there more stuff in the car?"

"No," Katy said. "I think we've got it all."

He reached out for his daughter's face. "Hey, pie," he said. She turned her head away, avoiding his touch. She lifted her bag of groceries and walked into the kitchen without a word. Ben tousled Matt's hair with his good hand. "It's nice to see you, pal."

Ben helped unpack the groceries and set the table while Katy got supper ready. She was making every effort to remain civil, but Ben could feel her anger, even on its short leash. It was not the time or place for a real talk.

Zoila and Roberto had left; Zoila's uncle had come that morning to pick them up and there was no indication when they were coming back, if ever. And just to top everything off, the parrot had escaped. No one knew quite how, but someone must have left the door to the cage ajar. The bird had flapped wildly around the kitchen before flying out a window and taking refuge in the top of the magnolia tree in the backyard. Matt had spent an hour trying to tempt him down with Oreos and slices of watermelon, without success.

Katy lifted the platter of chicken out of the oven. "I guess you can probably call the children."

"And Abby?" Ben said. "She didn't go to school today?"

"No. I called a woman at the University Counselling Service. I'm going to bring Abby in tomorrow."

Katy was determined to create a normal evening, even if it was a little like trying to cross Niagara Falls on a tightrope. Dinner was marked by long silences that she did her best to fill. Her mother had sent pictures from their summer visit and there were some wonderful ones. Matt needed to write her to say thank you for the check she'd sent for Matt's birthday and Abby needed to pick up her room.

Ben found himself growing increasingly cranky, even though he knew he had no right, not after what he'd put them through. All the same, who did Katy think she was protecting? Him? The children? Matt and Abby watched him eating left-handed. The chicken and the squash were manageable, but when he stabbed at his broccoli the green stalks skittered away from him. Without Zoila and Roberto the house felt too big, oddly spooky. Matt got up and went to the kitchen to pour himself more milk. When he got back, Ben put his knife down.

"I want to say something," he said. He saw the instant alarm on Katy's face. "I want to ask your forgiveness." Abby pulled the skin off, spinning it on her fork, banishing it to the edge of her plate. "You see, I found some money. I don't know how much Mom has told you. I found it in some coolers under the feedstore in our old neighborhood. It sounds a little like a fairy tale and I guess it was. But I couldn't give it up." Matt took a long drink of his milk, his eyes as wide as an owl's above his glass. "I kept it secret. I thought it was a chance to make things better for all of us. It was incredibly stupid, but I couldn't see what it would mean . . . how I would have to lie to your mother, how I would put Abby's life in danger."

"So will we get to keep it?" Abby said.

Startled, Ben looked across at his daughter. "The money? No. The money's disappeared."

"And will you go to jail?"

"Abby . . ." Katy said.

"No," Ben said. "I don't think so."

It had been a mistake, mentioning forgiveness. Abby brushed a strand of hair from in front of her eyes.

"When they had you down on the ground, I thought they were going to kill you," she said. "And you know what? I didn't even care."

"Abby!" Katy said.

Abby plunged on blindly, gesturing with her hands over her plate.

"I knew you must have deserved it, I mean, they wouldn't have done something like that for nothing. You know all I was thinking? That we'd have to move to a smaller house. . . ."

"Abby, you are not allowed to speak to your father like that!" Katy said.

Abby's chair scraped against the floor as she pushed away from the table. She stormed out of the room. Katy put her napkin to her lips, close to saying something, but she didn't. She folded the napkin carefully, set it next to her plate and then got up herself.

"Excuse me," she said. Ben watched her trip up the stairs. The room was suddenly just guys. They could hear the grandfather clock ticking in the hallway. Matt had not moved. Ben tried to smile at him.

"So does your hand hurt?" Matt said.

"It's O.K.," Ben said. "They gave me pills for it."

After dinner Ben and Matt went into the backyard to see if they could coax the parrot out of the magnolia tree. He was still there; they could catch glimpses of him through the canopy of great waxy leaves, strutting from branch to branch, looking back at them with his cock-eyed stare. They tried to talk him down at first, whistling and offering saltines, but their only reward was the bird's own repertoire of bizarre sounds: cacklings and mutterings, his imitation of a ringing phone and imperious cries for Zoila. The parrot would be lucky to survive the night out here—what did he know of hawks and owls and raccoons?—but he was not about to surrender his freedom.

They got the stepladder from the toolshed, Ben holding it in place so Matt could climb up with a long bamboo pole. Ben glanced back at the house. Katy was still in talking with Abby; his mind swarmed with the blackest thoughts. Matt rattled the pole slowly through the branches. With a shriek the parrot dove, a blur of green and yellow, sailing over to a neighboring elm. By the time they carried the ladder over to the elm and got it set, the parrot had flown back again, elusive as a genie out of his bottle.

Ben folded the paint-spattered ladder, staring into the magnolia. They were just going to have to wait him out. Ben couldn't even see the bird now. There was only the faintest shaking of the leaves and a mocking chortle that sounded like nothing so much as Sweeney's high-pitched laugh.

. . .

With only one good hand, Ben worked clumsily, moving wet laundry from the washer to the dryer. It was nearly ten-thirty and Katy was upstairs, saying goodnight to the children. Damp socks and underwear kept tumbling to the floor and he kept having to retrieve them, but the important thing was to stay busy, not to have to think.

He didn't hear Katy come into the kitchen. It wasn't until he punched the start button and turned that he saw her, standing at the refrigerator, putting away the milk. It give him a start. She closed the refrigerator door and stood up. For a moment neither of them knew what to say.

"Is she O.K.?" Ben said.

"She'll be fine."

"Should I go up to see her?"

"No, I think it would be better if you didn't right now." She wet a rag at the sink and began to wipe the counter. Without Zoila, all these tasks would be theirs again. "The things that Abby said . . . that isn't what she really thinks."

"I know that. Katy, I'm sorry. . . ."

"Please, don't say that. Please." He could see the reflection of her face wavering in the dark window; he could see her struggling. She rinsed out the rag and hung it over the spigot. "You know I thought a lot about what you said."

"What I said when?"

"Yesterday. About how you wanted me to have a home I could be proud of. I didn't need this house."

"Katy, I know that."

"I loved our life. I know we've had our struggles. Just like everybody else. But I could have gone back to work, we could have figured it out. But you didn't tell me, Ben. Why couldn't you tell me?"

He didn't know the answer; he was too battered and confused. The dryer whirred and knocked. "So you were the one who called the police yesterday?"

"No," she said.

"Then who did you call?"

"Sweeney."

He stared at her, dumfounded. It was impossible. Sweeney had to be long gone. "Sweeney!"

"There was no one else I could turn to."

"And you got hold of him?"

Her glance was resentful. "I called and left a message on his machine. He called me back maybe a half hour later."

"From where?"

"I have no idea." Branches raked the kitchen window. For just a second he was back there, in the van, the bat shattering the glass, Whale's face only inches from his own . . .

"And what did he say?"

"I explained what had happened. He said not to worry, I should just leave it to him, he would call the police. He said he thought he knew where they might have taken you. I tried to call him again this morning, but the phone's been cut off."

"I'll bet," Ben said. It was more than he could bear. To the bitter end, Sweeney had to have his cake and eat it too: rip him off and then ride to the rescue.

Katy pulled open the drawer and set the unused silverware back in its tray. "You have always been such a wonderful father to these children," she said. "And such a wonderful husband to me. But how are we going to get through this?"

"I don't know. But we're going to. I promise," Ben said. She stared at him, leaning back against the counter, the word *promise* floating between them like devalued currency.

Chapter Eighteen

Matt and his friends Stevie and Josh sat in the back seat, having an excited discussion of *Broken Arrow* while Ben drove. The boys all thought it was cool—exploding helicopters, fireballs mushrooming up tunnels, lots of broken glass and acrobatic karate, a thirteen year old's idea of a good movie. Under the bright overhead lights of the highway Ben could see the first patches of bluebonnets on the embankments, blooming in the March night.

Ben dropped Stevie off first and then Josh. Alone with his father in the car, Matt suddenly got quiet.

"So you liked the movie O.K.?" Ben said, glancing in the rear view mirror. Matt's eyes went wide and shy.

"Yeah."

"Your friend Josh is pretty funny."

"Yeah."

When they turned into the apartment complex there was a group of college students horsing around in the tiny pool, laughing and drinking beer. Matt opened the back door.

"Hey, pal," Ben said. He turned and grabbed Matt by the back of the neck with his right hand, the bad hand, the hand he would never be able to fully open or close. Matt didn't move, his head bowed. It was as much of an embrace as a thirteen year old boy could accept. "It was great seeing you."

"It was great seeing you, Dad."

"You have a good week at school, O.K.?"

"O.K."

Ben waited, watching Ben trip up the wooden steps to the second floor landing. It was several seconds before Katy came to open the door. She was visible only in silhouette, but Ben could see her hesitate for a second as Matt slipped past her. She knew Ben was out there. She raised a hand in greeting—after all this, she still had manners—and then the door closed.

By the time Ben got back on Mopac he was in a rage. This was impossible. This was not fair to anyone. They were a family: to go on like this would only continue to tear them apart.

The fall had been a siege, a series of hammer-blows. The story had been plastered across the front page of the newspaper, supplanting the tales of murderous baby-sitters and secessionist militias in West Texas. Photographers trampled through Rebecca's shrubbery to snap pictures and photographers waylaid the children outside of school.

It was more of a scandal than the University could handle. The department chair arranged for Ben to go on emergency sick leave for the semester and Katy's sister flew out to help. He went in once a week at night to pick up his mail, avoiding his colleagues. When he did run into them at the mall or one of the bookstores, they either pretended not to see him or went all bright and cheery with interest.

He met with a prosecutor from the financial crimes division of the Attorney General's office, a tenacious man who scoffed at the idea that Ben had just found the money (wasn't that the story he always heard?). He would have dearly loved to nail Ben, but after a month long investigation, including a couple of weeks when Ben was sure he was under surveillance, the prosecutor was reluctantly forced to conclude that Ben had committed no crime; he hadn't filed any false IRS returns and the records of his transactions with Sweeney were nowhere to be found.

Despite Ben's allegation, no charges were ever brought against Al Jackett. He had never received any money from anybody and as for the story that he had offer to launder Ben's money for him, it seemed, at least to the battery of lawyers involved, patently preposterous.

The only trial to take place was that of Ricardo Sanchez, Gustavo Santander and Donald Rodriquez (Doctor No's Christian name) for kidnapping and assault. Ben and Abby both had to take the stand, though the judge had not allowed him to hear his daughter's testimony. Ben had been forced to watch from the hallway, staring in through the narrow pane of glass in the courtroom door. He could not hear the questions or Abby's answers, but she seemed as composed as a Swiss choir girl in her sleeveless white linen blouse and blonde braid. The lawyers for both sides treated her with kid gloves and she only faltered a couple of times, biting her lip in confusion, looking over at her mother in the third row.

Ben's time on the stand did not go nearly so easily. The facts of the case were impossible to dispute; the only strategy the defense lad was to convince the jury that Ben was the one who should have been on trial, not the three teen-age boys.

"So tell me, Professor Lindberg, the afternoon that you learned that your daughter was missing, it was the first day of classes at the University?" The defense lawyer was a small man with a salt and pepper beard, sleepy eyes and a tone of acid contempt.

"Yes."

"And what had you been doing before that?"

"I'm sorry?"

"Until then. During the summer."

The three teen-age defendants, all in suits and ties, their hair cut short as military recruits, never took their eyes off Ben. Gustavo's left arm, still in a full cast, rested on the railing like a club. In the back row the relatives sat together. It was not hard to pick them out. They were all poor, all Mexican-American, their faces all taut with distress and distrust. A girl who couldn't have been older than Abby nursed an infant.

"I was working on my book," Ben said.

"So you didn't teach summer school?"

"No."

"So how long do you have off, three months? Four?"

The prosecutor shot to his feet. "Objection, your honor!"

"Objection sustained." The judge, in this room of flags and seriously varnished wood, had the muscly rectitude of a former Eagle Scout.

"So could you tell us what your book is about?"

"It's about the friendship between Ralph Waldo Emerson and Henry David Thoreau." Ricky, restless and bored, tipped back in his chair.

"Henry David Thoreau. One of America's most distinguished authors." The defense lawyer roamed the rail. He was a little too angry. Ben guessed that he had lost more than his share of cases; he lacked the ingratiating manner of a winner. "*Walden. Civil Disobedience.* The great inspiration for Gandhi and Martin Luther King."

"Yes."

"But you wouldn't consider yourself a real follower of the doc-trine of non-violent resistance, would you, Professor Lindberg? Considering that you smashed this boy's shoulder with a bat and shot a man in the face at point-blank range?"

The prosecutor was up again in an instant. "Objection, your honor!"

"Objection sustained!"

"I was protecting my daughter!" Ben said.

"Oh, and this is the way you protect your daughter, ripping off drug-dealers?"

The court erupted with the sounds of the gavel and shouts from the back of the room. Ben and the defense lawyer stared at one an-other. It was a pure moment. Whether the question was stricken or not, Ben had no answer.

Whatever card the defense lawyer thought he was playing, it back-fired. The three boys, being tried as adults in part because of their previous criminal records, were found guilty and sentenced to twenty-five years to life. Three days after the verdict was announced Katy and the children moved into the apartment on Enfield.

Headlights came up fast on Ben's right: a sleek red sports car. Mopac, since the speed limit had been raised, had suddenly turned into the Autobahn. Ben gradually increased his speed. There was no way he was going to let this guy cut him off. In his seven year old Maxima he didn't have a lot to lose. The sports car came up even with him—out of the corner of his eye Ben could see the driver checking him out—and, after a second, dropping back.

They had not put the separation to the kids as if it was going to be a permanent thing. It was just something for now, until things sorted out. It was as they just had to let the fever run its course. It had become sheer hell, the four of them under one roof—the glacial silences, the bursts of tears, the strangled courteous dinner conversations as if they were the newly-introduced guests at an English boarding house. They were all a little afraid of him after what had happened, spooked like earthquake survivors recoiling at the tinkling of ice in a glass. Abby would wake up at night, crying, and since she had started seeing her counsellor twice a week, had ceased speaking to Ben altogether. Matt remained loyal to his father, though Ben had started to notice he'd picked up an array of nervous tics and his grades were sliding.

He and Katy had been over the story so many times. Sometimes
he thought if he could have only pleaded temporary insanity or
chalked it off to a mid-life crisis, she might have been able to accept
it, but the truth was that Ben still believed that no one, faced with
those eight coolers in that spoor-ridden cellar, could have resisted.
That enraged her. What do you mean, no one could have resisted?
What an easy way out! Your daughter could have been killed. But I
couldn't see that, Ben would say. How could you not see it? Can't
you think? Only to a point, he would say. Only to a point.

She felt as if her heart had been sucked out of her. She needed for
there to be some lesson to be drawn. For the life of him, he could
find no lesson. It was like one of those nineteenth century Viennese
folk plays where the beggar wakes up in the king's bed. The beggar
was always brought low, and what lesson was that?

Financially it was a disaster trying to maintain two households.
Katy had found a job in an elementary school, but even with that
and the money her mother was sending her, they were just digging
themselves into a deeper hole. He was teaching again for the spring
semester, but there was no one in the department foolish enough to
suggest he had the remotest chance of being recommended for pro-
motion. He had one more year and then he was out. He'd sent letters to every college within two hundred miles, but he was not
hopeful. On Tuesday he was going in to interview for a state job,
something Tom Strickland had set up for him.

His life had become wonderfully simplified. He had a single pur-
pose: to dig out from under the rubble he'd caused. It didn't matter
how long it took, he wasn't going to give up. He struggled not to surrender to despair. He still saw Katy a couple of times a week—there
were still, after all, errands to be run, bills to go over, decisions about
the children to be made—but there was a look in her eye now, it
wasn't hatred or even sorrow, just something broken, and when he
saw that look all hope drained out of him, despite his resolves, and
he found himself thinking what he couldn't allow himself to think:
I had the gun in my hand; my mistake was using it on Whale; I
should have used it on myself.

He took the Steck exit. His apartment was just off the highway and
its only outstanding feature was its price. He rolled into his marked
parking place, locking the car when he got out. There was nothing
to steal, but he had come down one morning to find an empty Pop-
eye's box in the backseat and it had unnerved him.

Almost every balcony had its own barbecue grill and cheap plastic furniture. Someone had hung a rug over a railing to dry. It was the sort of complex where the tenants kept to themselves. In seven months he had only met two people. One was the creepy fertilizer salesman who, whenever Ben made the mistake of asking him how he was, would always reply, "Delicious." The other was his next door neighbor, a quiet, constantly worried older woman who was a secretary for Motor Vehicle.

He opened his door and turned on the light. The day's mail lay strewn across the floor. He bent down to gather it up. He flipped through it quickly, hoping for a letter from one of the colleges, but no such luck. The only thing of interest was a bulky manila envelope with a Canadian postmark and no return address.

He walked into the kitchen. The concrete arches of the cloverleaf, the interchange of One Eighty-three and Mopac loomed though his back window like the bowed legs of giant cowboys. When he flipped on the lights a roach scurried frantically for the back of the refrigerator. He dumped all the junk mail in the waste basket and sat down at the table.

The envelope made a scratchy sound when he squeezed it. He tore it open and then turned it upside down. Pine needles sprayed across the table and a half dozen color photos slithered out. Ben peered inside the envelope and pulled free a small pine bough.

He spread the pictures in front of him with his stiff right hand. There was one of a moose in a driving rainstorm, another of a red fox playing on a stump, a third he needed to look at for a few seconds before he realized it was of a grizzly wading in a distant stream.

He did not understand. He could hear his neighbor's television playing through the thin walls. He checked the envelope again and spied the letter inside. He tugged it out. It was typed on what must have been the world's oldest typewriter.

Dear Ben,

So here I am, up where the roads end. There's no point trying to find me. They don't put places like this on any of the maps. About the only people I see are bush pilots and a few crazy fishermen.

I killed a moose, can you believe that? Talk about ribs! You can eat on those things for months. Winter up here is unbelievable. Fifty degrees below zero and the sun never gets more than a few inches above the horizon. Sort of a shock for an old

Houston boy. At least Thoreau had his mother to bring him pies. All I got is some Eskimo dropping by with lynx meat stew. But it's good to get away from the rat race once in a while and get back to basics. Not that I don't miss those UT coeds.

I've thought about it a lot, the way things ended between you and me, and it never makes me happy. I know I wasn't exactly a saint, but I swear to God it could have worked if you hadn't gone all squirrely on me. Jackett's the real thing, he could have saved your ass, and the money. But you just couldn't trust me, could you? Did you really think I was so stupid I wasn't going to figure out that you were lying to me? I've had people try to run games on me before, but never my Thoreau professor. I'll confess, it sort of pissed me off. But I guess that's all so much water under the bridge now, huh?

I hope everything has worked out with Katy. I was kind of worried about you guys.

I probably won't be coming back to Texas soon, so drink a Shiner for me.

The big P, Paranoia, it'll get you every time.

> All the best,
> Daniel Sweeney

P.S. I'm sending along a little something to help with the bills. More to follow.

Ben stared at the P.S. What was Sweeney talking about? He picked up the envelope. There was still some balled-up newspaper in the bottom and when he pulled it out more pine needles sprinkled the table and then two packets of one hundred dollar bills tumbled out. One of the packets fell to the floor. Ben retrieved it and set it on the table, next to its twin. He could hear the theme music from *Saturday Night Live* coming through the walls. The evergreen made the tiny kitchen smell like Christmas. The two stacks of bills sat in front of him like a freshly cut pack of cards. He did not move.